My Weird School
graphic Novel

WITHDRAWN

Dorks in New York!

New York Times Bestselling Author
Dan Gutman

Pictures by
Jim Paillot

HARPER alley
An imprint of HarperCollins Publishers

THERE ARE EIGHT MILLION STORIES IN THE NAKED CITY.

THIS IS ONE OF THEM.

ONE WAY

EEK!

HE SAID NAKED!

THAT'S A BAD WORD!

HELP!

I'M NOT READING THAT!

HarperAlley is an imprint of HarperCollins Publishers.
My Weird School Graphic Novel: Dorks in New York!
Text copyright © 2023 by Dan Gutman
Illustrations copyright © 2023 by Jim Paillot
All rights reserved. Manufactured in Italy.
No part of this book may be used or reproduced in any manner whatsoever without written permission except in the case of brief quotations embodied in critical articles and reviews. Products, pictures, and trademarks are used fictitiously throughout this story to give it a sense of authenticity. No endorsement of this book is given by the owners of such products, pictures, and trademarks, and no endorsement is implied by their inclusion in this book. For information address HarperCollins Children's Books, a division of HarperCollins Publishers, 195 Broadway, New York, NY 10007.
www.harperalley.com

Library of Congress Control Number: 2022935789
ISBN 978-0-06-322971-6 (pbk. bdg.) — ISBN 978-0-06-322972-3 (hardcover bdg.)

Typography by Martha Maynard
22 23 24 25 26   RTLO   10 9 8 7 6 5 4 3 2 1
❖
First Edition

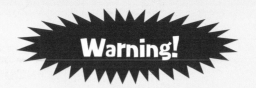

Warning!

THIS BOOK CONTAINS SCENES OF GRAPHIC VIOLINS, AS WELL AS CAR CRASHES, WILD RAMPAGING ANIMALS, THROWING THINGS OFF TALL BUILDINGS, ROBBERY, DUMB STUNTS, PEOPLE FALLING INTO OPEN MANHOLES, GROWN-UPS BEHAVING VERY POORLY, OBNOXIOUS CHILDREN, THE TOTAL DESTRUCTION OF PRICELESS OBJECTS, DISTORTED HISTORY, BAD JOKES, SWORD FIGHTING, IMPLAUSIBLE SITUATIONS, AND PEOPLE WALKING INTO DOORS.

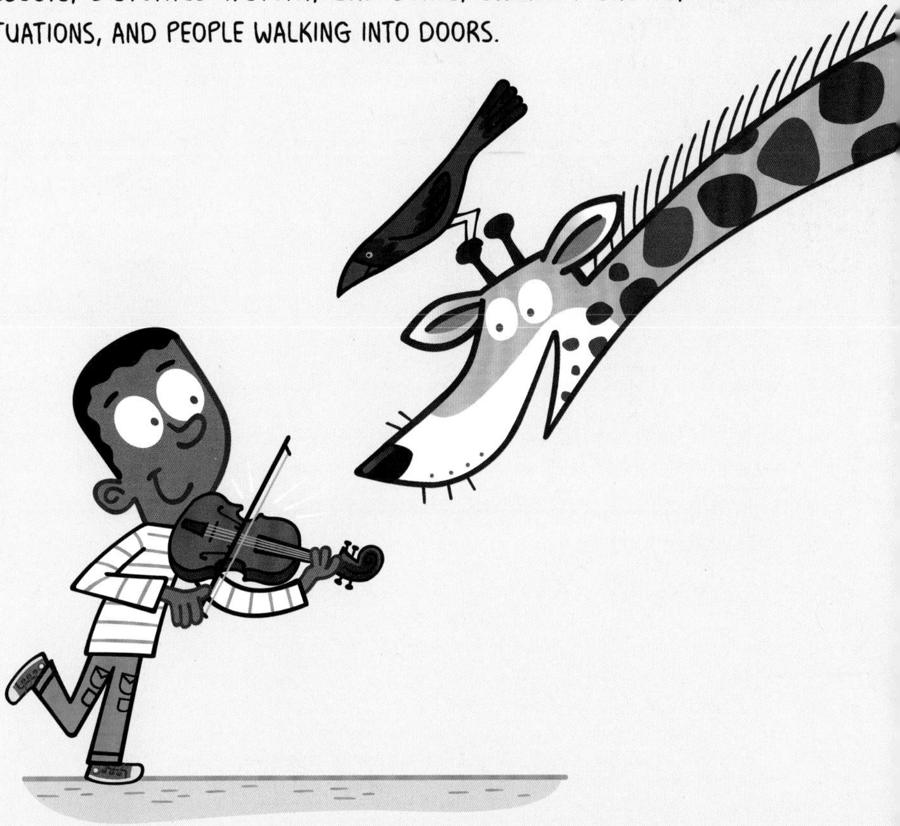

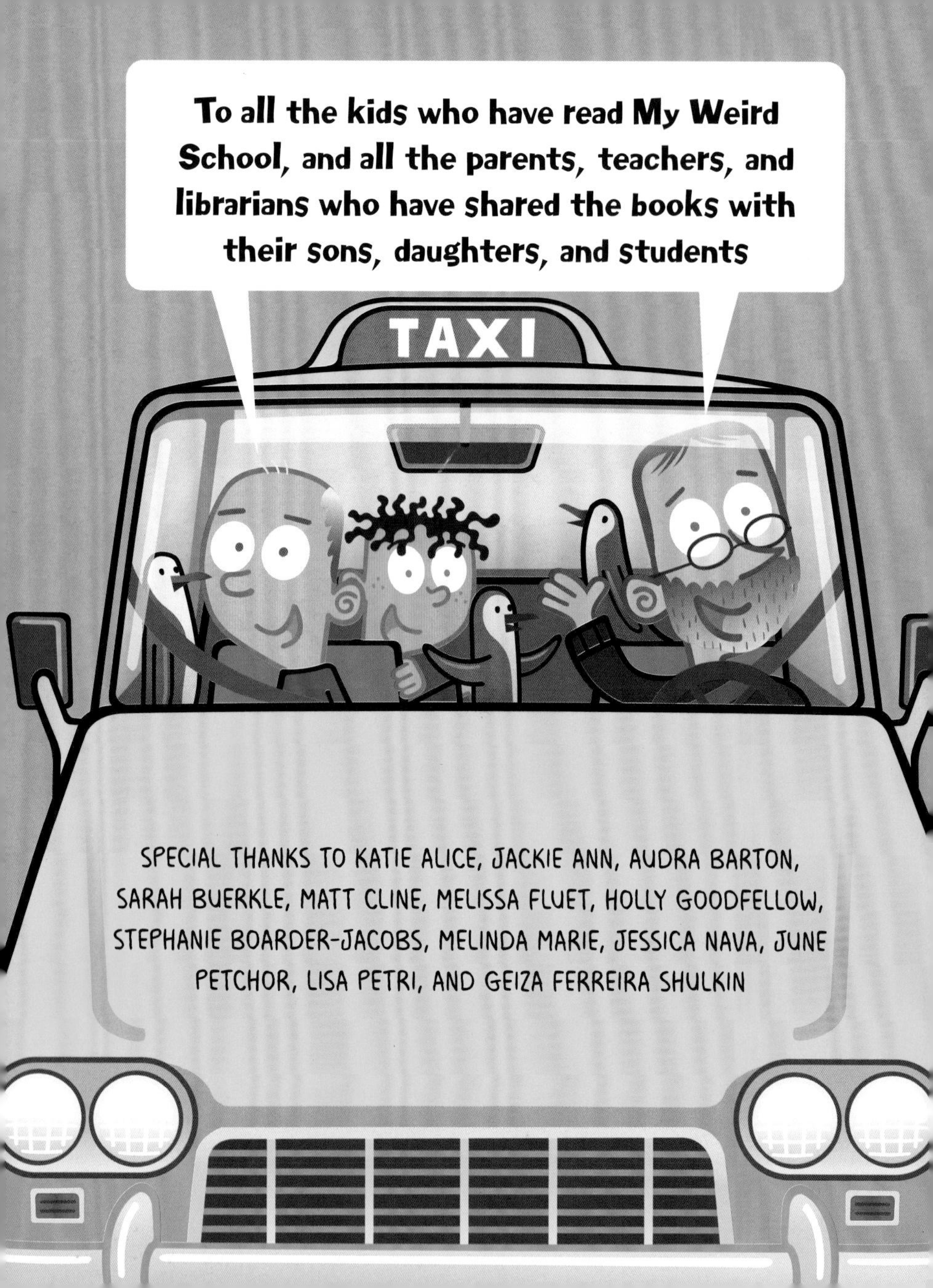
To all the kids who have read **My Weird School**, and all the parents, teachers, and librarians who have shared the books with their sons, daughters, and students
TAXI
SPECIAL THANKS TO KATIE ALICE, JACKIE ANN, AUDRA BARTON, SARAH BUERKLE, MATT CLINE, MELISSA FLUET, HOLLY GOODFELLOW, STEPHANIE BOARDER-JACOBS, MELINDA MARIE, JESSICA NAVA, JUNE PETCHOR, LISA PETRI, AND GEIZA FERREIRA SHULKIN

Table of Dis-Contents

THAT STUFF DRIVES ME CRAZY!

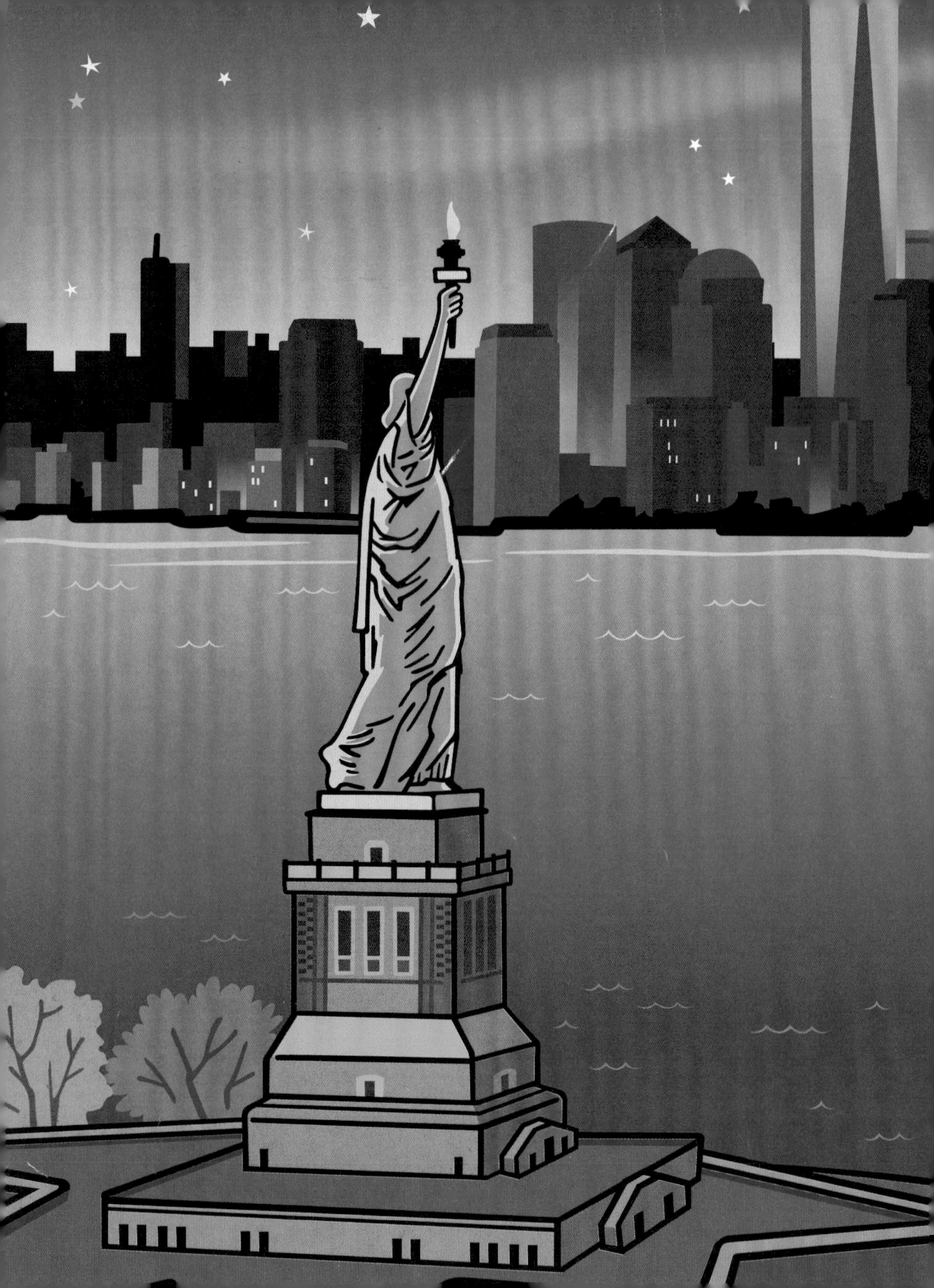

CHAPTER 1

People Who Leave Their Shopping Carts in the Middle of the Parking Lot

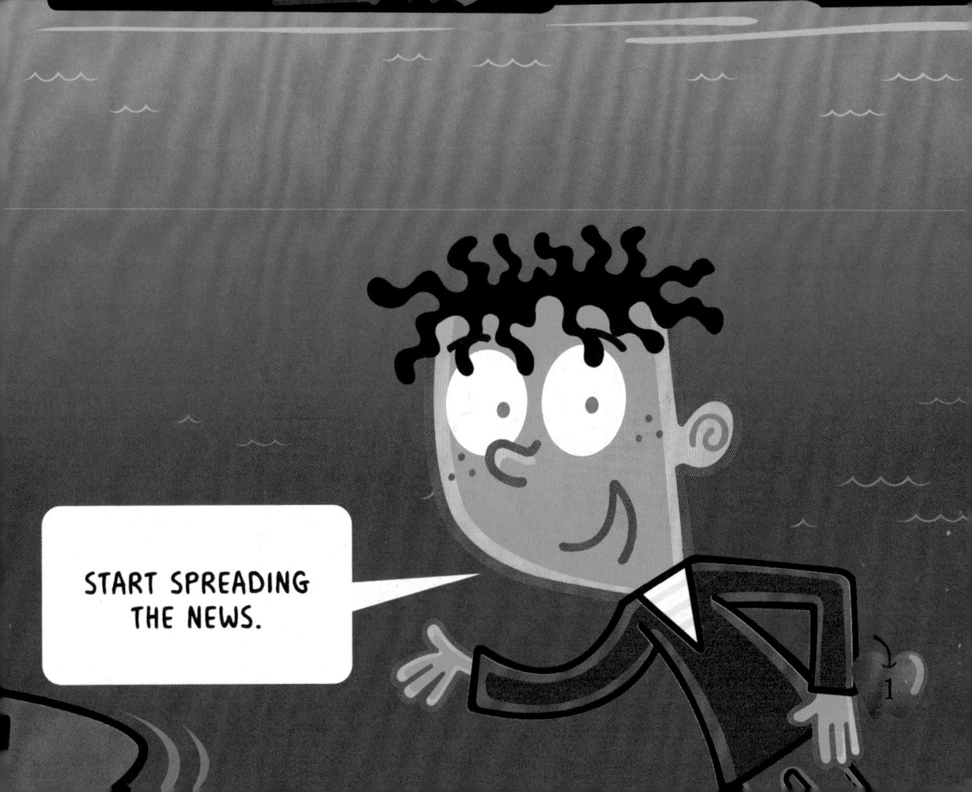
START SPREADING THE NEWS.

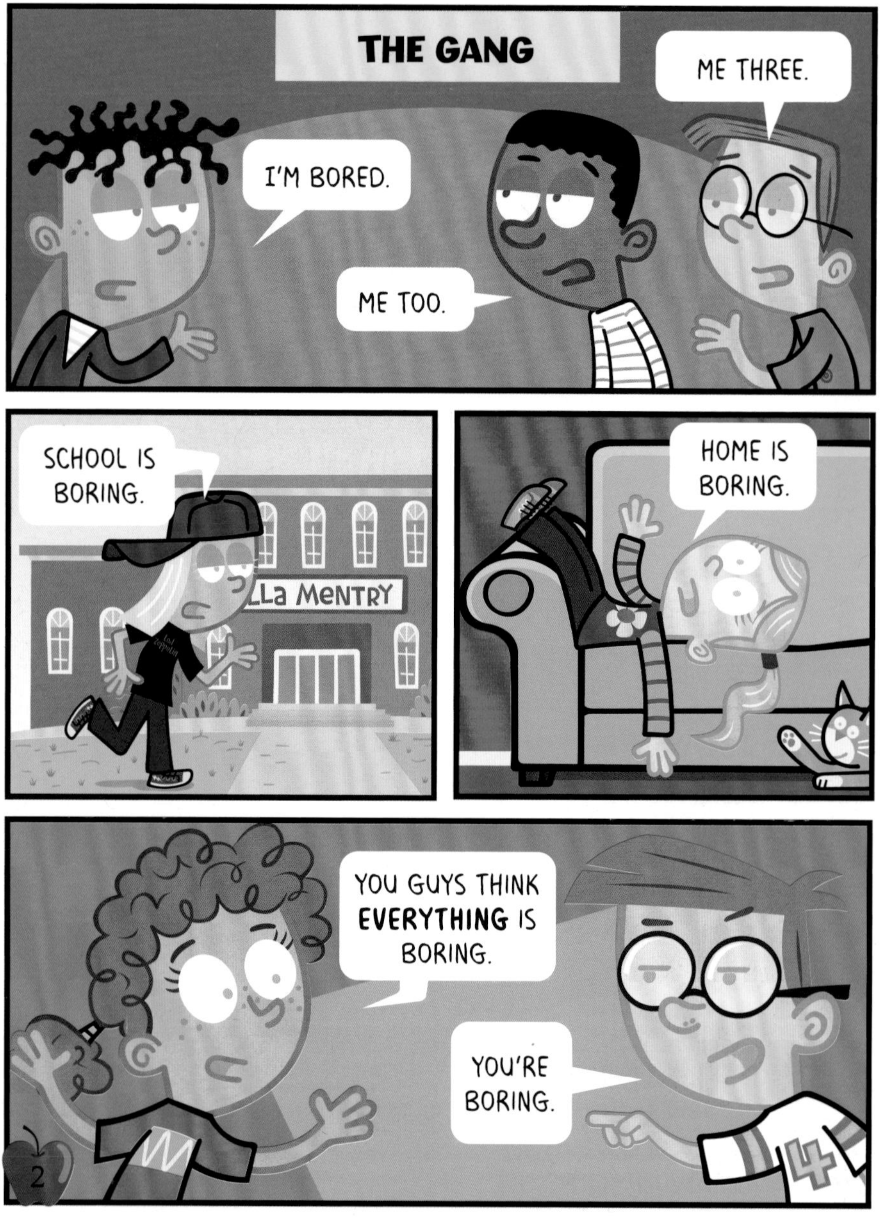

THE GANG
I'M BORED.
ME TOO.
ME THREE.
SCHOOL IS BORING.
LLa MENTRY
HOME IS BORING.
YOU GUYS THINK **EVERYTHING** IS BORING.
YOU'RE BORING.

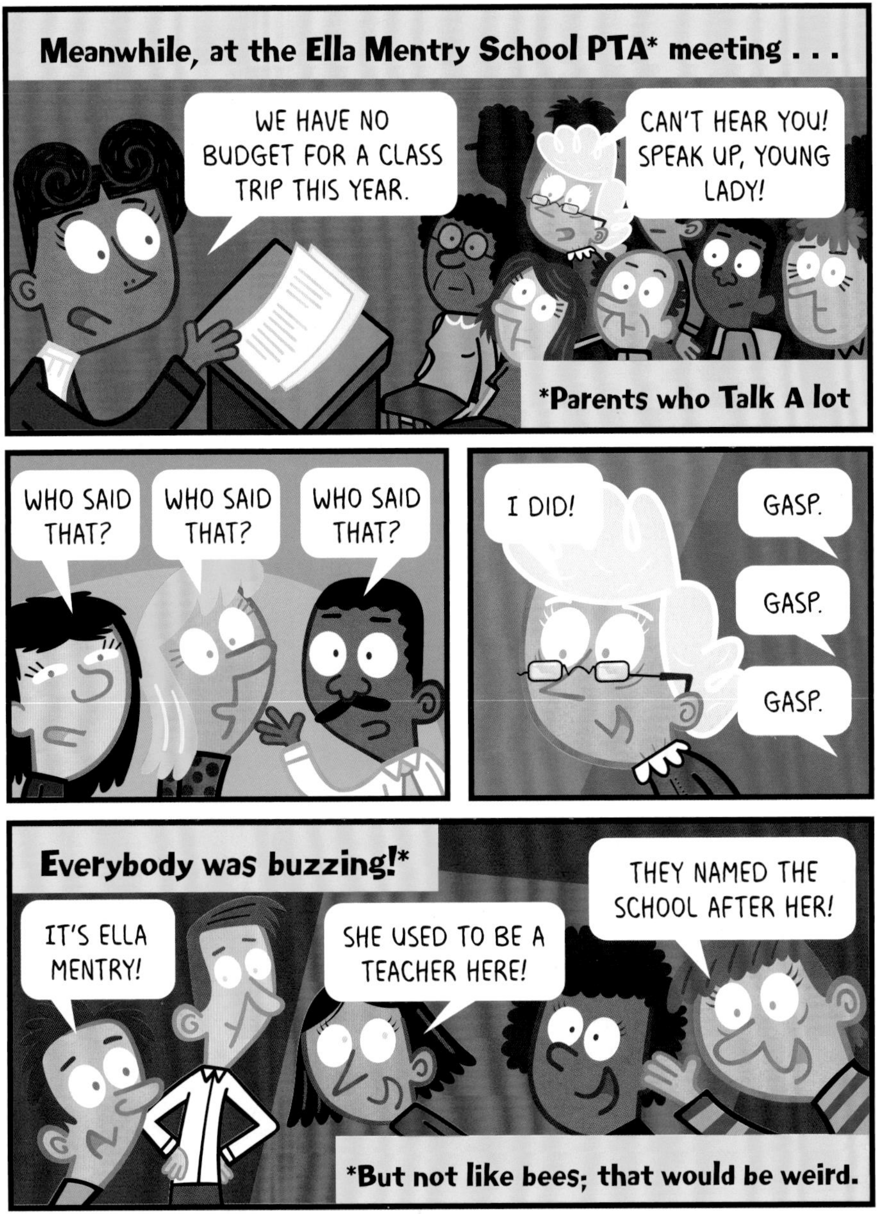
Meanwhile, at the Ella Mentry School PTA* meeting . . .
WE HAVE NO BUDGET FOR A CLASS TRIP THIS YEAR.
CAN'T HEAR YOU! SPEAK UP, YOUNG LADY!
*Parents who Talk A lot
WHO SAID THAT?
WHO SAID THAT?
WHO SAID THAT?
I DID!
GASP.
GASP.
GASP.
Everybody was buzzing!*
IT'S ELLA MENTRY!
SHE USED TO BE A TEACHER HERE!
THEY NAMED THE SCHOOL AFTER HER!
*But not like bees; that would be weird.

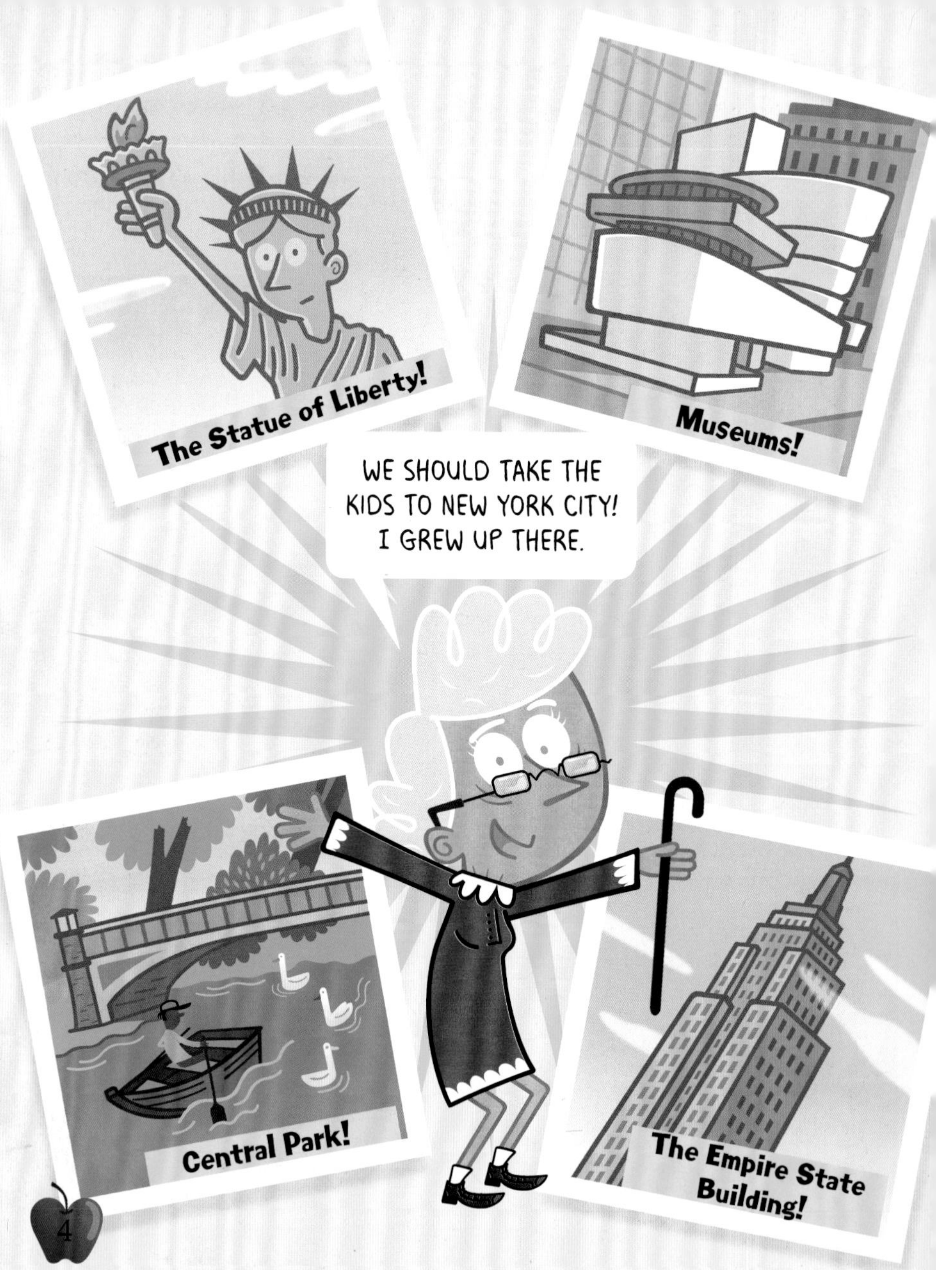
The Statue of Liberty!
Museums!
WE SHOULD TAKE THE KIDS TO NEW YORK CITY! I GREW UP THERE.
Central Park!
The Empire State Building!

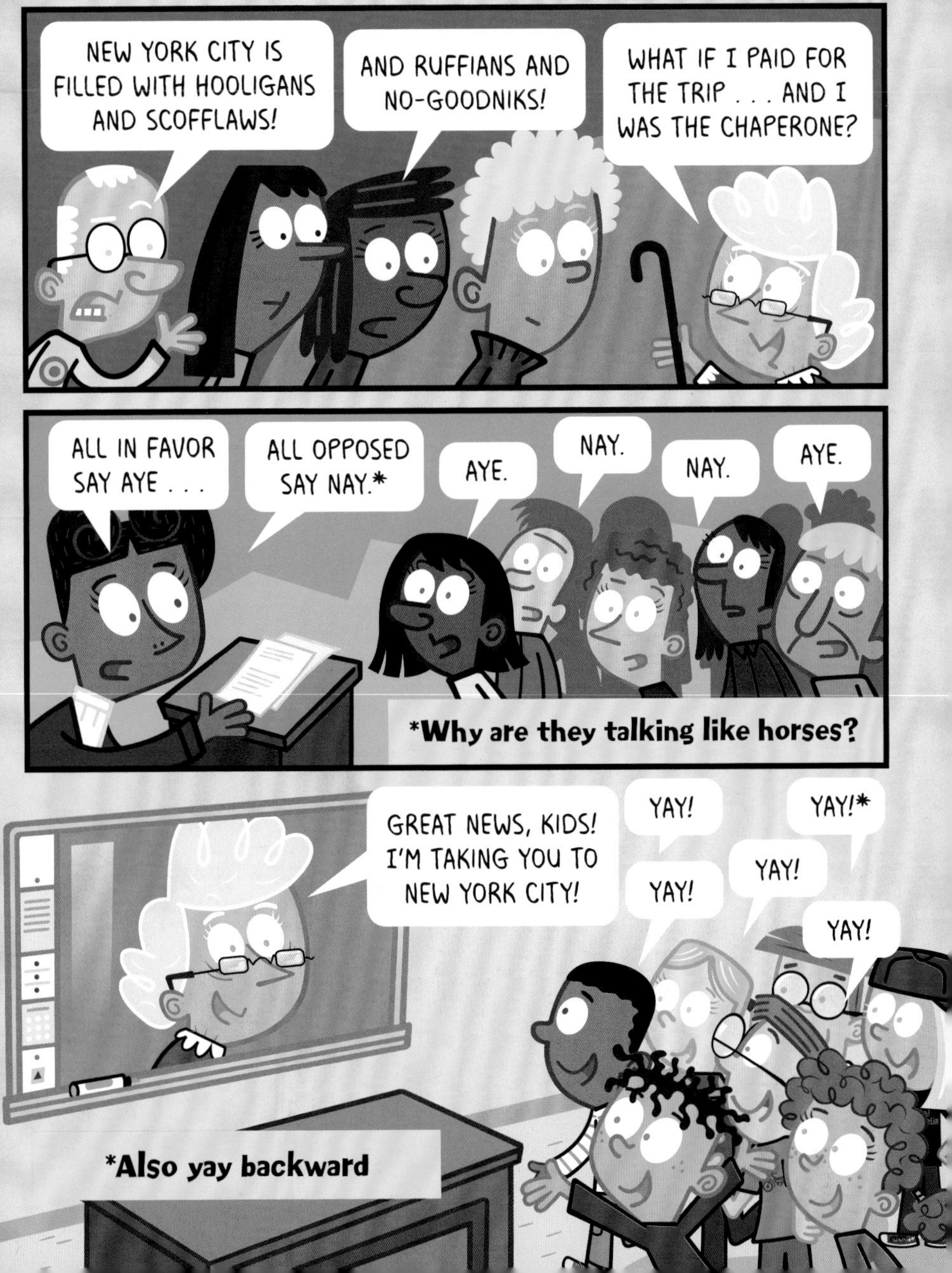
NEW YORK CITY IS FILLED WITH HOOLIGANS AND SCOFFLAWS!
AND RUFFIANS AND NO-GOODNIKS!
WHAT IF I PAID FOR THE TRIP . . . AND I WAS THE CHAPERONE?
ALL IN FAVOR SAY AYE . . .
ALL OPPOSED SAY NAY.*
AYE.
NAY.
NAY.
AYE.
*Why are they talking like horses?
GREAT NEWS, KIDS! I'M TAKING YOU TO NEW YORK CITY!
YAY!
YAY!*
YAY!
YAY!
YAY!
*Also yay backward

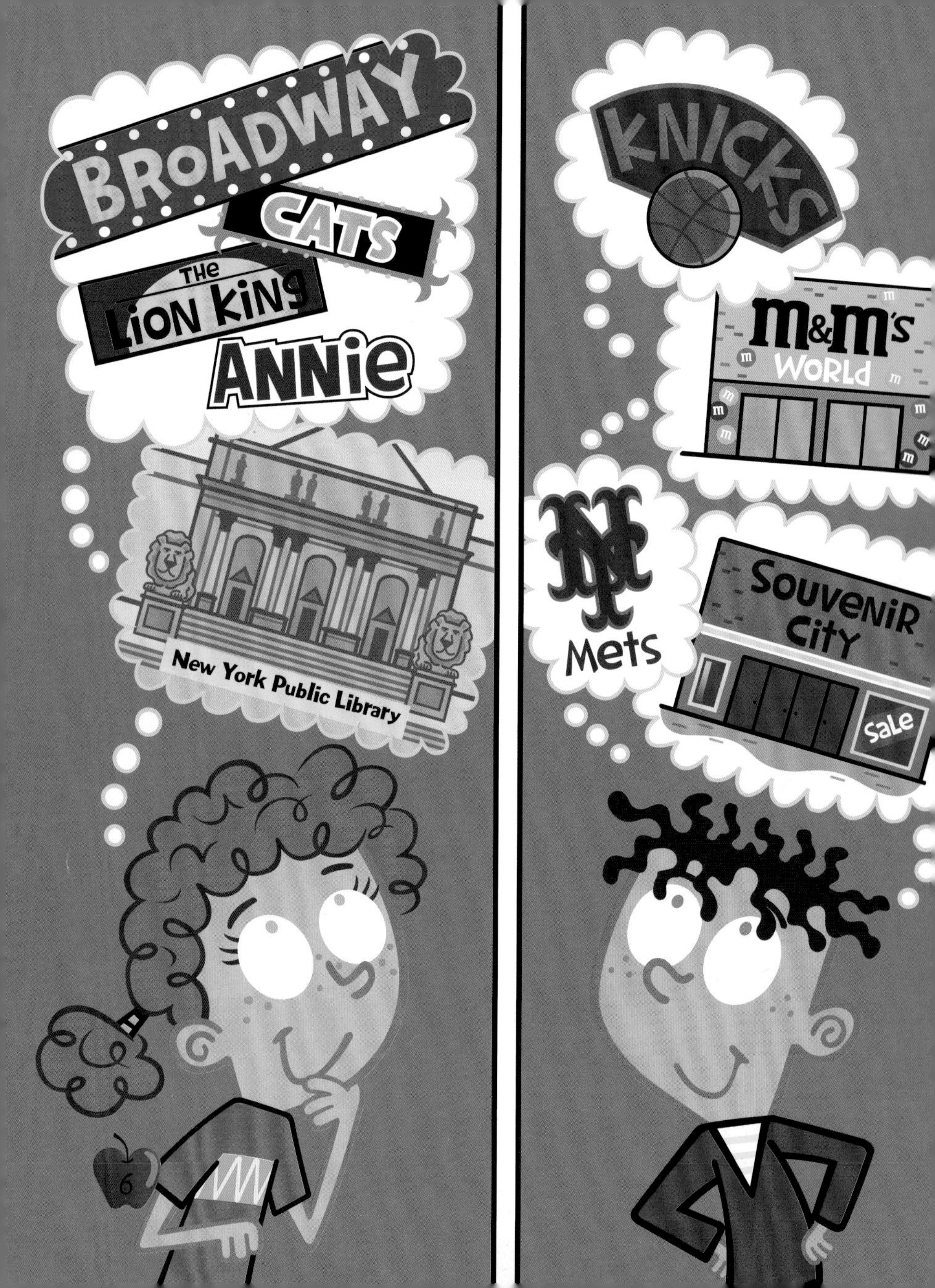
BROADWAY
CATS
THE LION KING
ANNIE
New York Public Library
KNICKS
M&M's WORLD
NY
Mets
SOUVENIR CITY
SALE

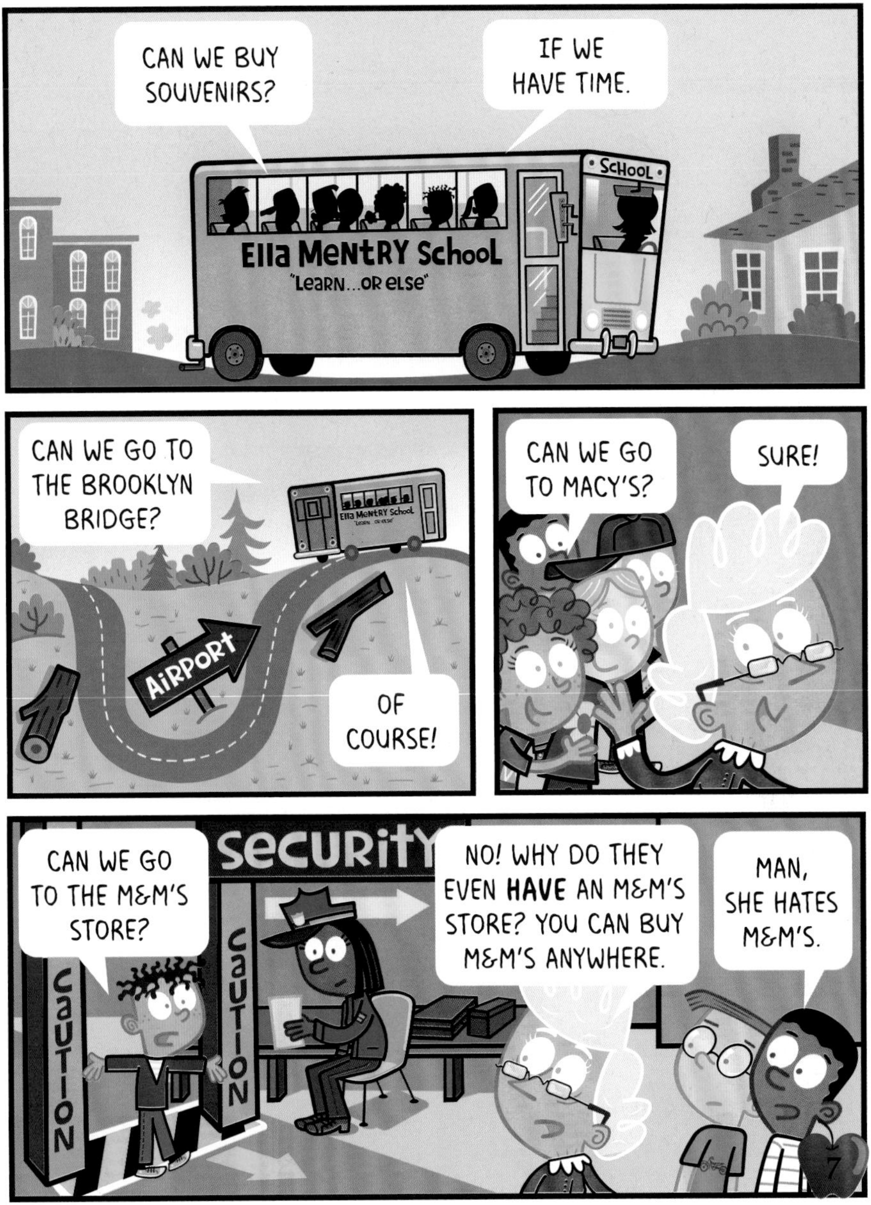
CAN WE BUY SOUVENIRS?
IF WE HAVE TIME.
SCHOOL
Ella MenTRY School
"LearN...OR eLSe"
CAN WE GO TO THE BROOKLYN BRIDGE?
Ella MenTRY School
AIRPORT
OF COURSE!
CAN WE GO TO MACY'S?
SURE!
CAN WE GO TO THE M&M'S STORE?
SECURITY
CAUTION
CAUTION
NO! WHY DO THEY EVEN **HAVE** AN M&M'S STORE? YOU CAN BUY M&M'S ANYWHERE.
MAN, SHE HATES M&M'S.

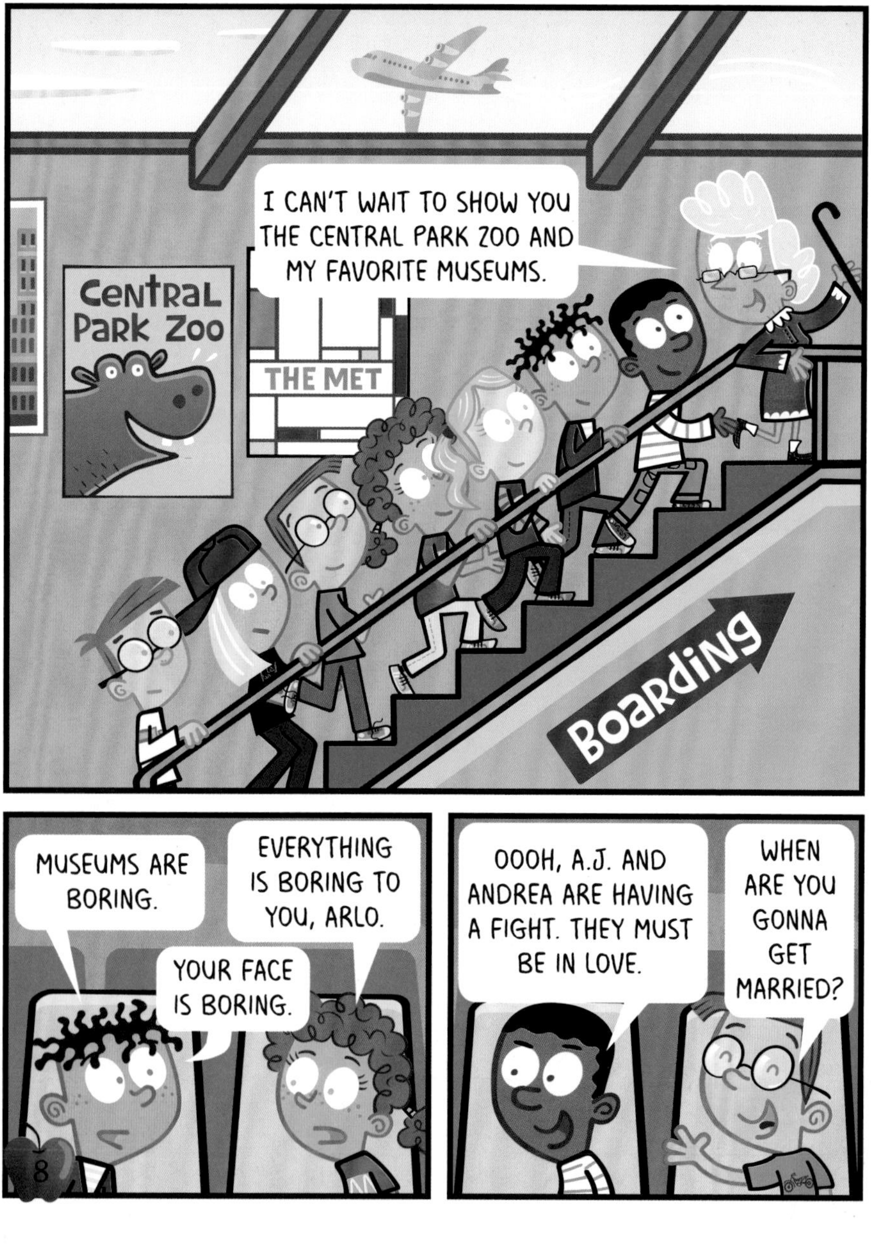

Central Park Zoo
THE MET
I CAN'T WAIT TO SHOW YOU THE CENTRAL PARK ZOO AND MY FAVORITE MUSEUMS.
Boarding
MUSEUMS ARE BORING.
EVERYTHING IS BORING TO YOU, ARLO.
YOUR FACE IS BORING.
OOOH, A.J. AND ANDREA ARE HAVING A FIGHT. THEY MUST BE IN LOVE.
WHEN ARE YOU GONNA GET MARRIED?

Weird Stuff about New York

IT'S A MISDEMEANOR TO FART IN NEW YORK CITY CHURCHES.

ALBERT EINSTEIN'S EYEBALLS ARE STORED IN A SAFE DEPOSIT BOX IN THE CITY.

THE EMPIRE STATE BUILDING HAS ITS OWN ZIP CODE.

MORE THAN 800 LANGUAGES ARE SPOKEN IN NEW YORK CITY.

NEW YORK CITY WAS THE FIRST CAPITAL OF THE UNITED STATES, IN 1789.

ONE OUT OF EVERY 38 PEOPLE IN THE UNITED STATES LIVES IN NEW YORK CITY.

TIMES SQUARE WAS NAMED AFTER THE *NEW YORK TIMES*.

MORE PUERTO RICANS LIVE IN NEW YORK THAN IN ANY CITY IN PUERTO RICO.

THE FEDERAL RESERVE BANK HAS 7,000 TONS OF GOLD BARS, THE LARGEST GOLD STORAGE IN THE WORLD.

275 SPECIES OF BIRDS HAVE BEEN SPOTTED IN CENTRAL PARK.

INVENTED IN NEW YORK: ENGLISH MUFFINS, JELL-O, POTATO CHIPS, TOILET PAPER, AIR-CONDITIONING, THE TUXEDO, EGGS BENEDICT, CHEWING GUM, TEDDY BEARS, SCRABBLE, HOT DOGS, HIP-HOP, MR. POTATO HEAD

THAT'S WEIRD.

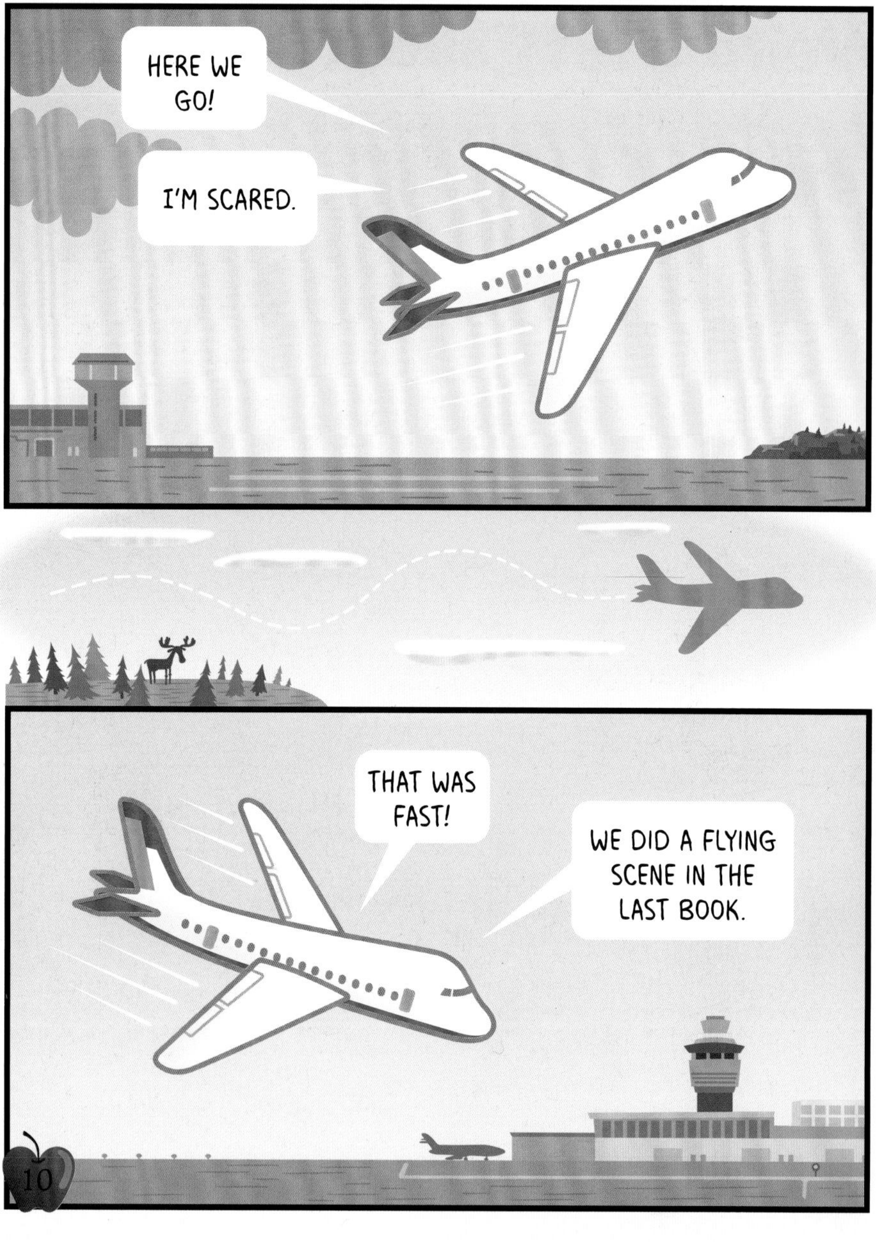
HERE WE GO!
I'M SCARED.
THAT WAS FAST!
WE DID A FLYING SCENE IN THE LAST BOOK.

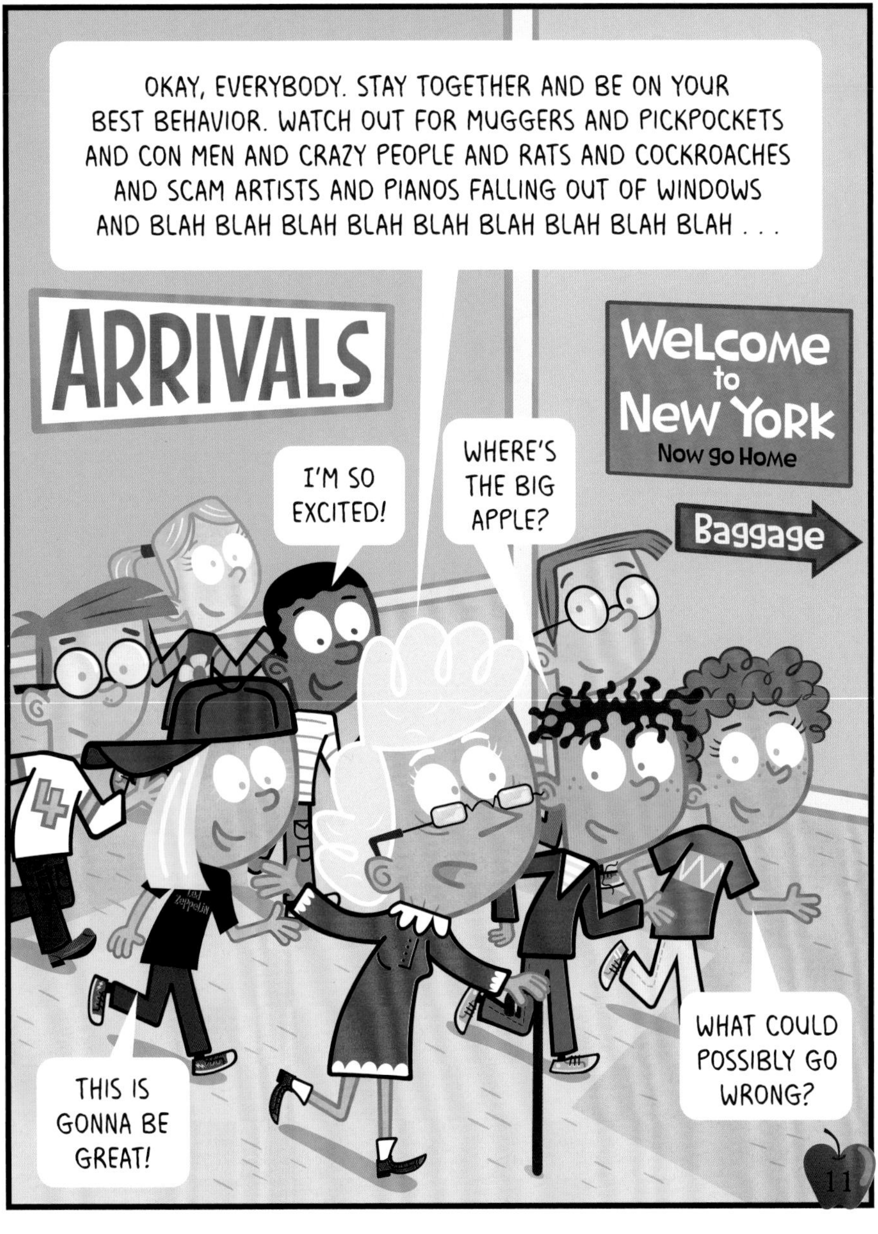
OKAY, EVERYBODY. STAY TOGETHER AND BE ON YOUR BEST BEHAVIOR. WATCH OUT FOR MUGGERS AND PICKPOCKETS AND CON MEN AND CRAZY PEOPLE AND RATS AND COCKROACHES AND SCAM ARTISTS AND PIANOS FALLING OUT OF WINDOWS AND BLAH BLAH BLAH BLAH BLAH BLAH BLAH BLAH BLAH . . .
ARRIVALS
Welcome to New York
Now go Home
I'M SO EXCITED!
WHERE'S THE BIG APPLE?
Baggage
THIS IS GONNA BE GREAT!
WHAT COULD POSSIBLY GO WRONG?

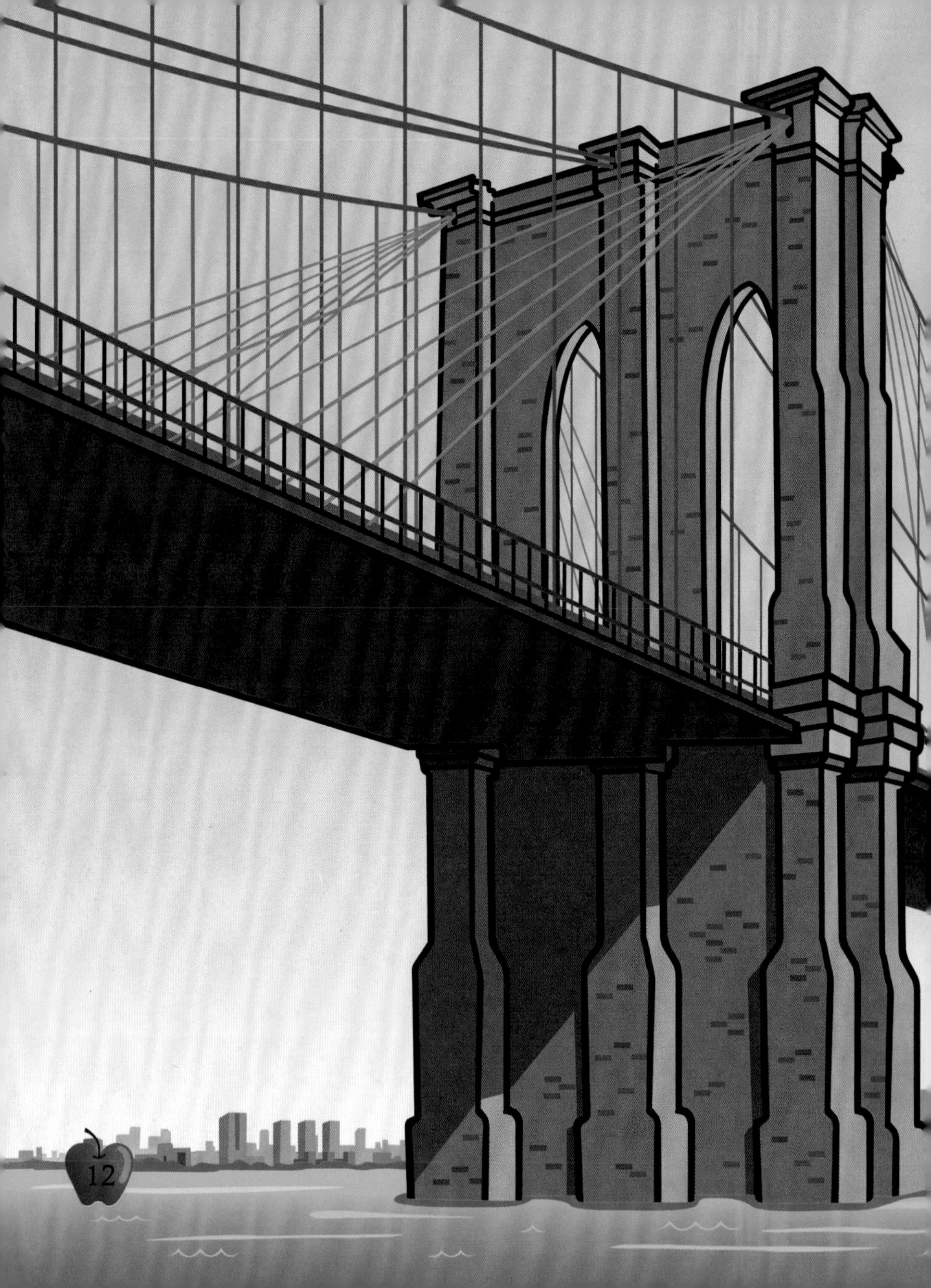

CHAPTER 2

People Who Don't Flush the Toilet

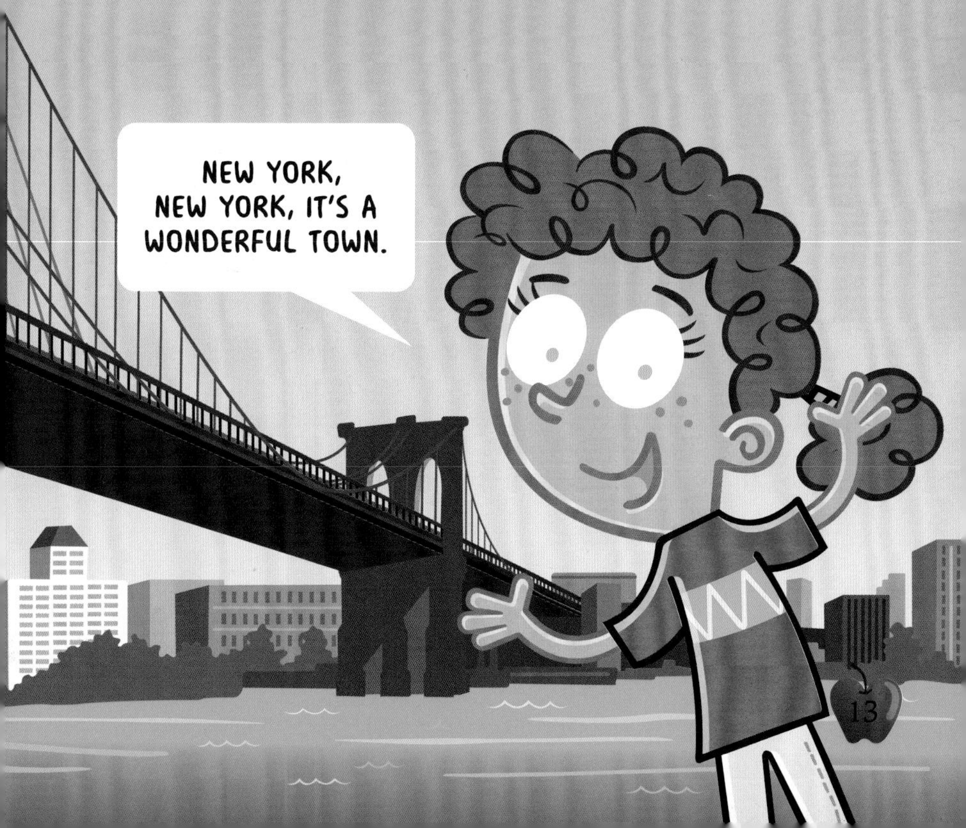
NEW YORK, NEW YORK, IT'S A WONDERFUL TOWN.

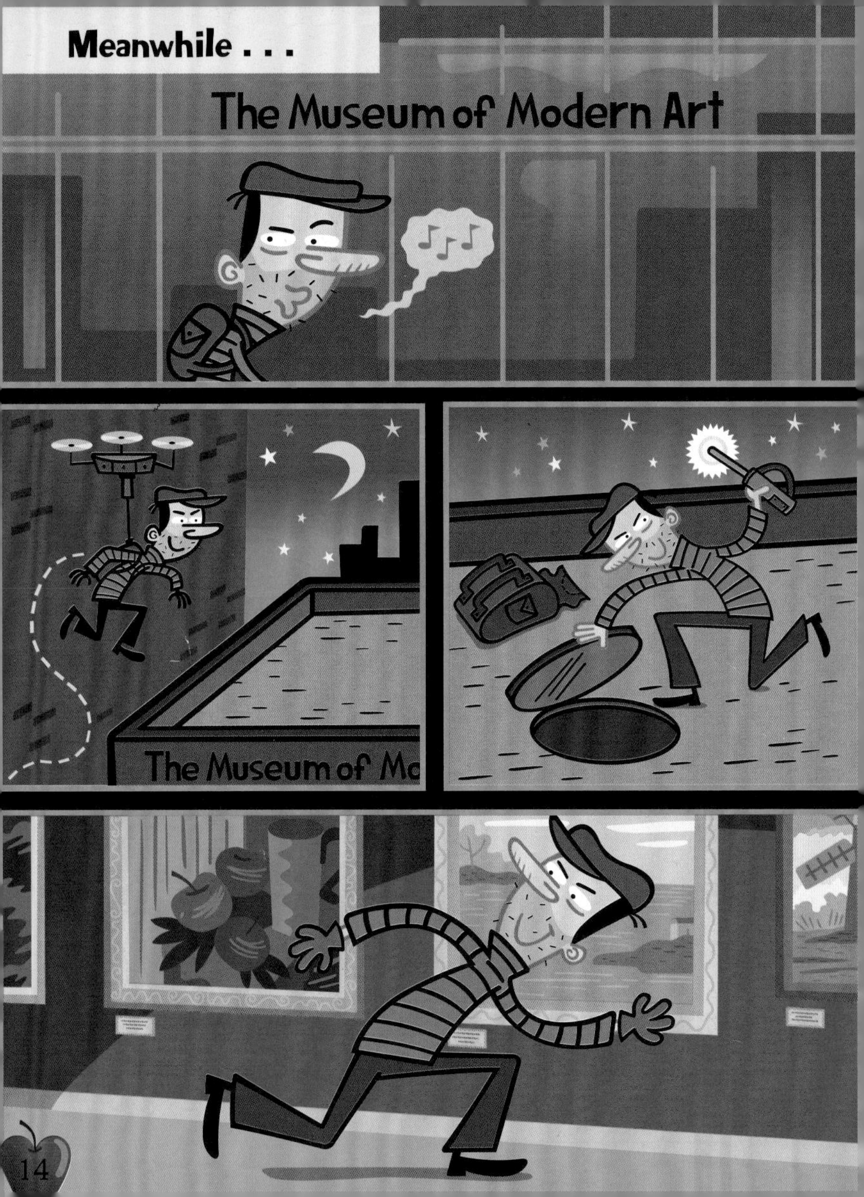
Meanwhile . . .
The Museum of Modern Art
The Museum of Mo

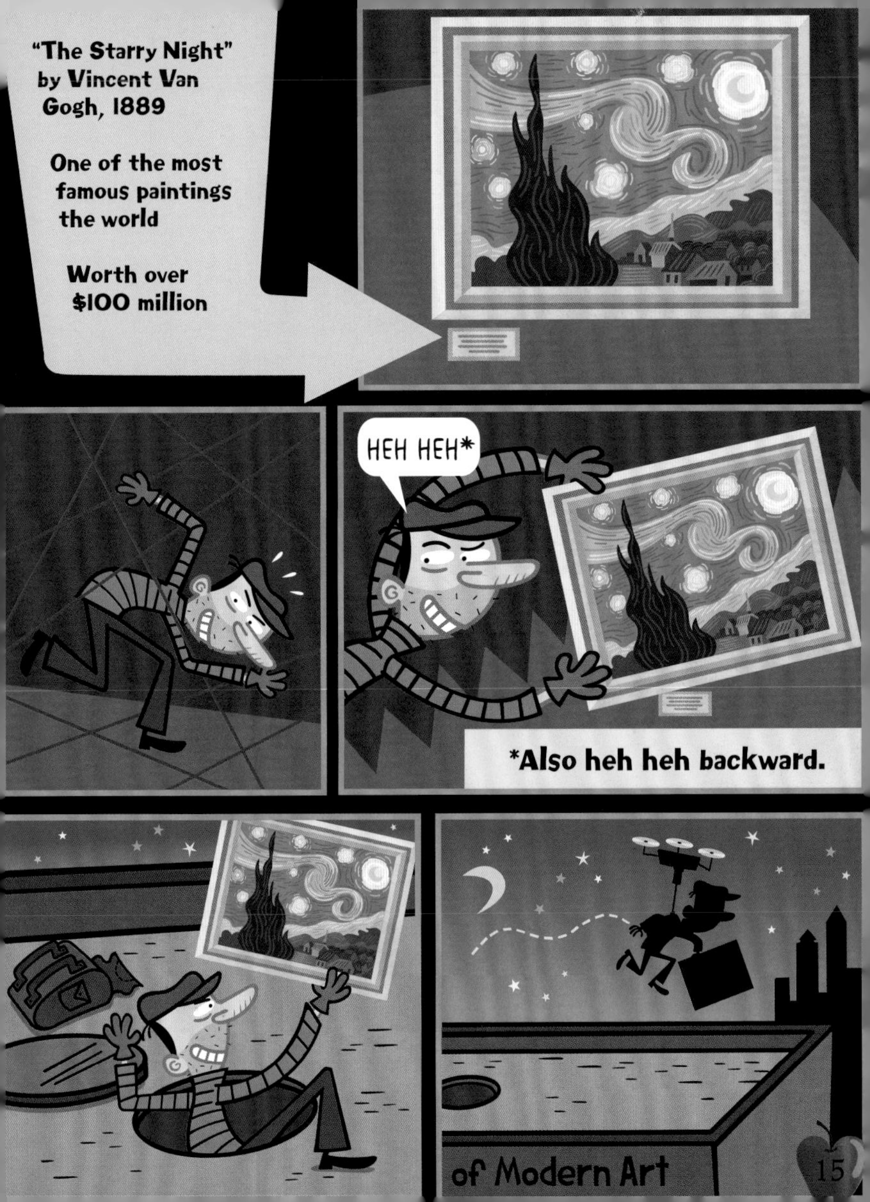
"The Starry Night" by Vincent Van Gogh, 1889
One of the most famous paintings the world
Worth over $100 million
HEH HEH*
*Also heh heh backward.
of Modern Art

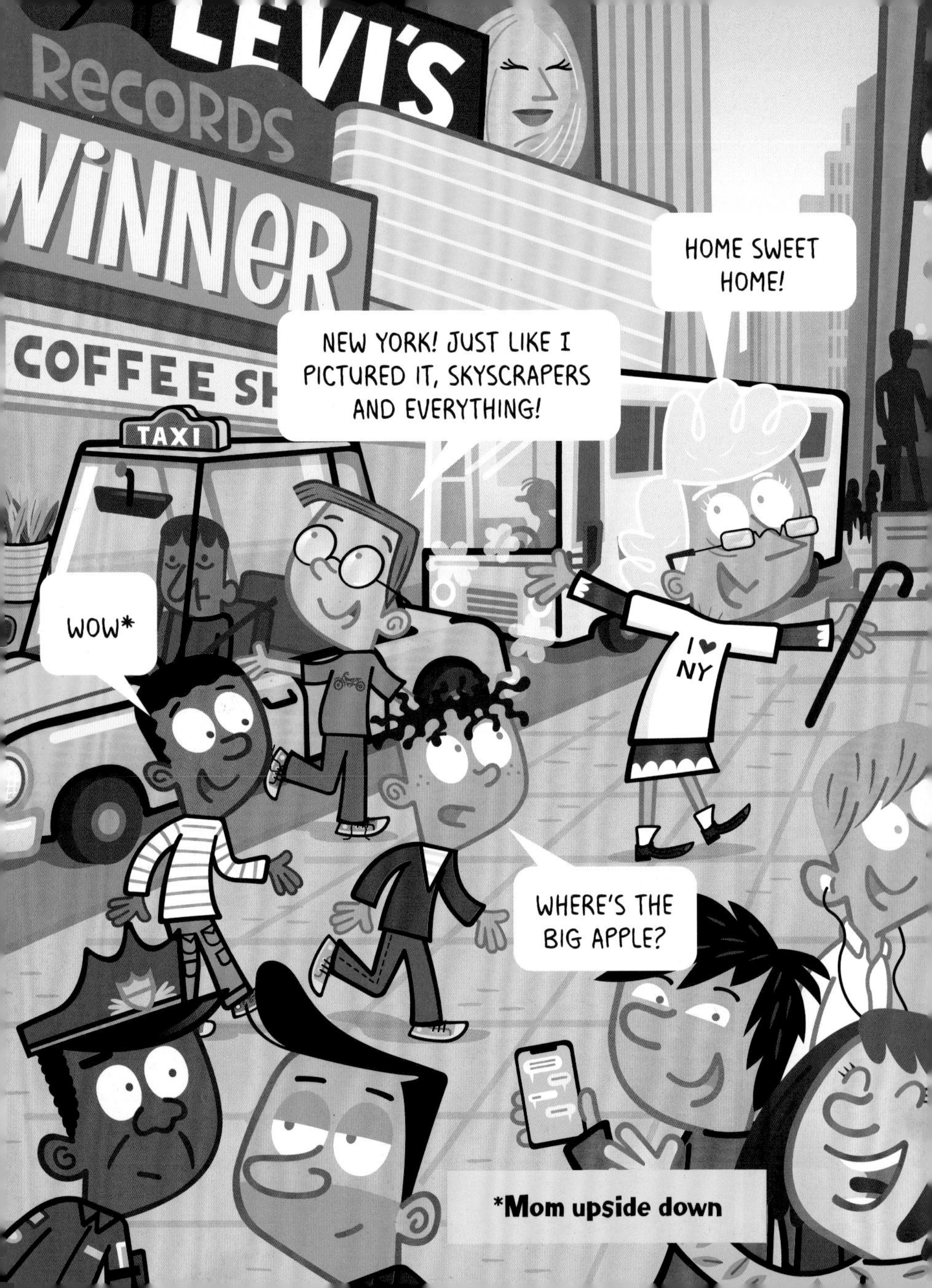
LEVI'S
RECORDS
WINNER
COFFEE SH
TAXI
HOME SWEET HOME!
NEW YORK! JUST LIKE I PICTURED IT, SKYSCRAPERS AND EVERYTHING!
WOW*
I ♥ NY
WHERE'S THE BIG APPLE?
*Mom upside down

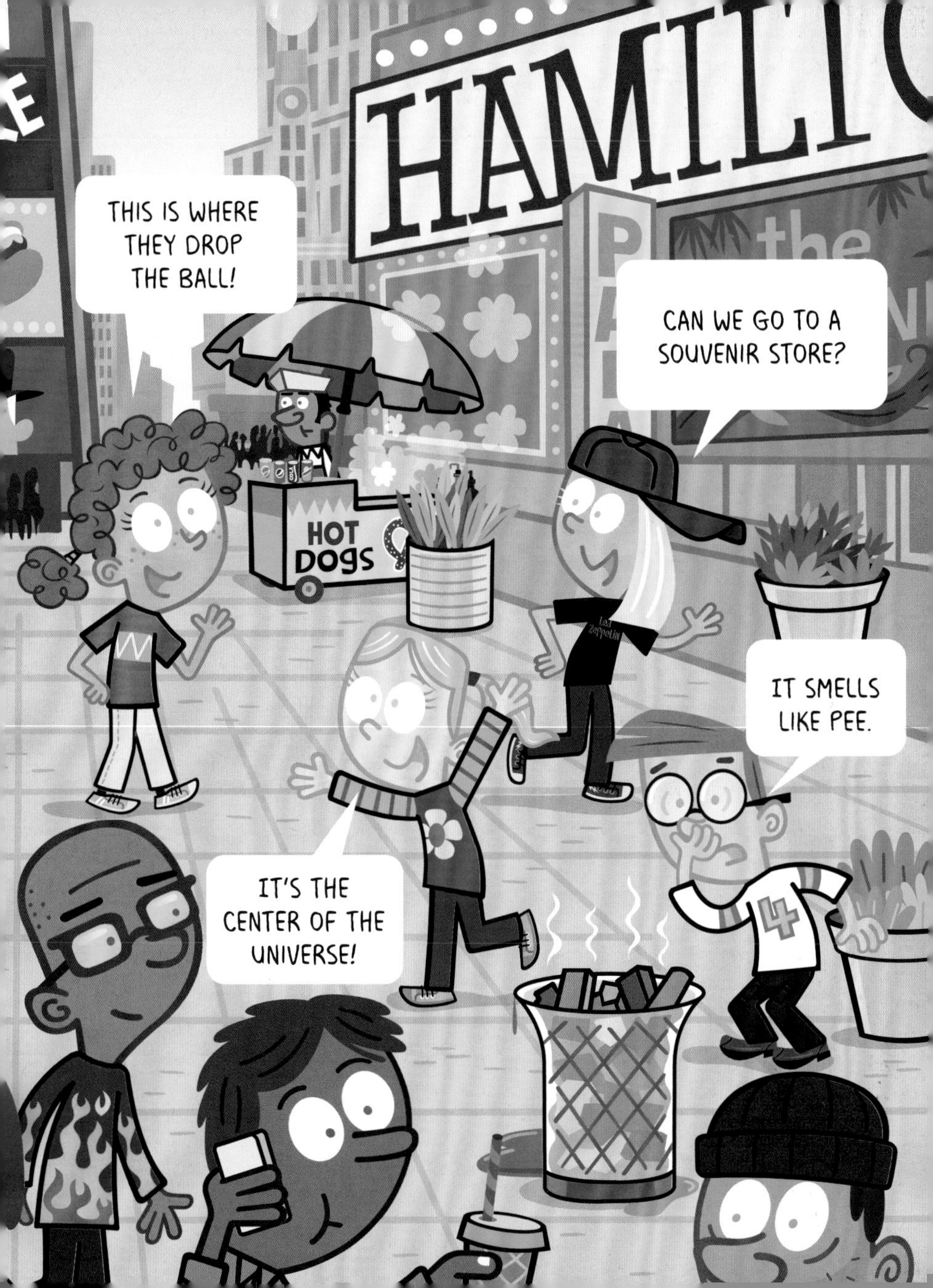
HAMILT
THIS IS WHERE THEY DROP THE BALL!
CAN WE GO TO A SOUVENIR STORE?
HOT DOGS
IT'S THE CENTER OF THE UNIVERSE!
IT SMELLS LIKE PEE.

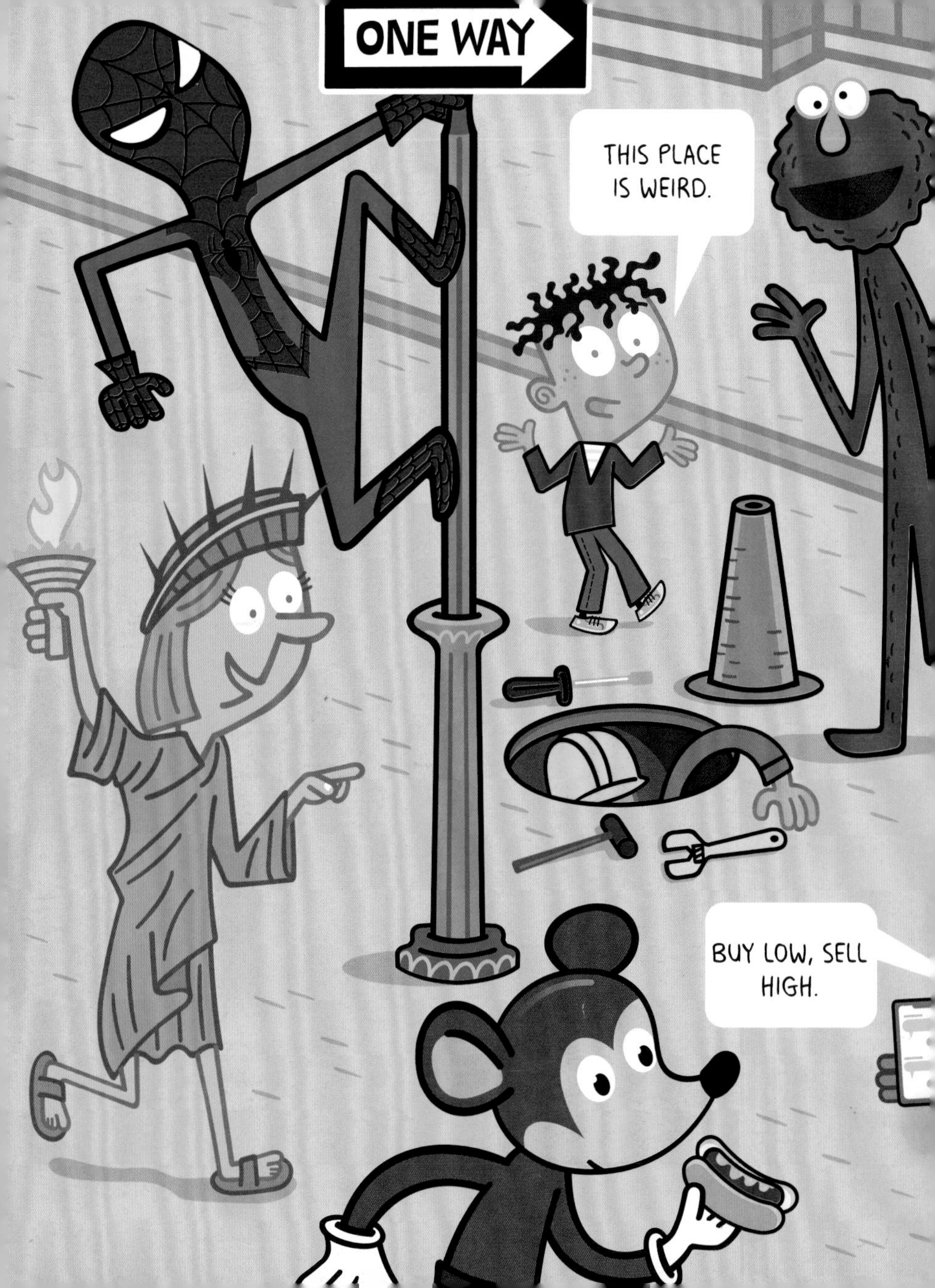
ONE WAY
THIS PLACE IS WEIRD.
BUY LOW, SELL HIGH.

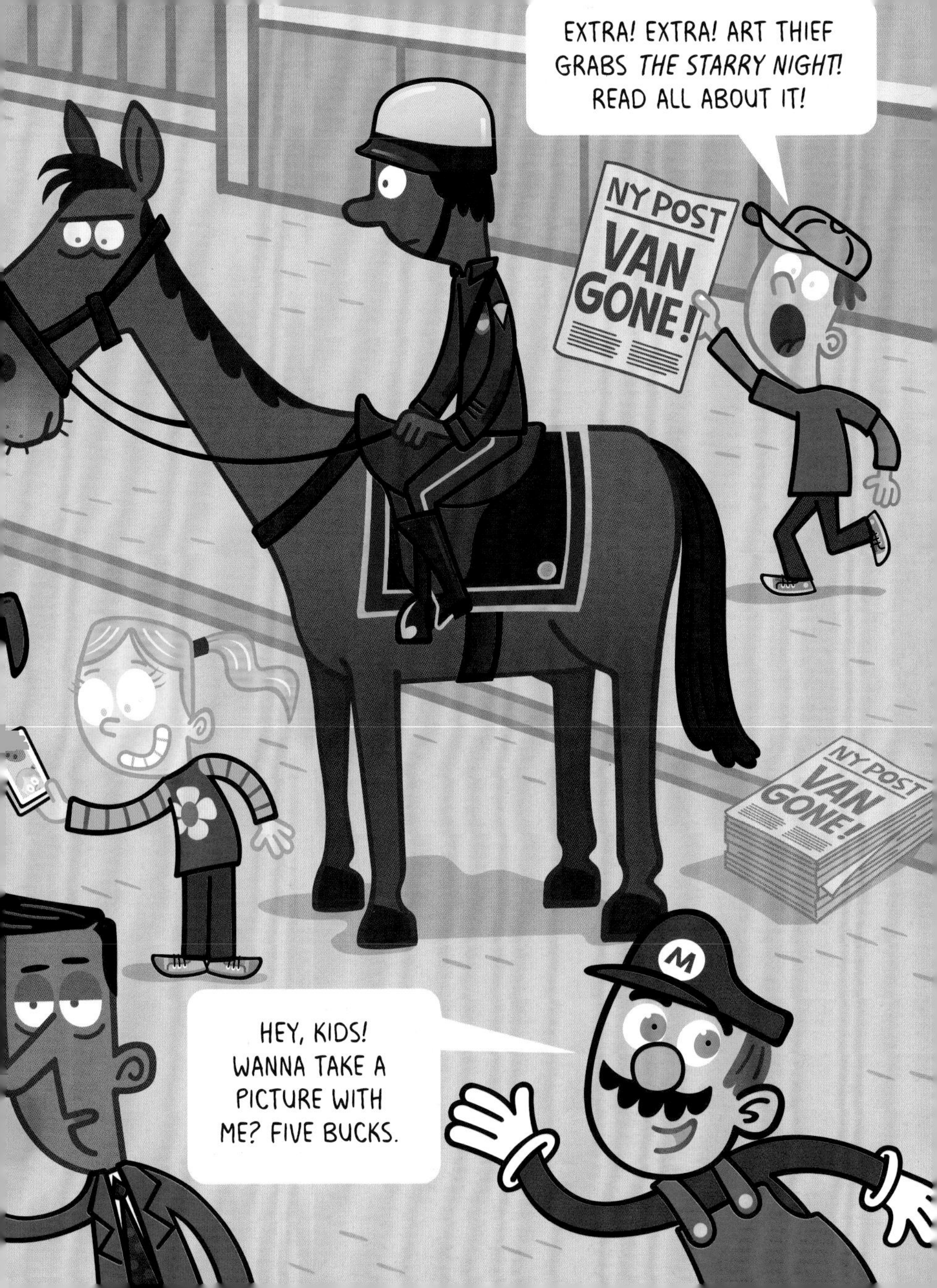
EXTRA! EXTRA! ART THIEF GRABS *THE STARRY NIGHT*! READ ALL ABOUT IT!
NY POST
VAN GONE!
NY POST
VAN GONE!
HEY, KIDS! WANNA TAKE A PICTURE WITH ME? FIVE BUCKS.

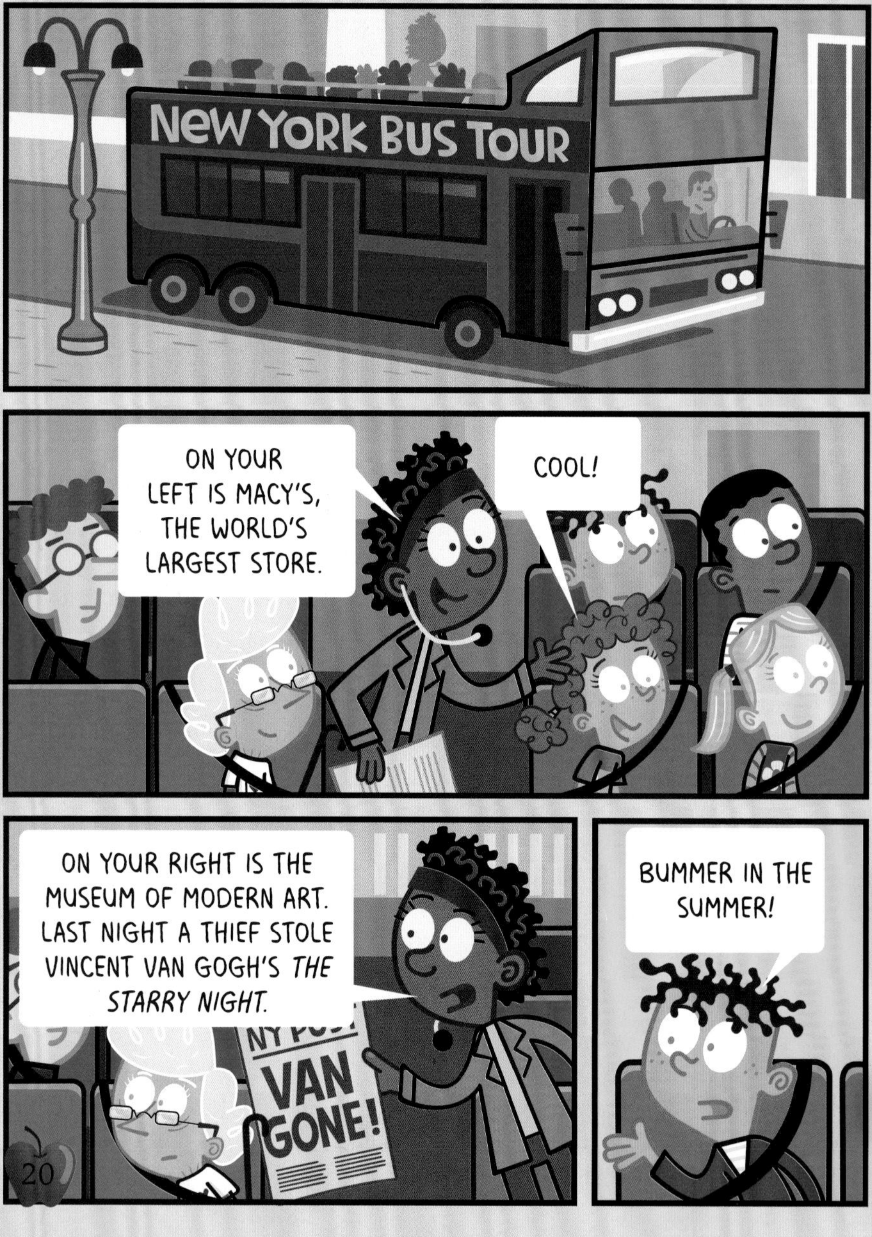
NEW YORK BUS TOUR
ON YOUR LEFT IS MACY'S, THE WORLD'S LARGEST STORE.
COOL!
ON YOUR RIGHT IS THE MUSEUM OF MODERN ART. LAST NIGHT A THIEF STOLE VINCENT VAN GOGH'S *THE STARRY NIGHT*.
VAN GONE!
BUMMER IN THE SUMMER!

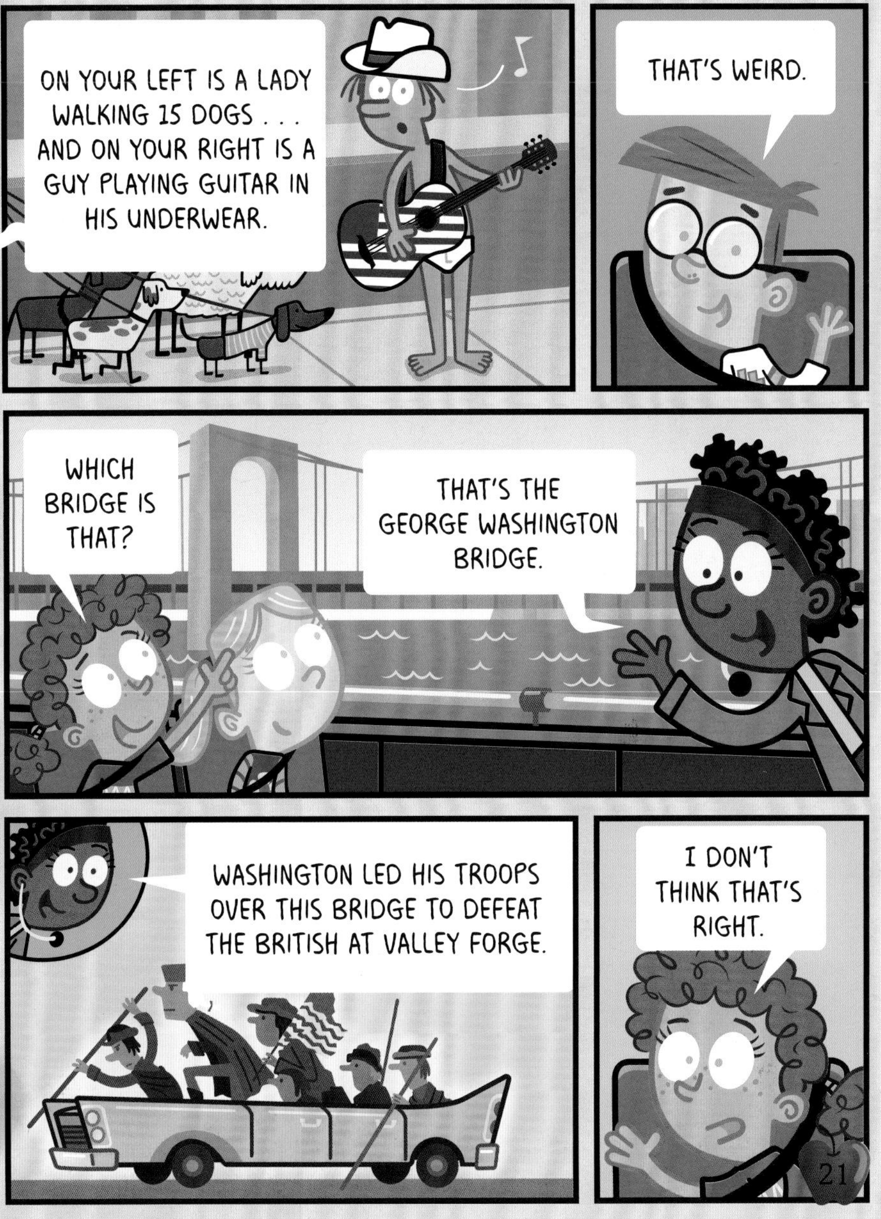
ON YOUR LEFT IS A LADY WALKING 15 DOGS . . . AND ON YOUR RIGHT IS A GUY PLAYING GUITAR IN HIS UNDERWEAR.
THAT'S WEIRD.
WHICH BRIDGE IS THAT?
THAT'S THE GEORGE WASHINGTON BRIDGE.
WASHINGTON LED HIS TROOPS OVER THIS BRIDGE TO DEFEAT THE BRITISH AT VALLEY FORGE.
I DON'T THINK THAT'S RIGHT.

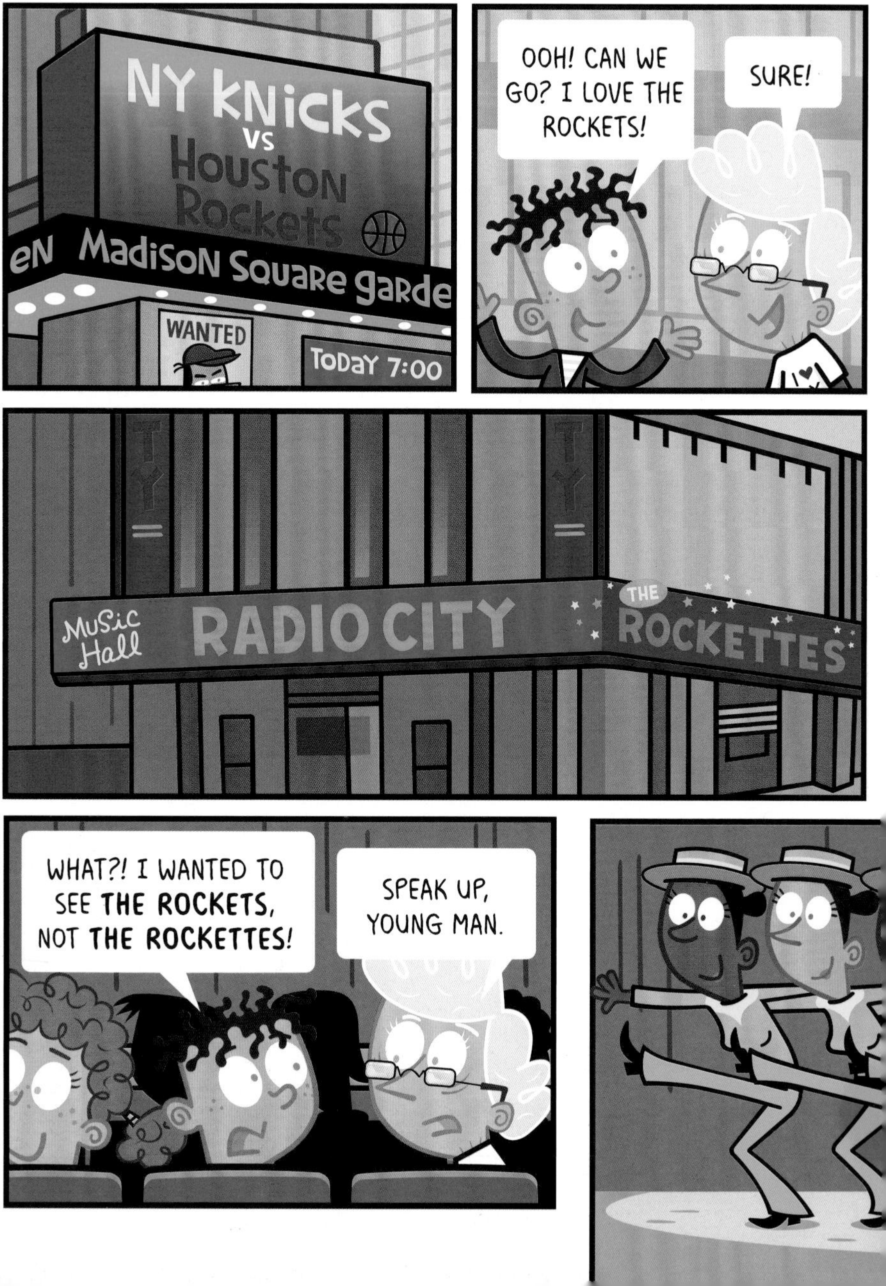
NY KNICKS VS HOUSTON ROCKETS
EN MADISON SQUARE GARDE
WANTED
TODAY 7:00
OOH! CAN WE GO? I LOVE THE ROCKETS!
SURE!
MUSIC HALL
RADIO CITY
THE ROCKETTES
WHAT?! I WANTED TO SEE **THE ROCKETS**, NOT **THE ROCKETTES**!
SPEAK UP, YOUNG MAN.

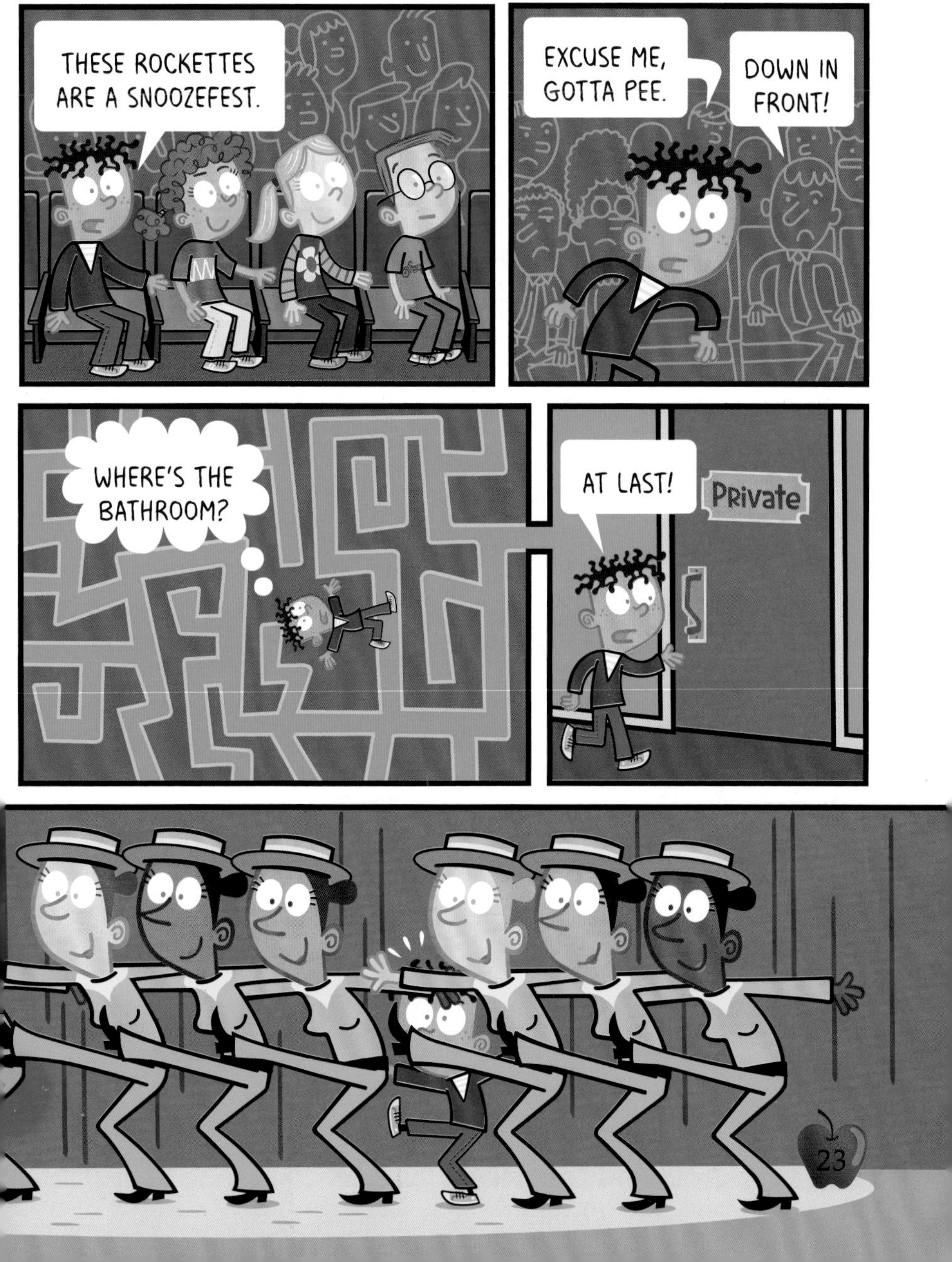
THESE ROCKETTES ARE A SNOOZEFEST.
EXCUSE ME, GOTTA PEE.
DOWN IN FRONT!
WHERE'S THE BATHROOM?
AT LAST!
PRIVATE

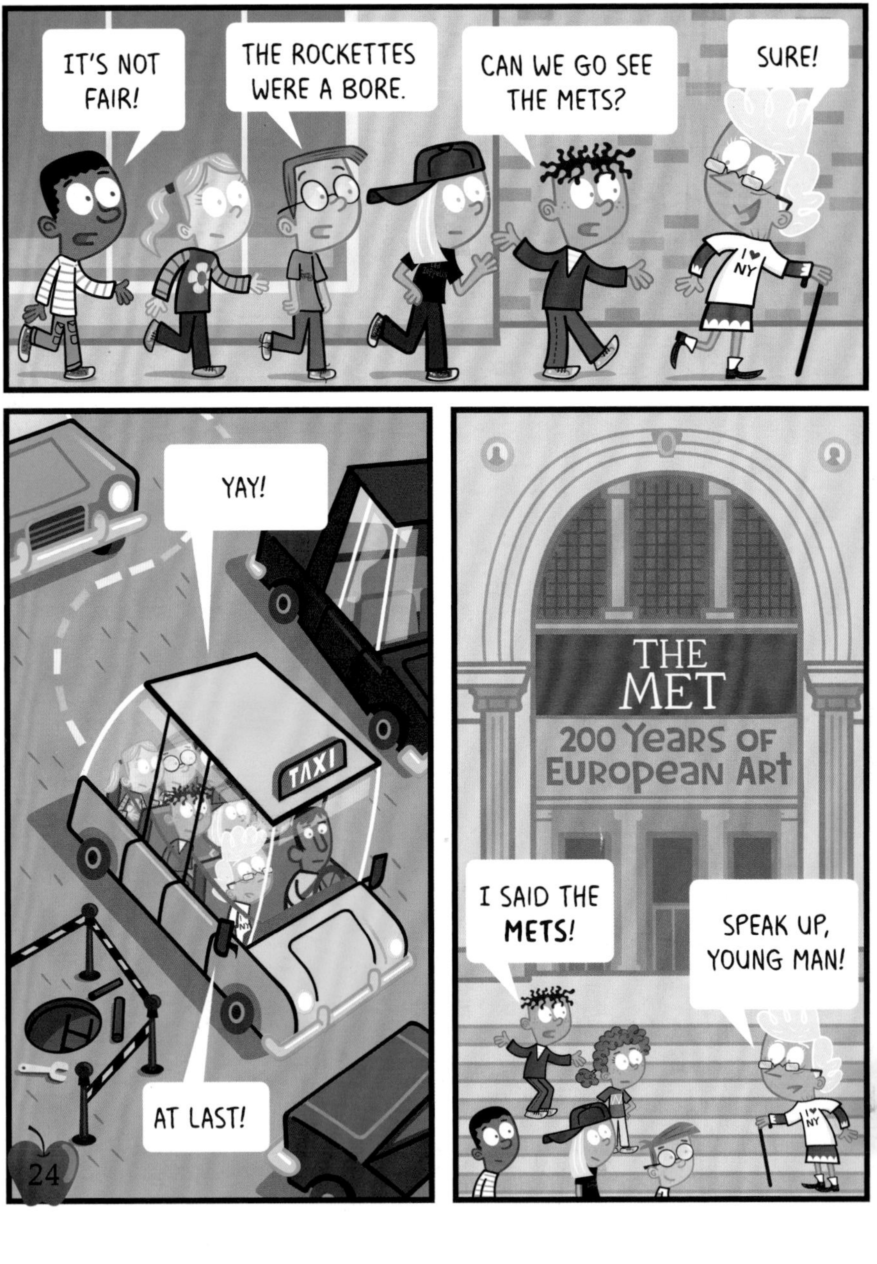
IT'S NOT FAIR!
THE ROCKETTES WERE A BORE.
CAN WE GO SEE THE METS?
SURE!
I ♥ NY
YAY!
TAXI
AT LAST!
THE MET
200 Years of European Art
I SAID THE **METS!**
SPEAK UP, YOUNG MAN!

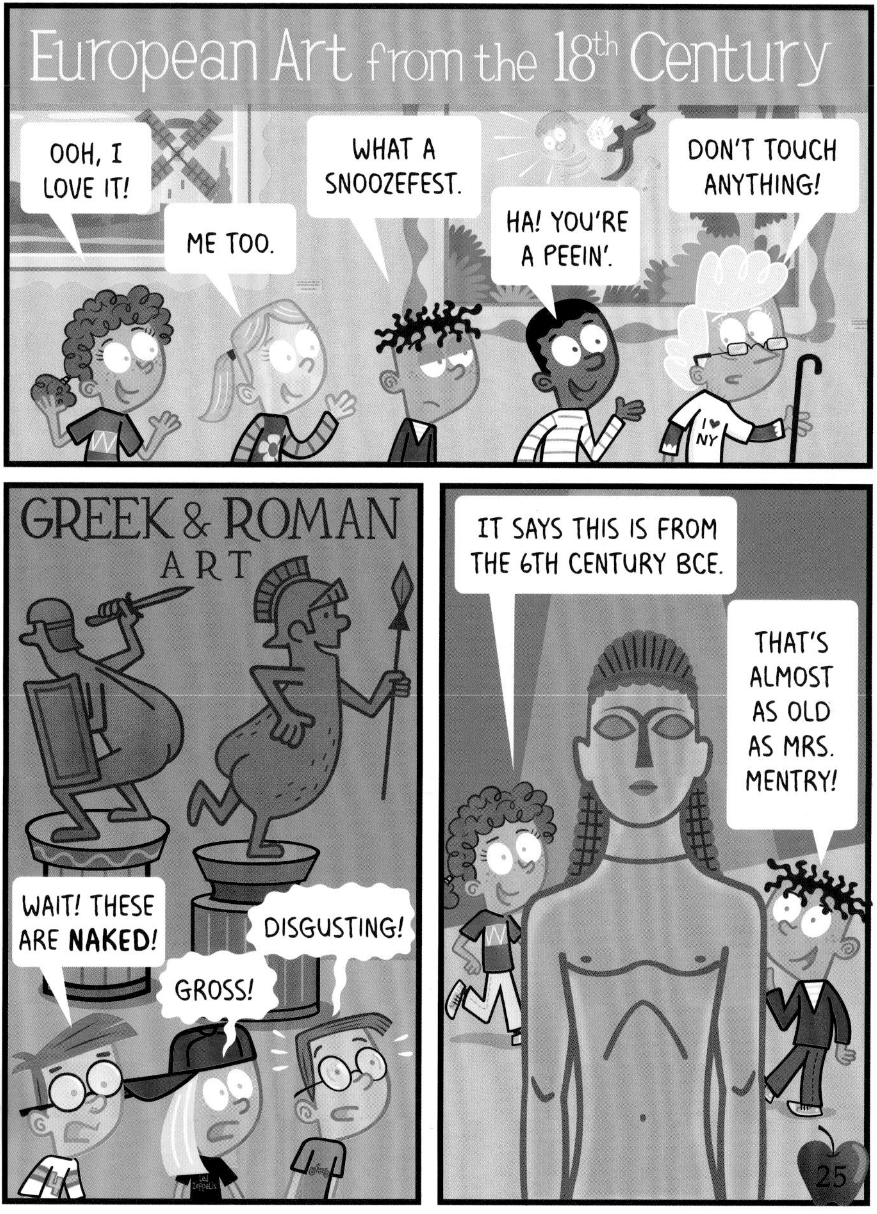

European Art from the 18th Century
OOH, I LOVE IT!
ME TOO.
WHAT A SNOOZEFEST.
HA! YOU'RE A PEEIN'.
DON'T TOUCH ANYTHING!
GREEK & ROMAN ART
WAIT! THESE ARE **NAKED!**
GROSS!
DISGUSTING!
IT SAYS THIS IS FROM THE 6TH CENTURY BCE.
THAT'S ALMOST AS OLD AS MRS. MENTRY!

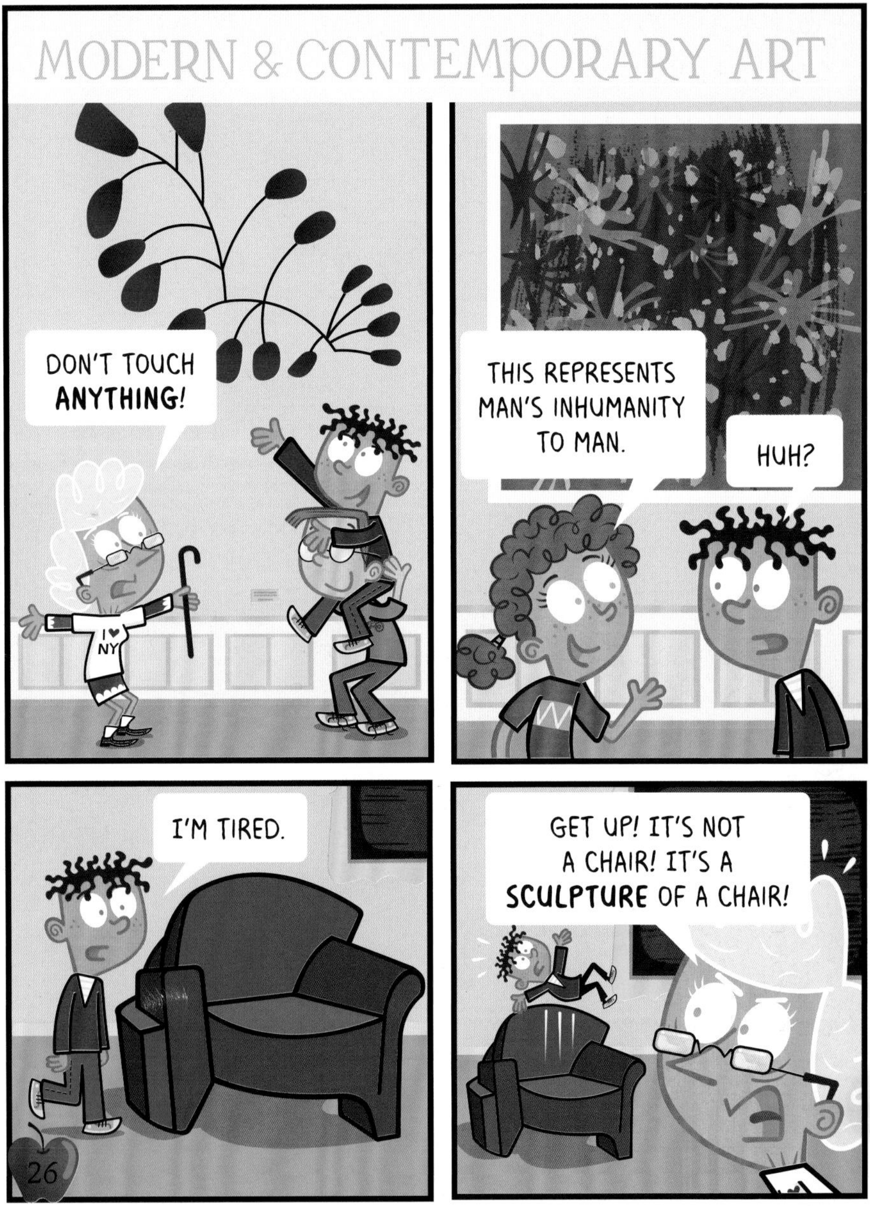
MODERN & CONTEMPORARY ART
DON'T TOUCH **ANYTHING**!
THIS REPRESENTS MAN'S INHUMANITY TO MAN.
HUH?
I'M TIRED.
GET UP! IT'S NOT A CHAIR! IT'S A **SCULPTURE** OF A CHAIR!

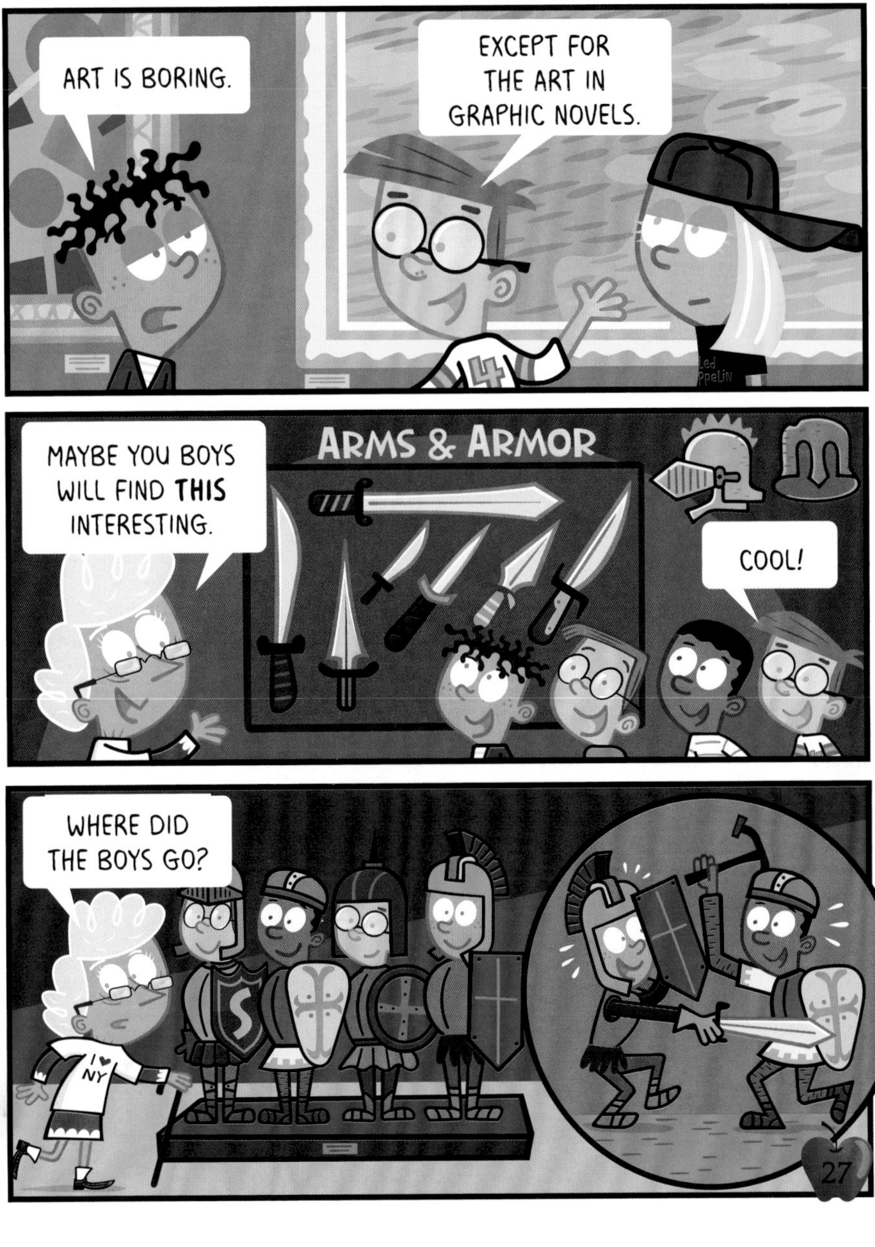
ART IS BORING.
EXCEPT FOR THE ART IN GRAPHIC NOVELS.
Led Zeppelin
MAYBE YOU BOYS WILL FIND **THIS** INTERESTING.
ARMS & ARMOR
COOL!
WHERE DID THE BOYS GO?
I ♥ NY

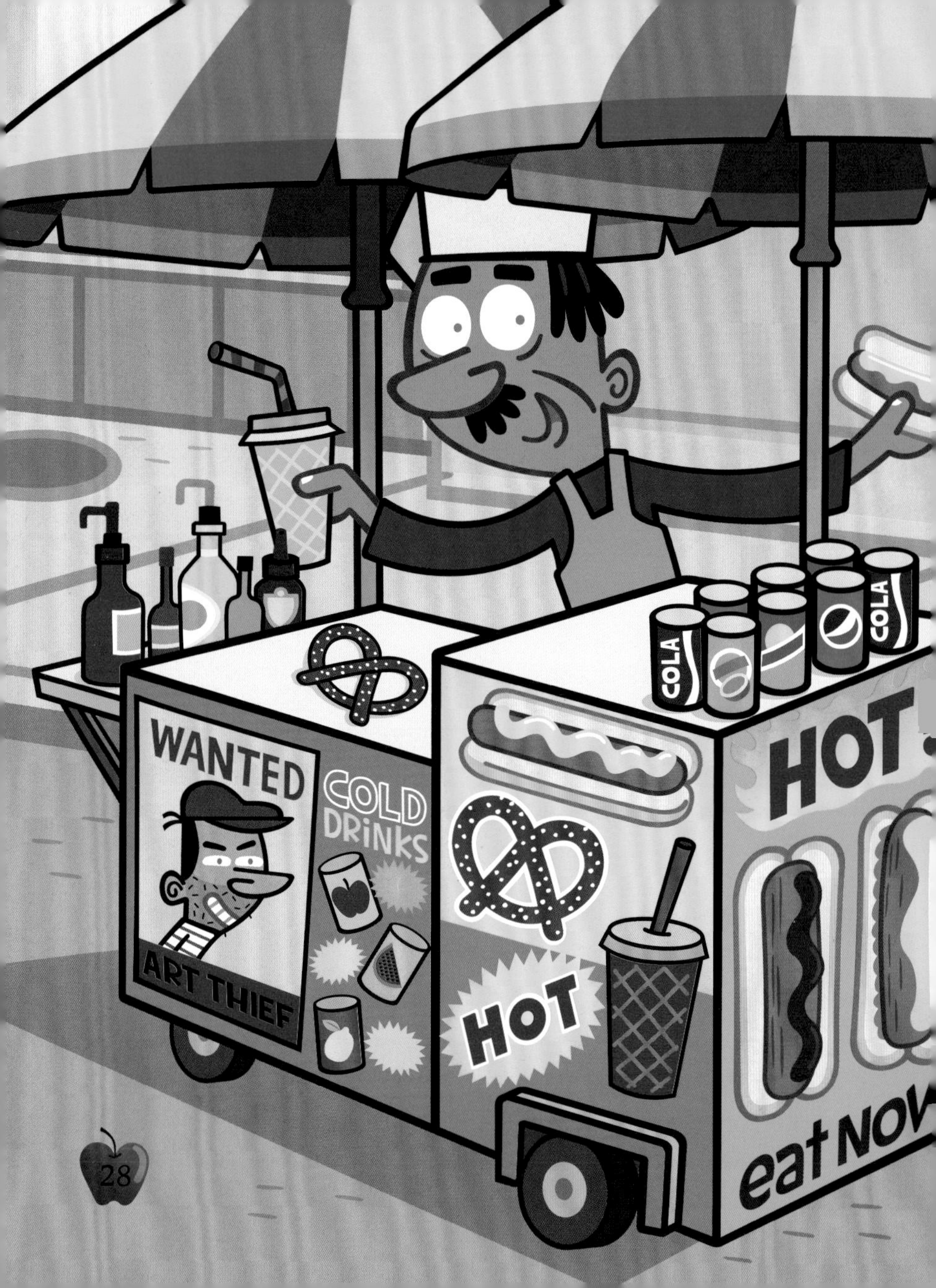
WANTED
ART THIEF
COLD DRINKS
COLA
COLA
HOT
HOT
eat NOW

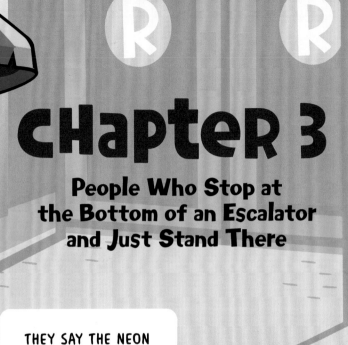

CHAPTER 3

People Who Stop at the Bottom of an Escalator and Just Stand There

THEY SAY THE NEON LIGHTS ARE BRIGHT ON BROADWAY.

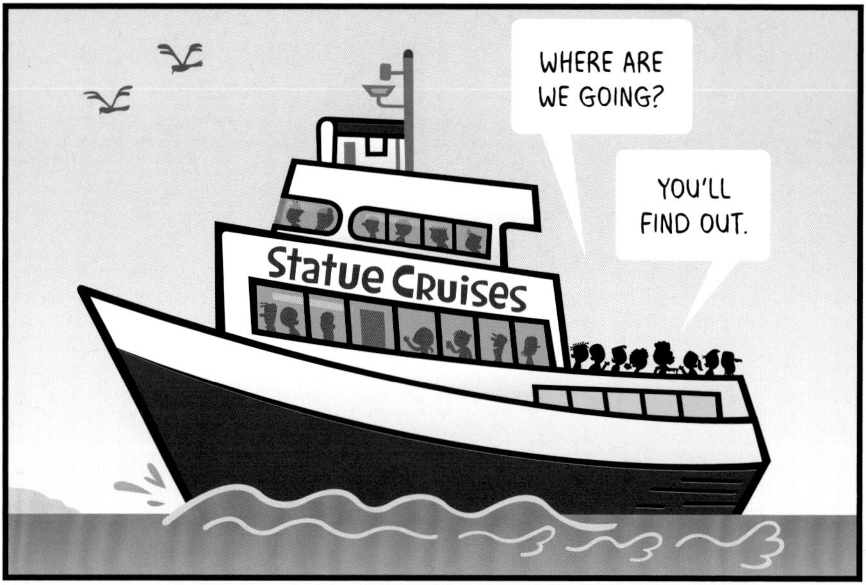
WHERE ARE WE GOING?
YOU'LL FIND OUT.
Statue Cruises

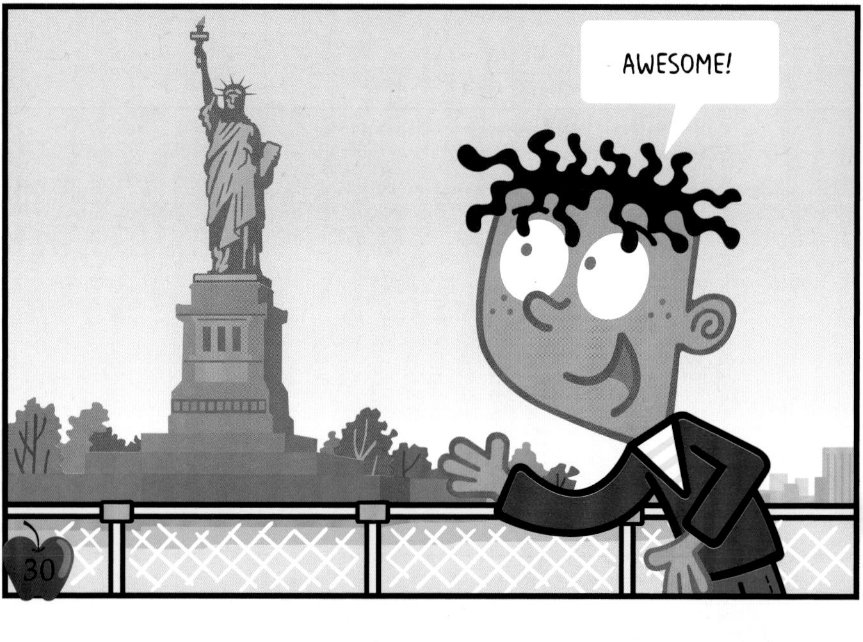
AWESOME!

Weird Stuff about the Statue of Liberty

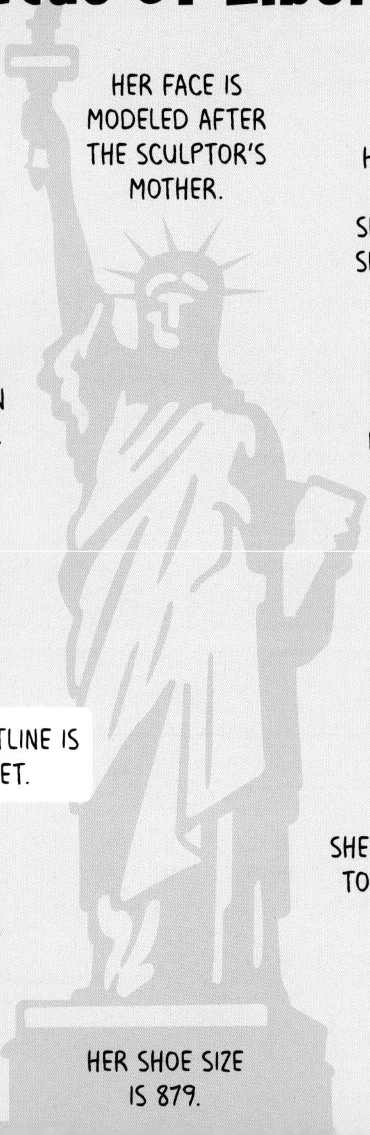

HER FACE IS MODELED AFTER THE SCULPTOR'S MOTHER.

SHE GETS STRUCK BY LIGHTNING 600 TIMES A YEAR.

HER SPIKY CROWN REPRESENTS THE SEVEN OCEANS AND SEVEN CONTINENTS.

THE SHIP CARRYING HER ALMOST SANK ON ITS WAY TO AMERICA.

SHE'S GREEN BECAUSE OF THE OXIDATION OF COPPER.

IN 1886, SHE WAS THE TALLEST IRON STRUCTURE IN THE WORLD.

IN HIGH WINDS, SHE CAN SWAY THREE INCHES.

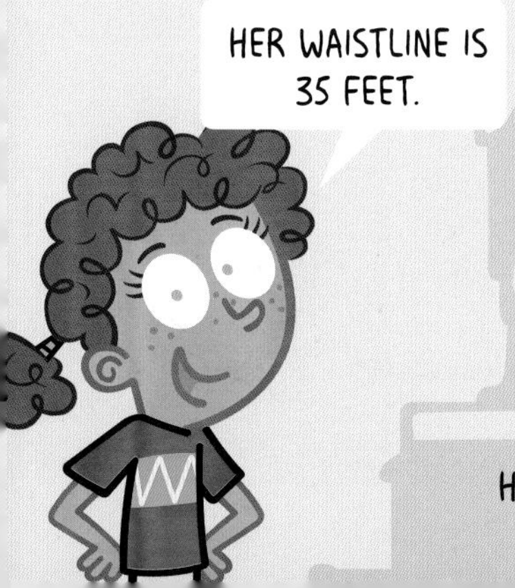
HER WAISTLINE IS 35 FEET.

SHE'S ACTUALLY CLOSER TO NEW JERSEY THAN NEW YORK.

HER SHOE SIZE IS 879.

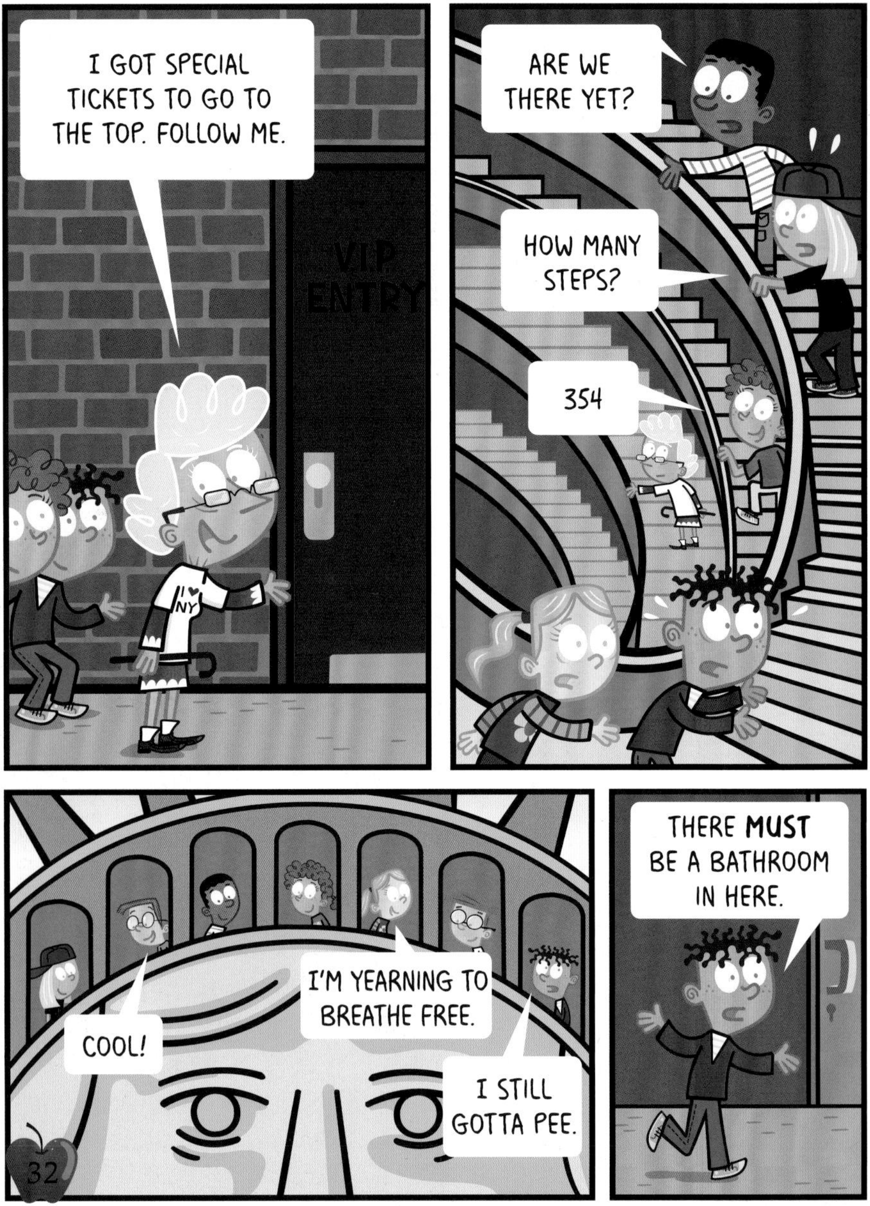
I GOT SPECIAL TICKETS TO GO TO THE TOP. FOLLOW ME.
V.I.P. ENTRY
I ♥ NY
ARE WE THERE YET?
HOW MANY STEPS?
354
COOL!
I'M YEARNING TO BREATHE FREE.
I STILL GOTTA PEE.
THERE **MUST** BE A BATHROOM IN HERE.

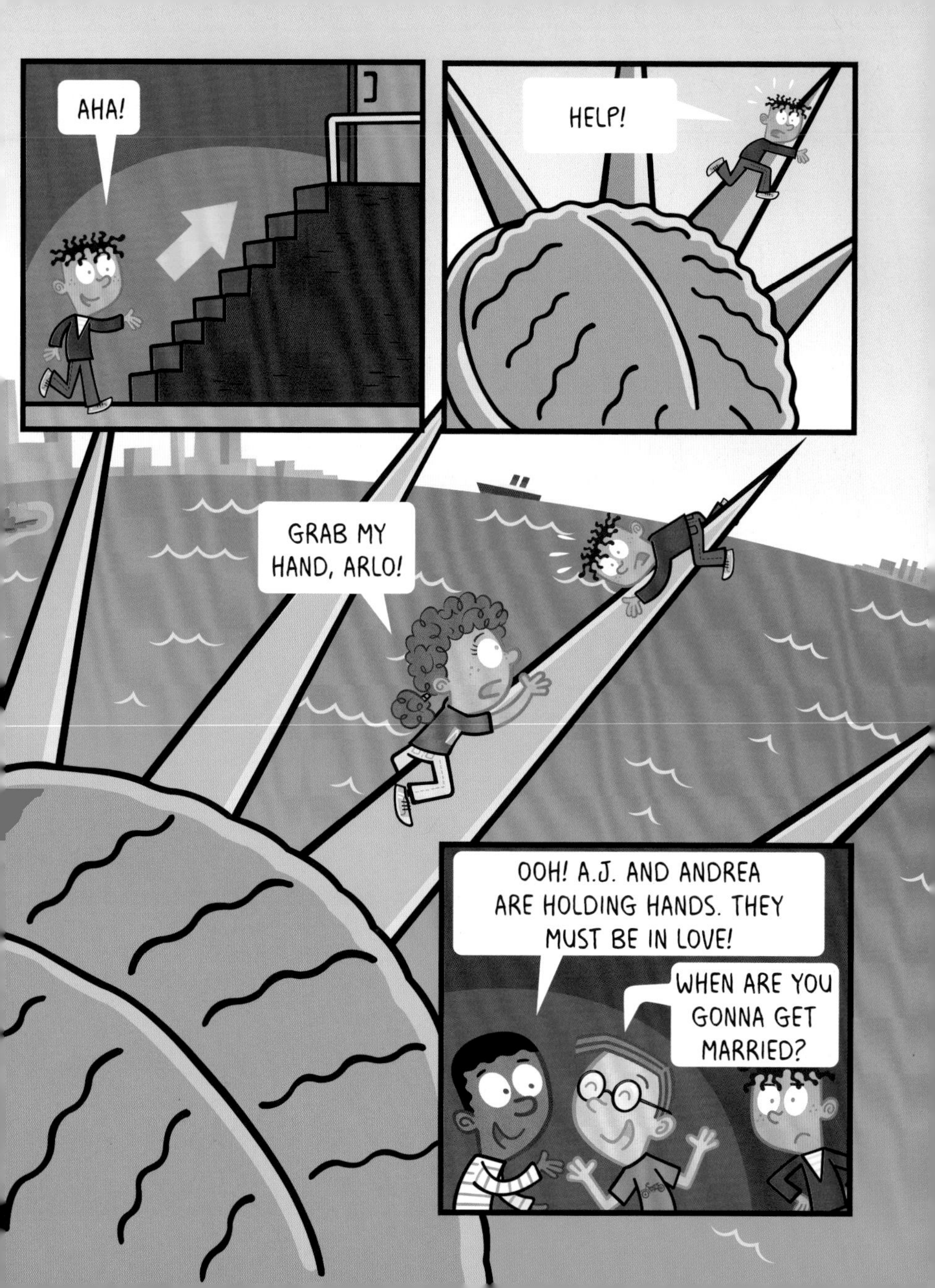
AHA!
HELP!
GRAB MY HAND, ARLO!
OOH! A.J. AND ANDREA ARE HOLDING HANDS. THEY MUST BE IN LOVE!
WHEN ARE YOU GONNA GET MARRIED?

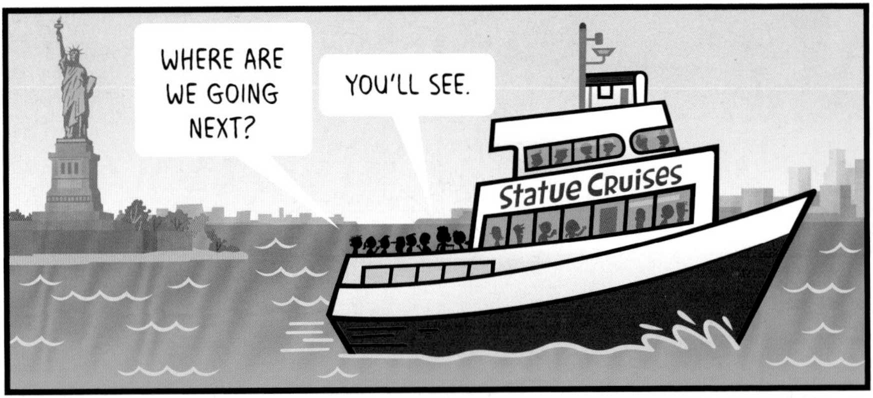
WHERE ARE WE GOING NEXT?
YOU'LL SEE.
Statue Cruises

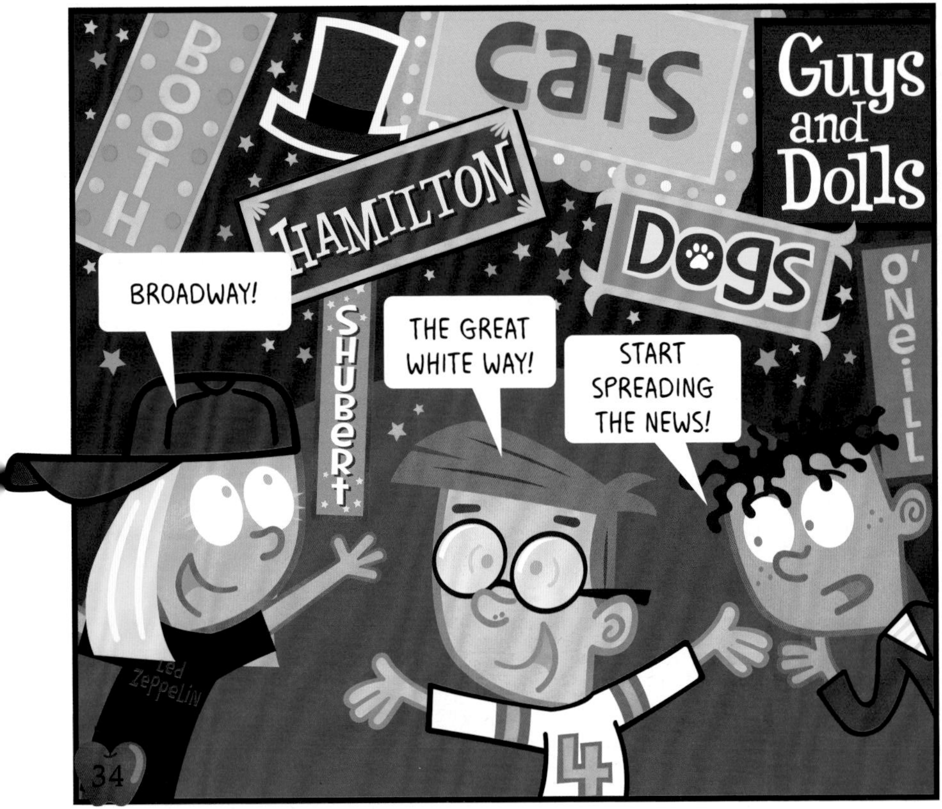
BOOTH
Cats
Guys and Dolls
HAMILTON
Dogs
O'NEILL
SHUBERT
BROADWAY!
THE GREAT WHITE WAY!
START SPREADING THE NEWS!
Led Zeppelin
4

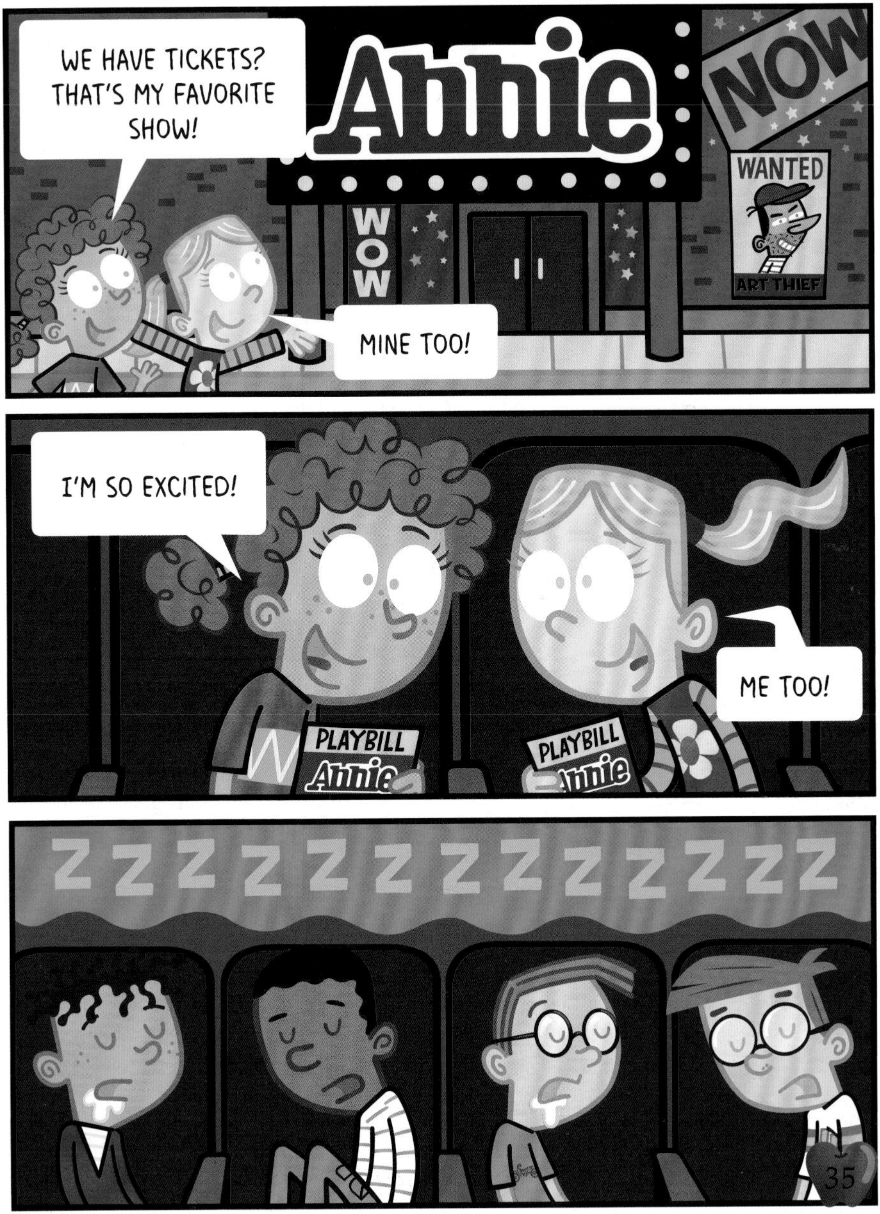
WE HAVE TICKETS? THAT'S MY FAVORITE SHOW!
Annie
NOW
WOW
WANTED
ART THIEF
MINE TOO!
I'M SO EXCITED!
ME TOO!
PLAYBILL
PLAYBILL
Z Z Z Z Z Z Z Z Z Z Z Z

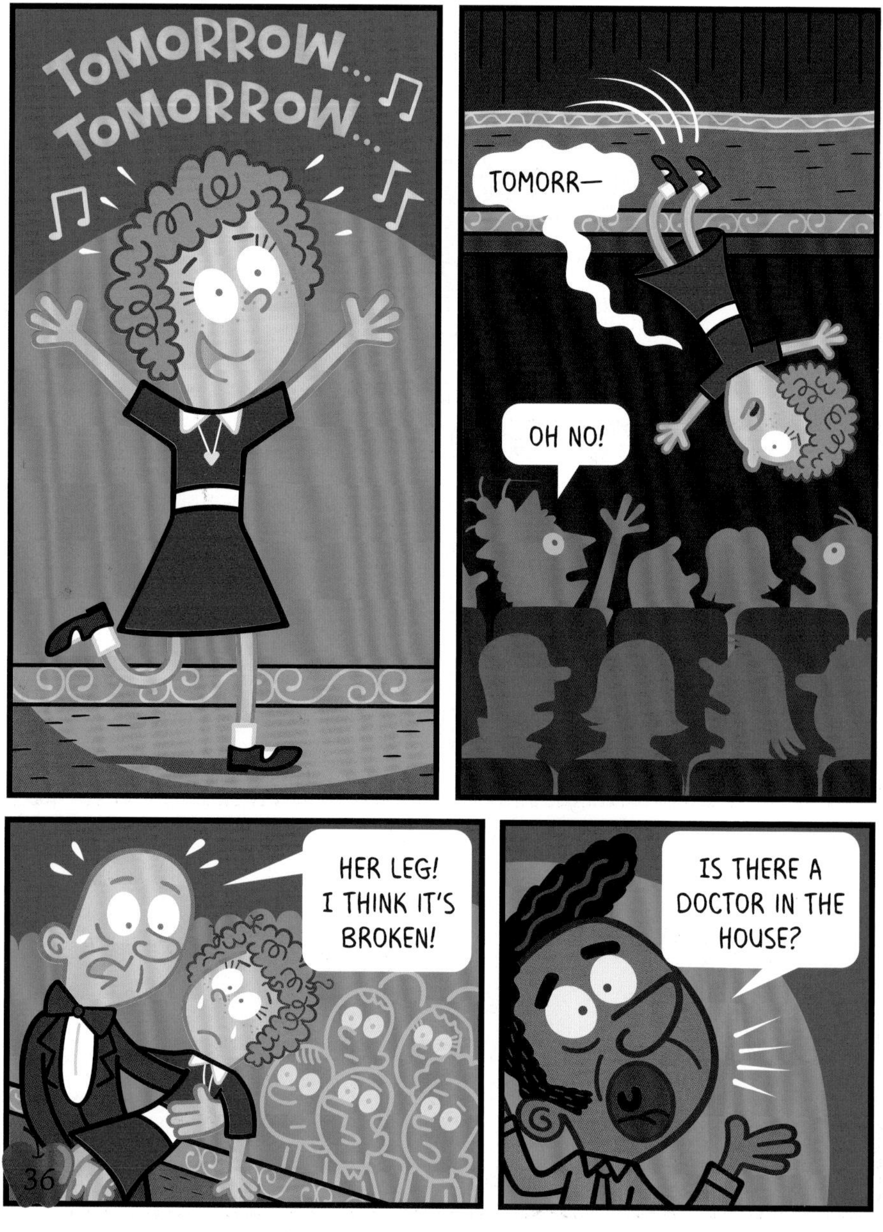
TOMORROW... TOMORROW...
TOMORR—
OH NO!
HER LEG! I THINK IT'S BROKEN!
IS THERE A DOCTOR IN THE HOUSE?

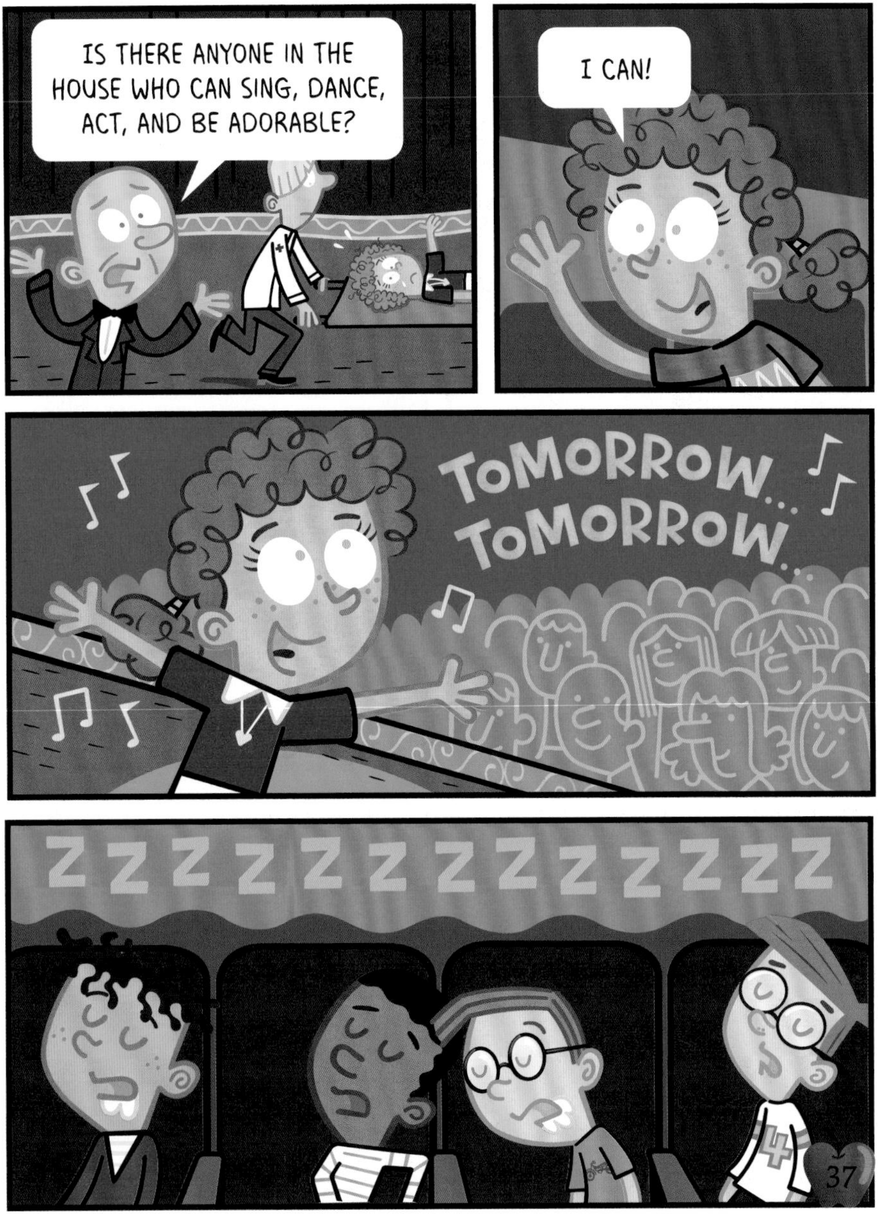
IS THERE ANYONE IN THE HOUSE WHO CAN SING, DANCE, ACT, AND BE ADORABLE?
I CAN!
TOMORROW... TOMORROW...
ZZZZZZZZZZZZ
4

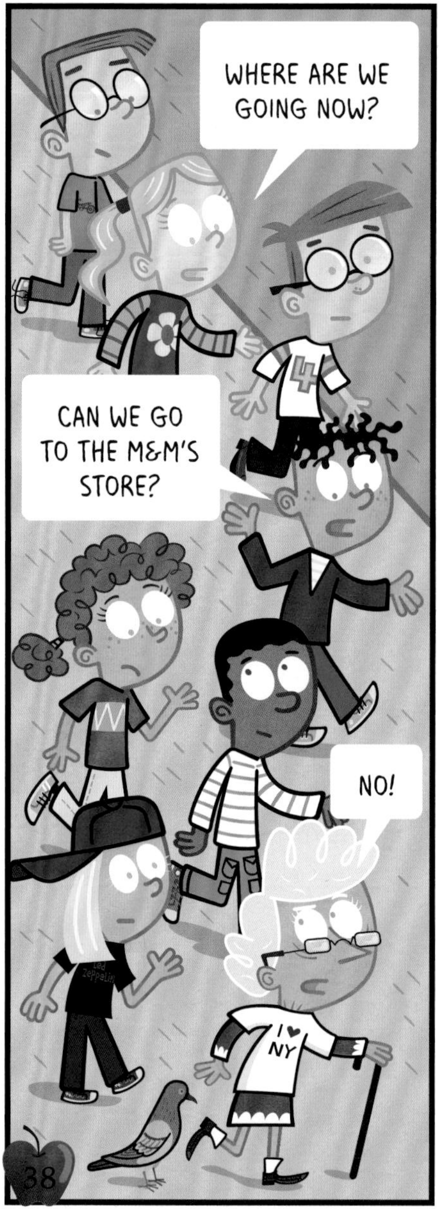
WHERE ARE WE GOING NOW?
CAN WE GO TO THE M&M'S STORE?
NO!
Led Zeppelin
I ♥ NY

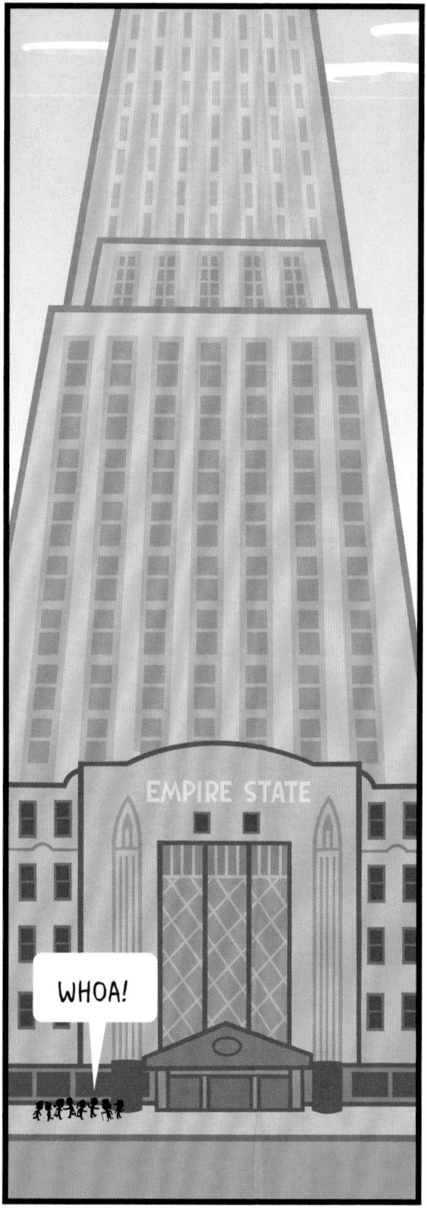
EMPIRE STATE
WHOA!

Weird Stuff about the Empire State Building

IT TOOK JUST 410 DAYS TO BUILD.

IT WAS ORIGINALLY GOING TO BE USED AS A BLIMP DOCKING STATION.

ON A CLEAR DAY, YOU CAN SEE UP TO 80 MILES FROM THE TOP.

IN 1986, TWO GUYS PARACHUTED OFF THE 86TH FLOOR OBSERVATION DECK.

IT WAS THE TALLEST BUILDING IN THE WORLD FOR NEARLY FORTY YEARS.

IT HAS ITS OWN ZIP CODE: 10118

THERE'S AN ANNUAL RACE TO RUN UP 1,576 STEPS TO THE 86TH FLOOR.

YOU CAN GET MARRIED ON THE 80TH FLOOR.

BECAUSE OF STATIC ELECTRICITY, COUPLES CAN GET A SHOCK WHILE KISSING AT HIGH LEVELS.

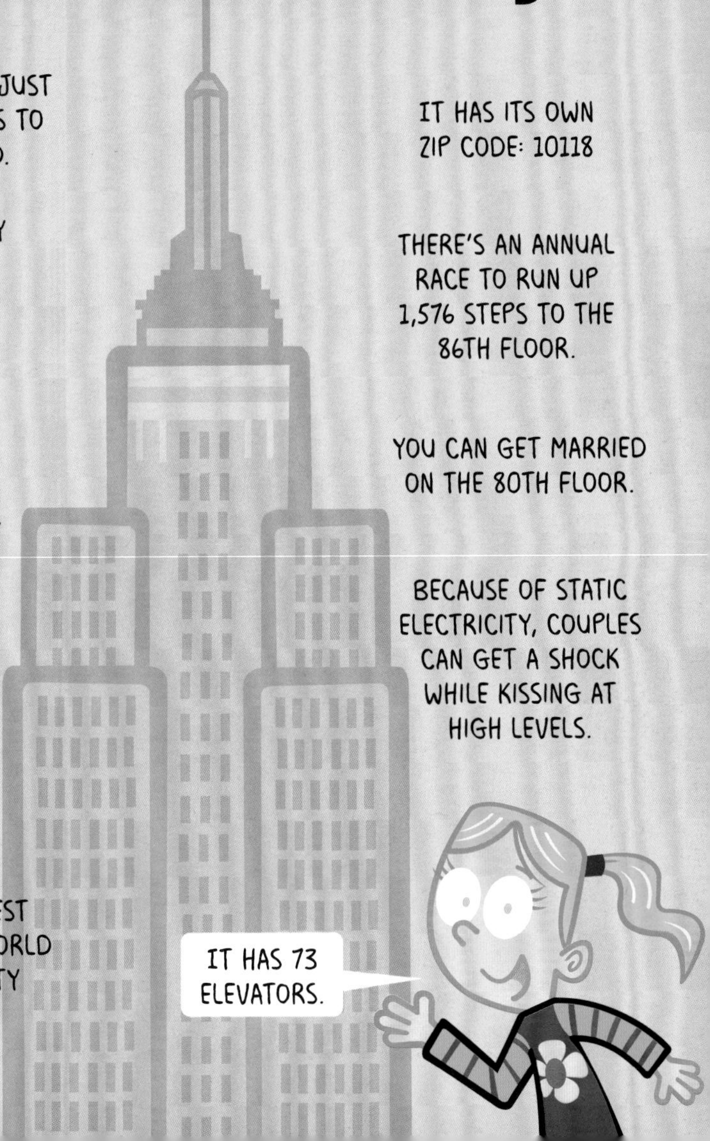
IT HAS 73 ELEVATORS.

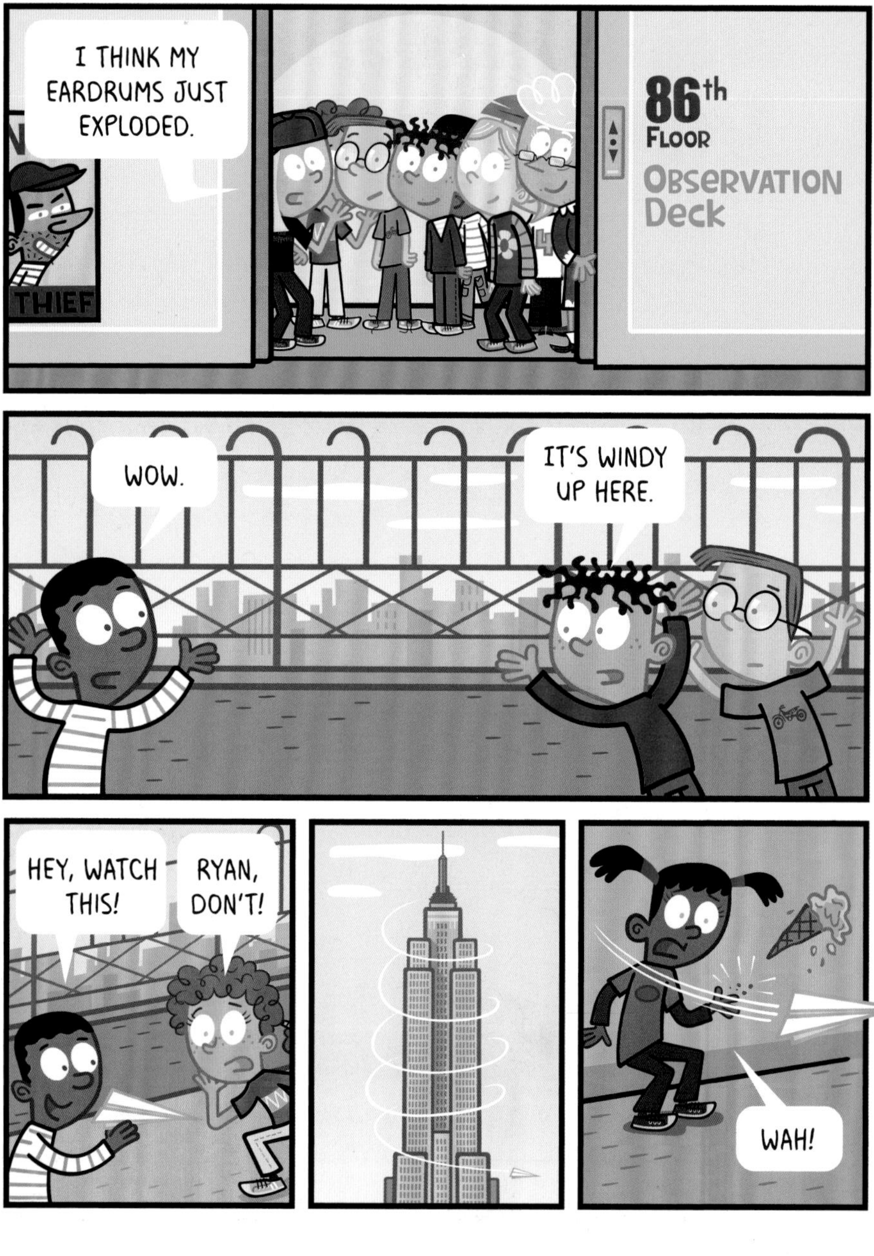
I THINK MY EARDRUMS JUST EXPLODED.
THIEF
86th FLOOR
OBSERVATION Deck
WOW.
IT'S WINDY UP HERE.
HEY, WATCH THIS!
RYAN, DON'T!
WAH!

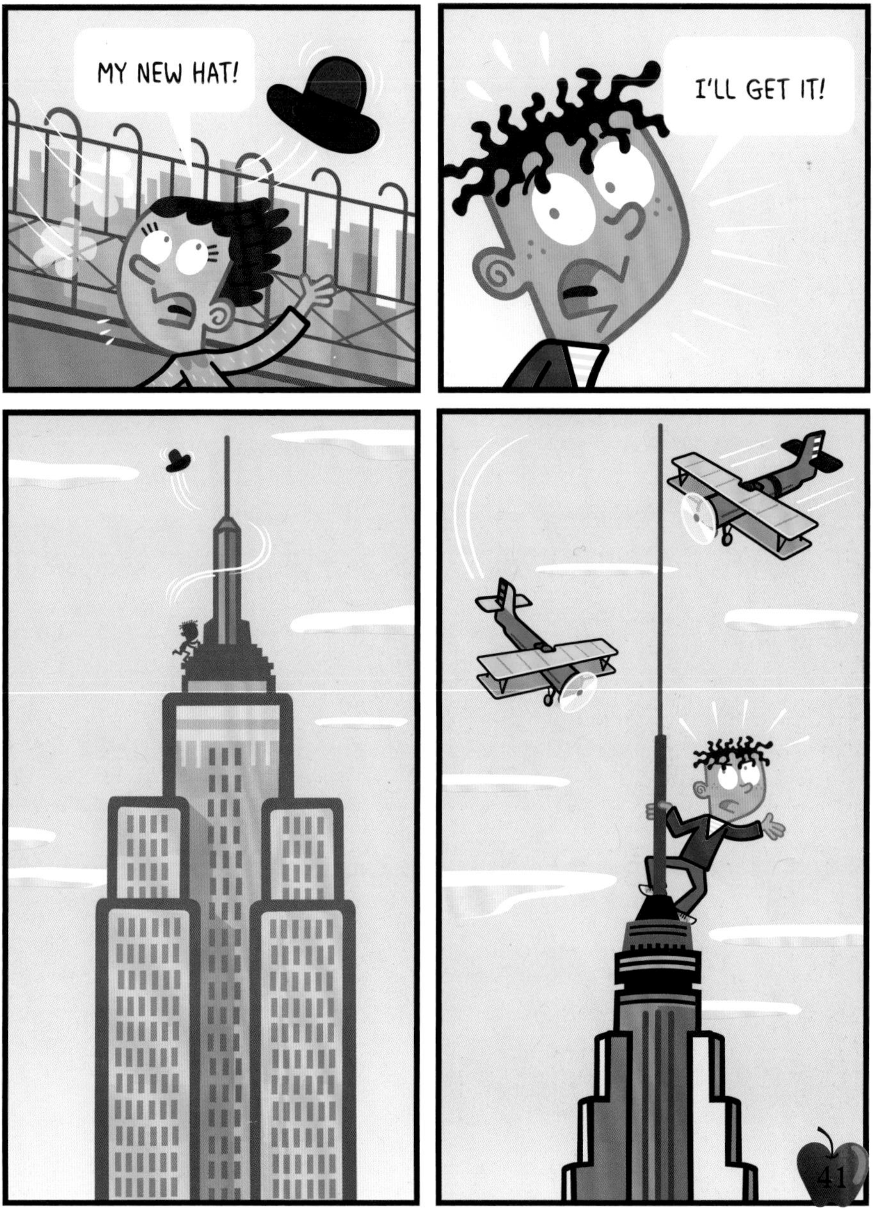
MY NEW HAT!
I'LL GET IT!

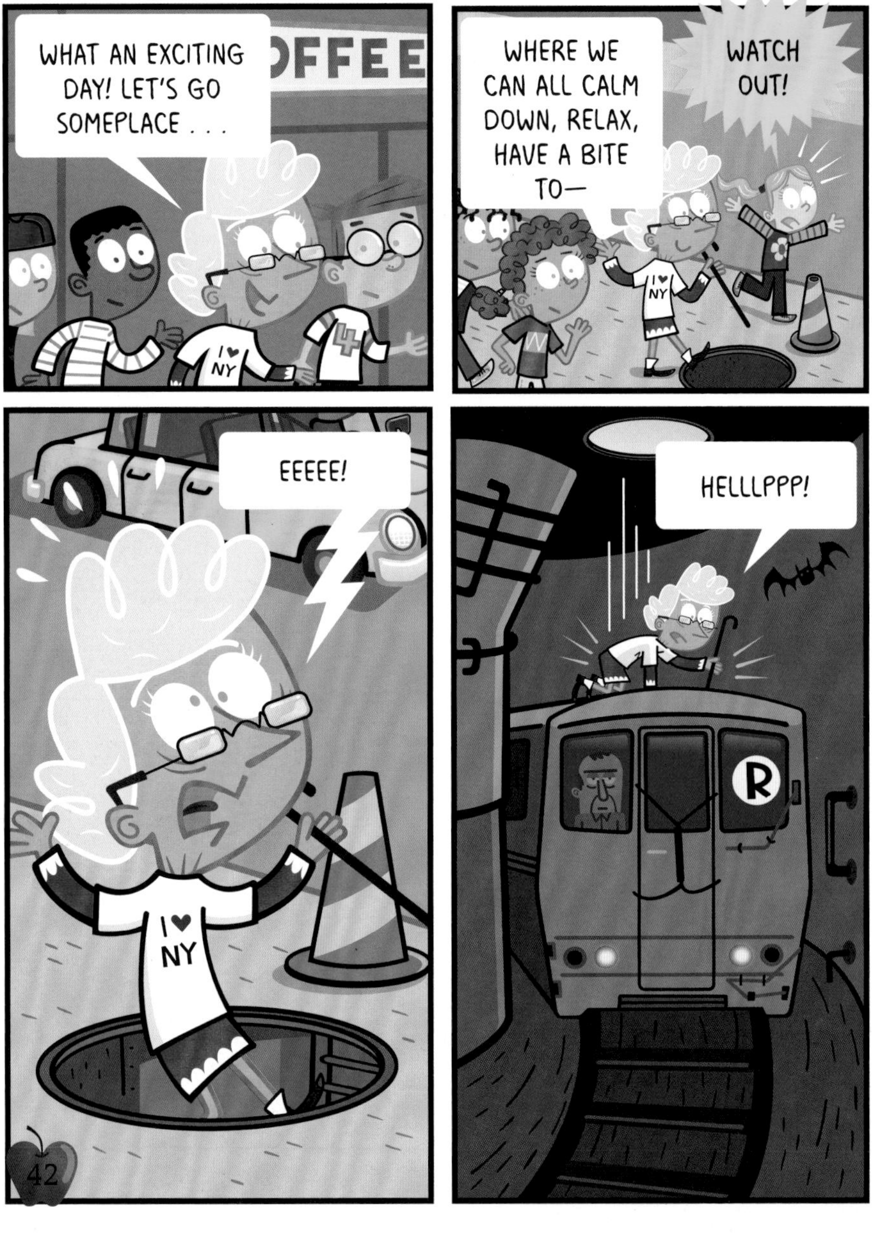
OFFEE
WHAT AN EXCITING DAY! LET'S GO SOMEPLACE . . .
I ♥ NY
WHERE WE CAN ALL CALM DOWN, RELAX, HAVE A BITE TO—
WATCH OUT!
EEEEE!
HELLLPPP!
R

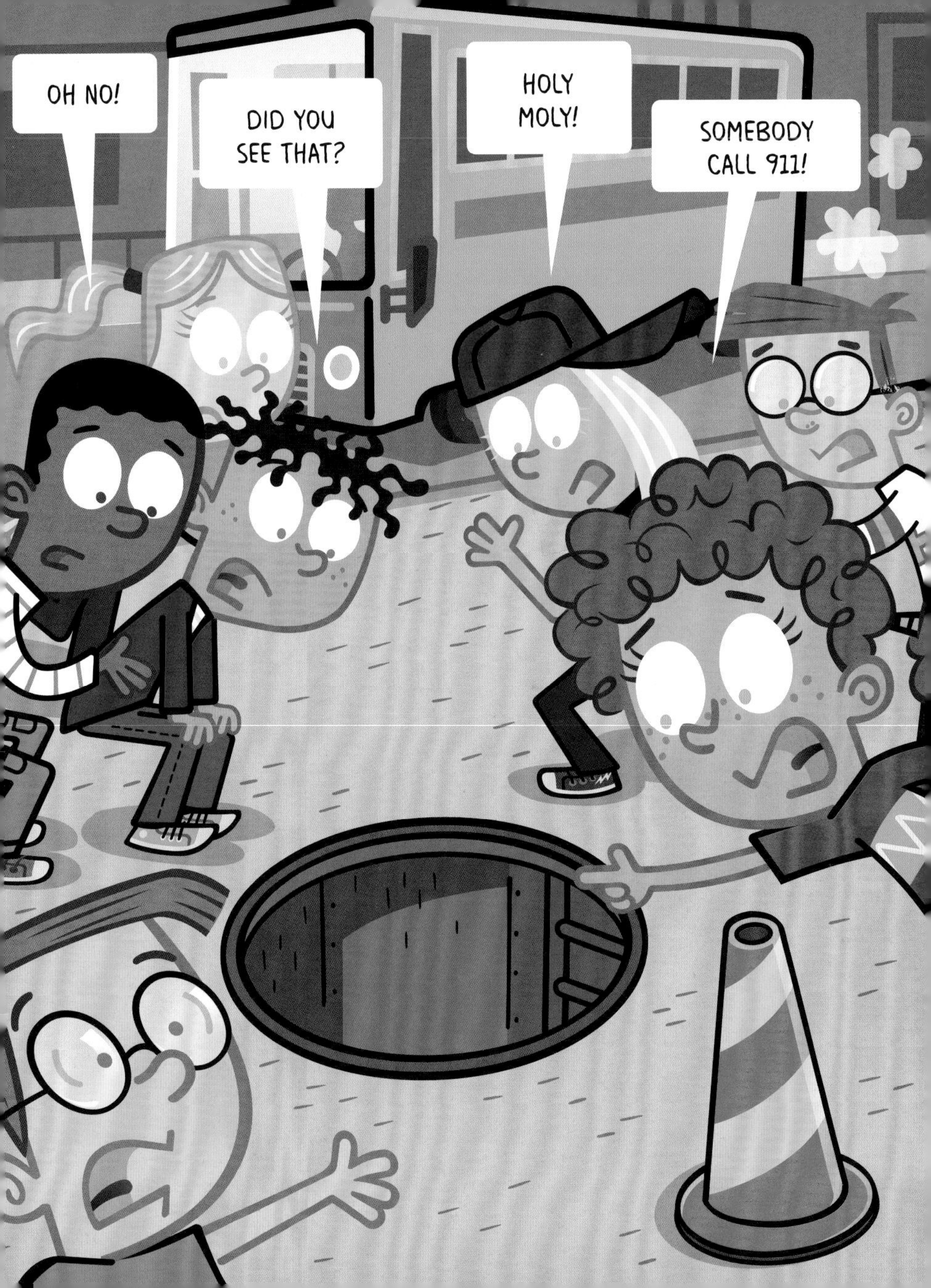
OH NO!
DID YOU SEE THAT?
HOLY MOLY!
SOMEBODY CALL 911!

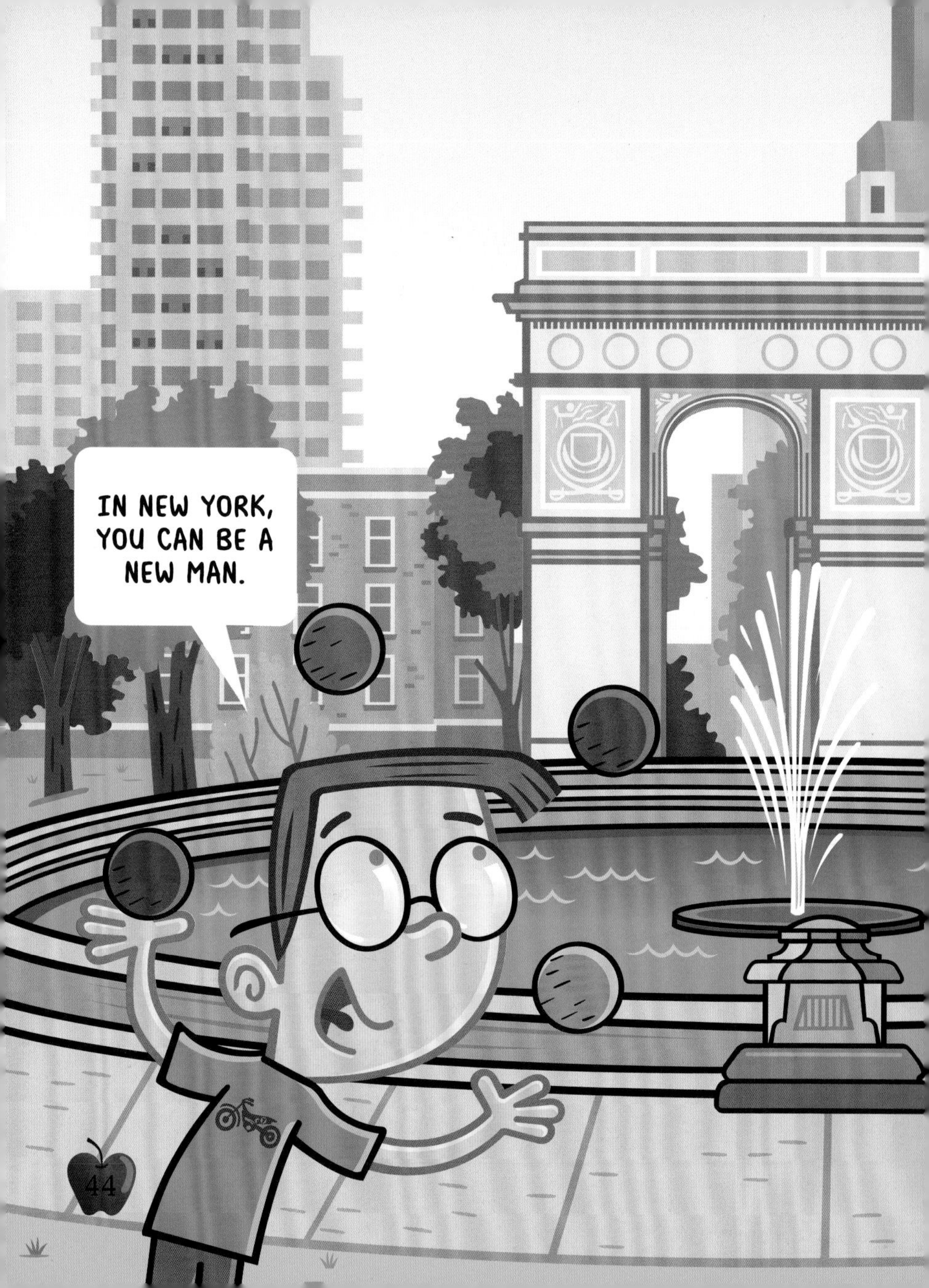
IN NEW YORK, YOU CAN BE A NEW MAN.

CHAPTER 4

People Who Chew with Their Mouths Open

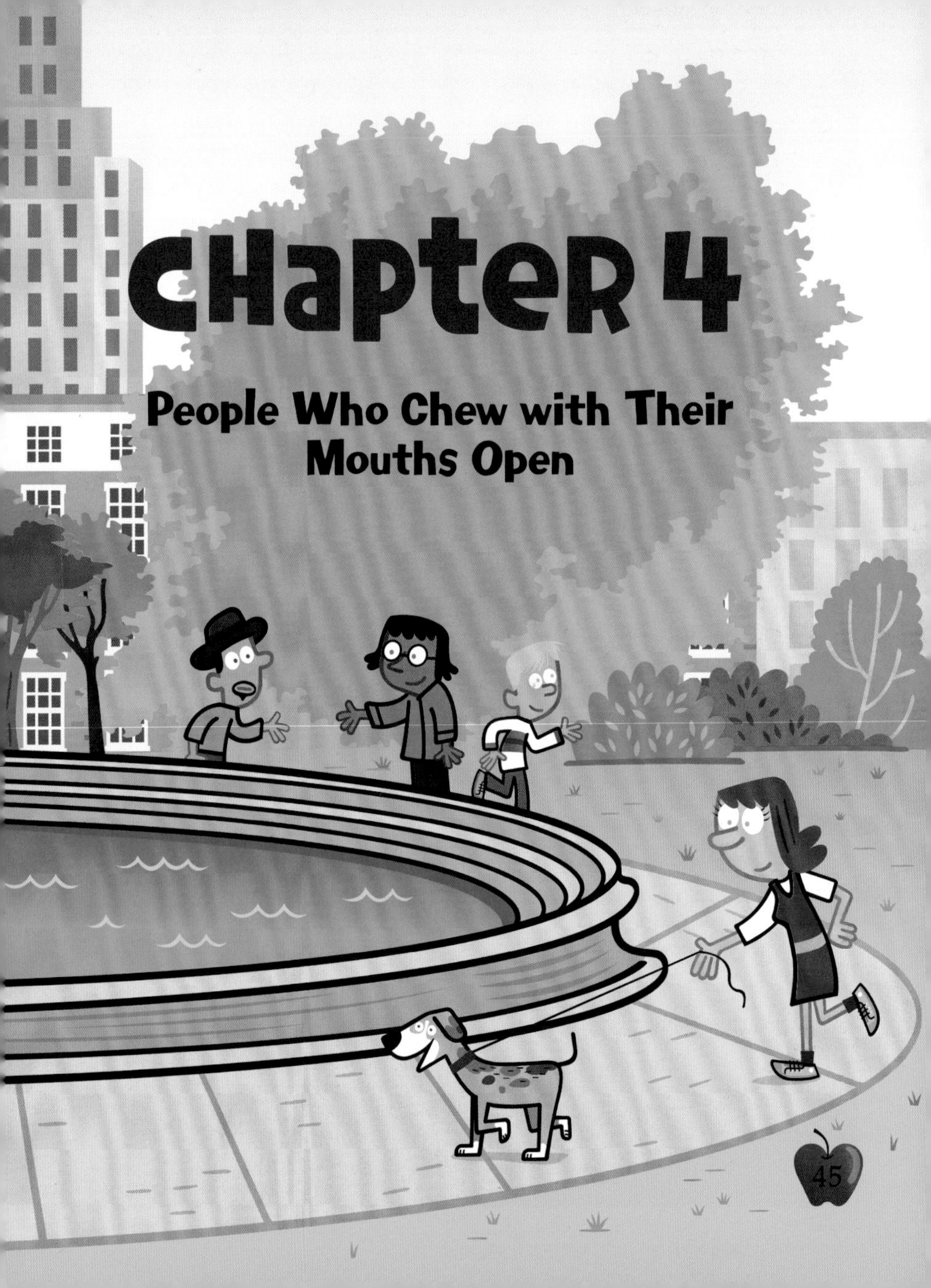

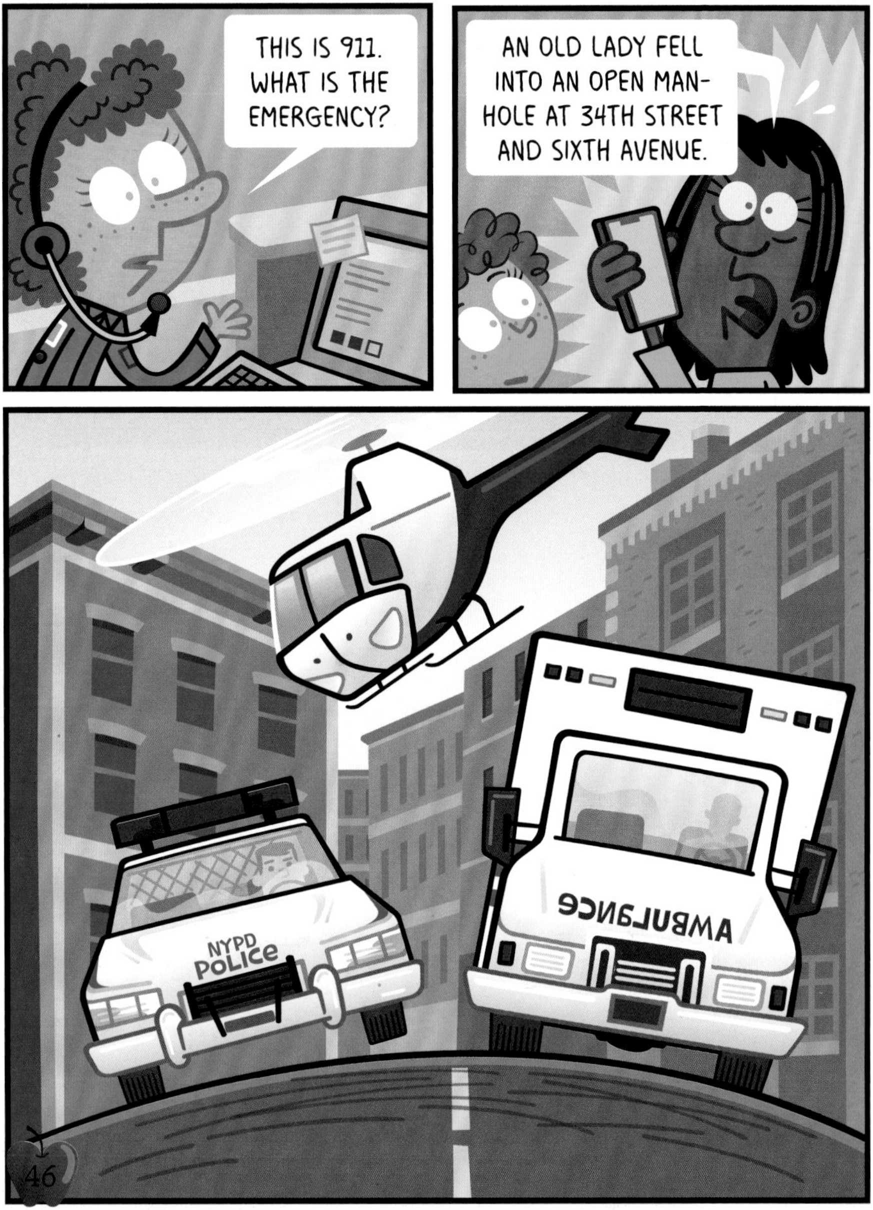
THIS IS 911. WHAT IS THE EMERGENCY?
AN OLD LADY FELL INTO AN OPEN MAN-HOLE AT 34TH STREET AND SIXTH AVENUE.
NYPD POLICE
AMBULANCE

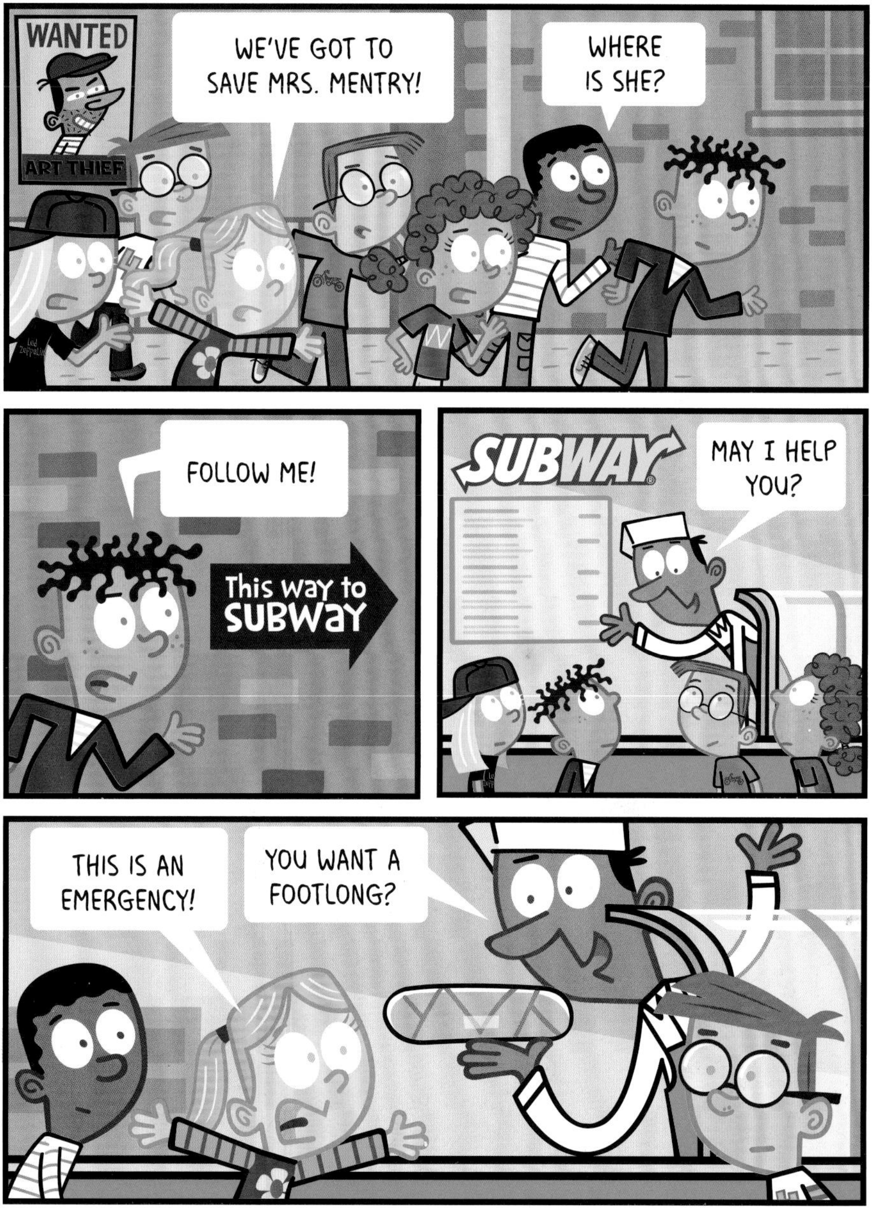
WANTED
ART THIEF
WE'VE GOT TO SAVE MRS. MENTRY!
WHERE IS SHE?
Led Zeppelin
FOLLOW ME!
This way to SUBWAY
SUBWAY
MAY I HELP YOU?
THIS IS AN EMERGENCY!
YOU WANT A FOOTLONG?

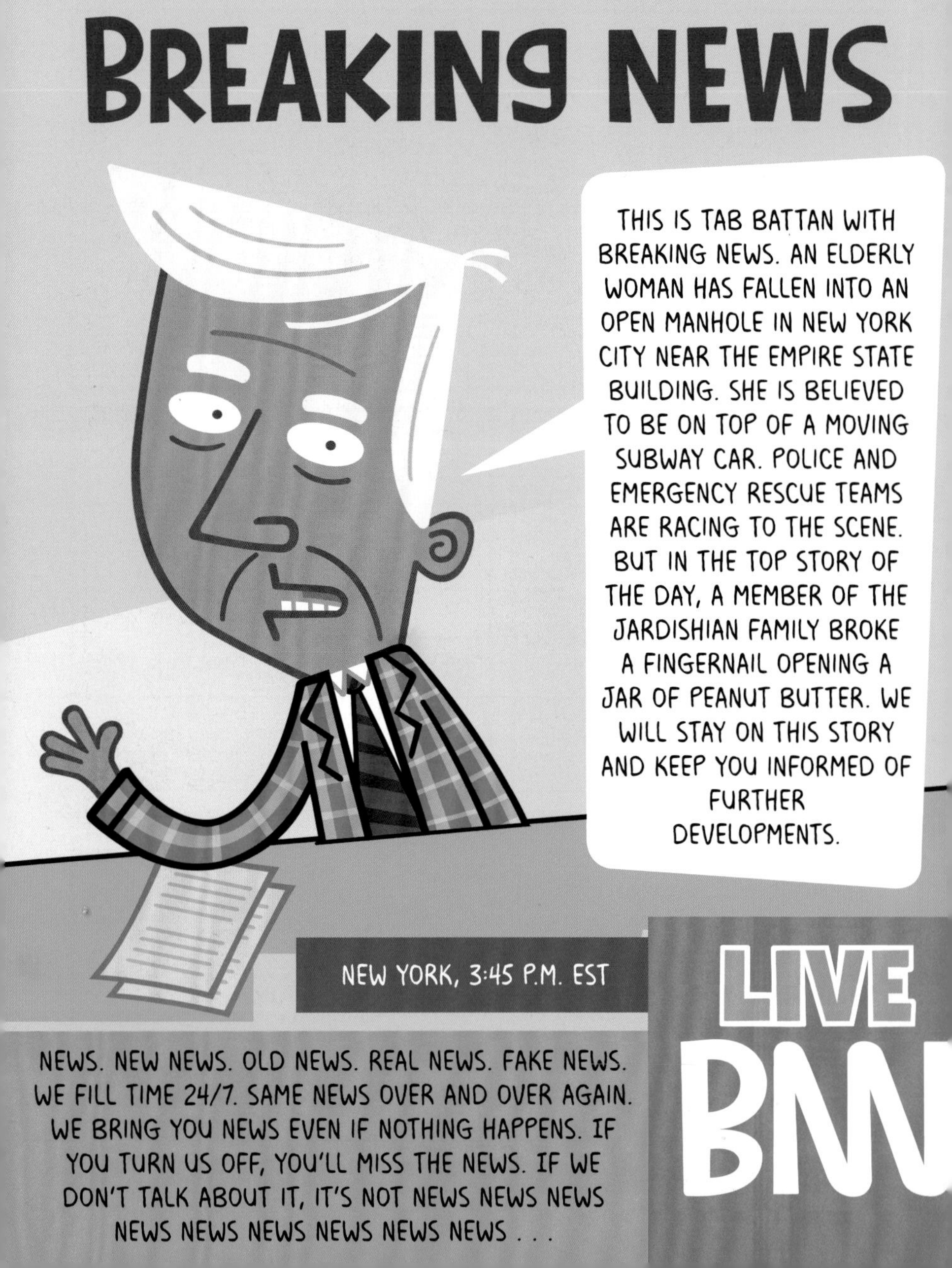

BREAKING NEWS
THIS IS TAB BATTAN WITH BREAKING NEWS. AN ELDERLY WOMAN HAS FALLEN INTO AN OPEN MANHOLE IN NEW YORK CITY NEAR THE EMPIRE STATE BUILDING. SHE IS BELIEVED TO BE ON TOP OF A MOVING SUBWAY CAR. POLICE AND EMERGENCY RESCUE TEAMS ARE RACING TO THE SCENE. BUT IN THE TOP STORY OF THE DAY, A MEMBER OF THE JARDISHIAN FAMILY BROKE A FINGERNAIL OPENING A JAR OF PEANUT BUTTER. WE WILL STAY ON THIS STORY AND KEEP YOU INFORMED OF FURTHER DEVELOPMENTS.
NEW YORK, 3:45 P.M. EST
LIVE
BNN
NEWS. NEW NEWS. OLD NEWS. REAL NEWS. FAKE NEWS. WE FILL TIME 24/7. SAME NEWS OVER AND OVER AGAIN. WE BRING YOU NEWS EVEN IF NOTHING HAPPENS. IF YOU TURN US OFF, YOU'LL MISS THE NEWS. IF WE DON'T TALK ABOUT IT, IT'S NOT NEWS NEWS NEWS NEWS NEWS NEWS NEWS NEWS NEWS . . .

Mrs. Mentry is lost. What are the kids going to do now?

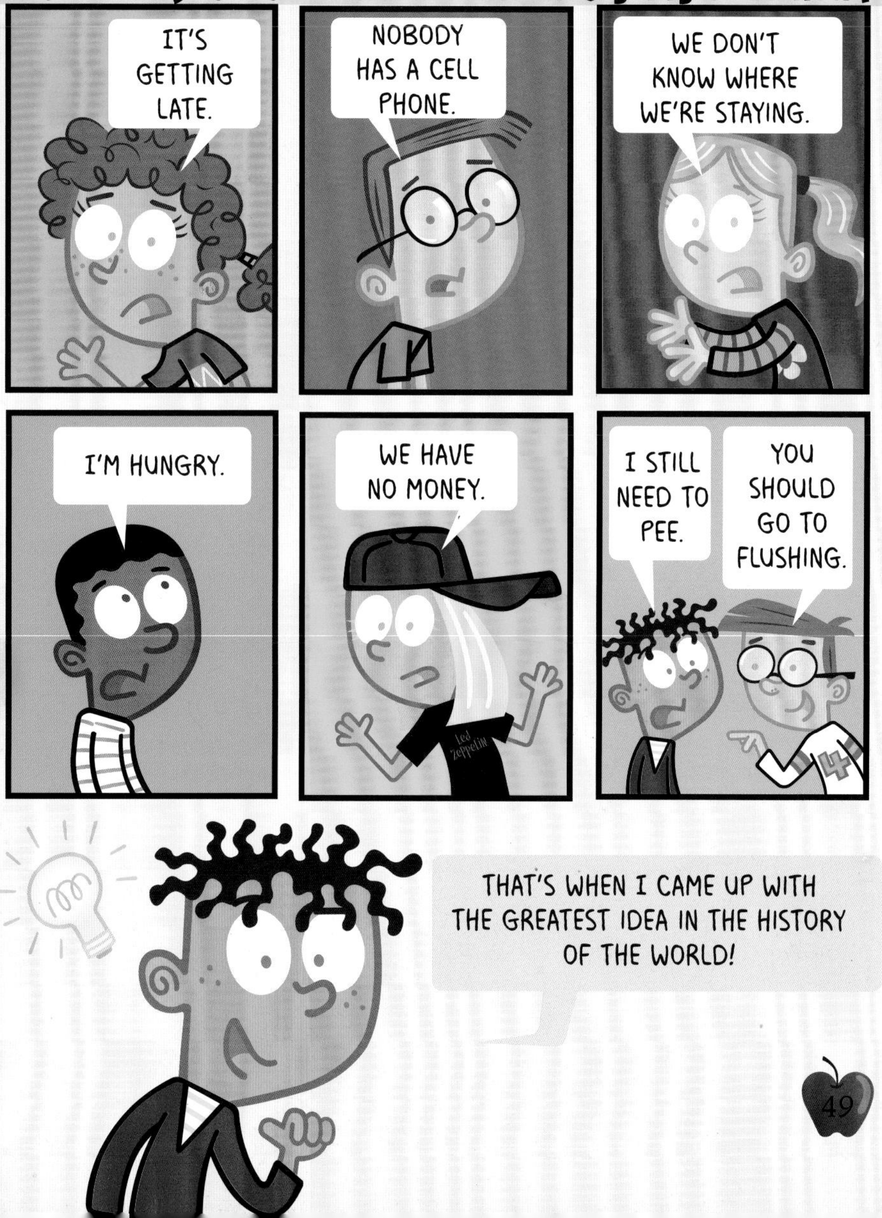
IT'S GETTING LATE.
NOBODY HAS A CELL PHONE.
WE DON'T KNOW WHERE WE'RE STAYING.
I'M HUNGRY.
WE HAVE NO MONEY.
I STILL NEED TO PEE.
YOU SHOULD GO TO FLUSHING.
THAT'S WHEN I CAME UP WITH THE GREATEST IDEA IN THE HISTORY OF THE WORLD!

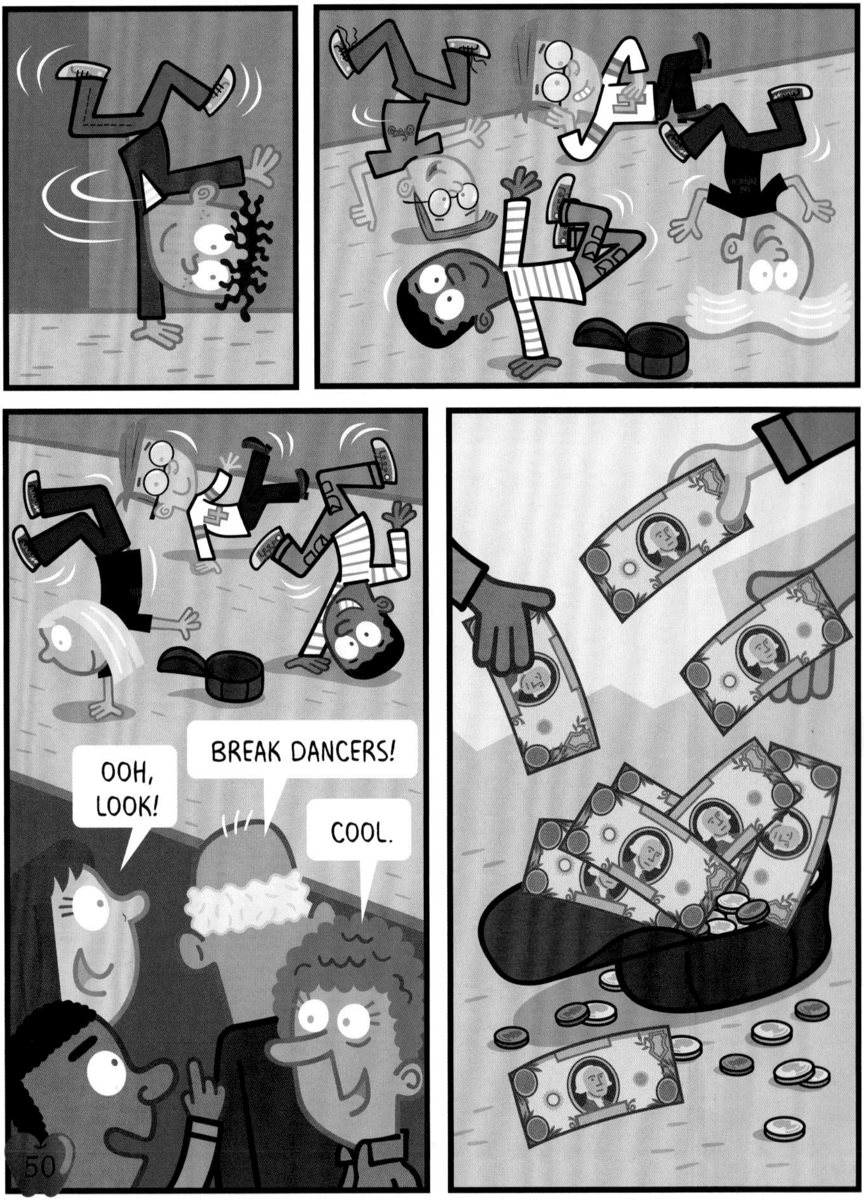
OOH, LOOK!
BREAK DANCERS!
COOL.

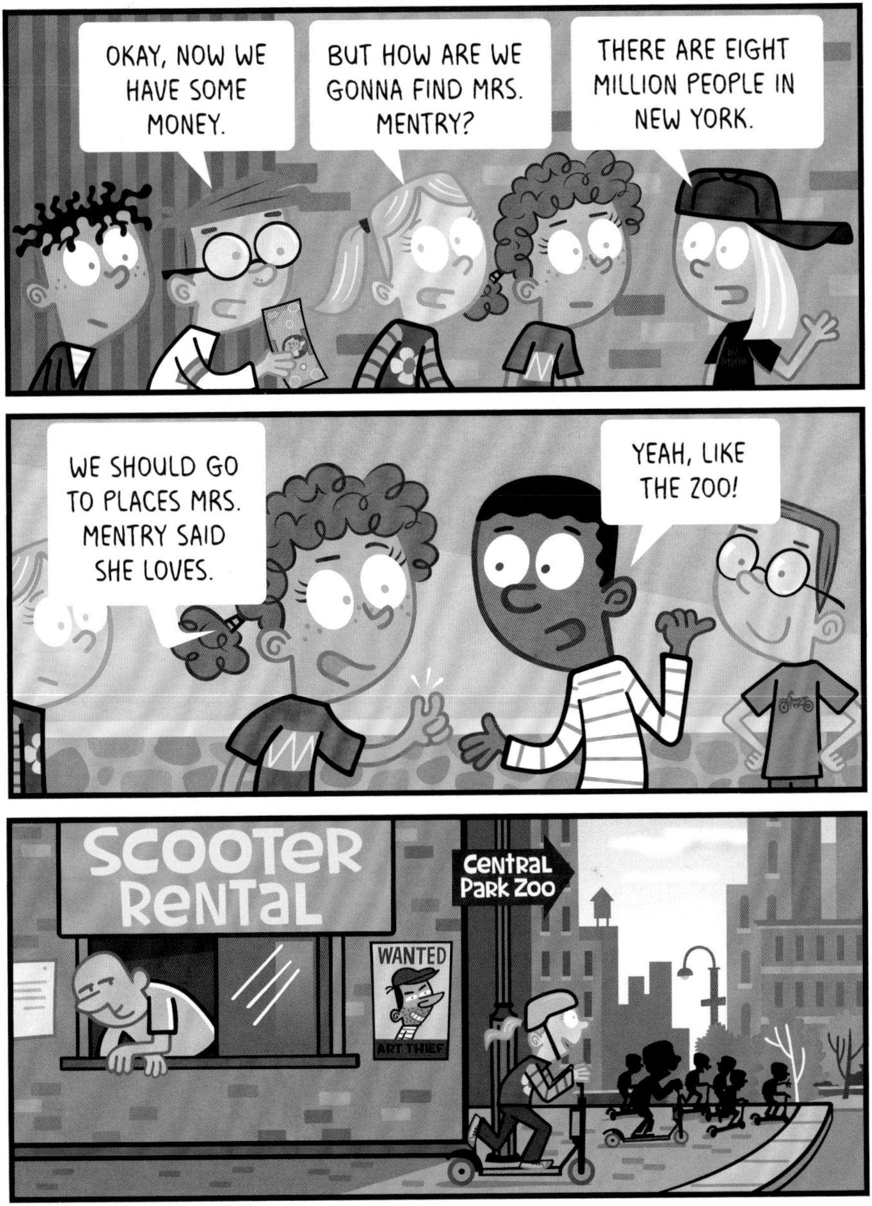
OKAY, NOW WE HAVE SOME MONEY.
BUT HOW ARE WE GONNA FIND MRS. MENTRY?
THERE ARE EIGHT MILLION PEOPLE IN NEW YORK.
WE SHOULD GO TO PLACES MRS. MENTRY SAID SHE LOVES.
YEAH, LIKE THE ZOO!
SCOOTER RENTAL
Central Park Zoo
WANTED
ART THIEF

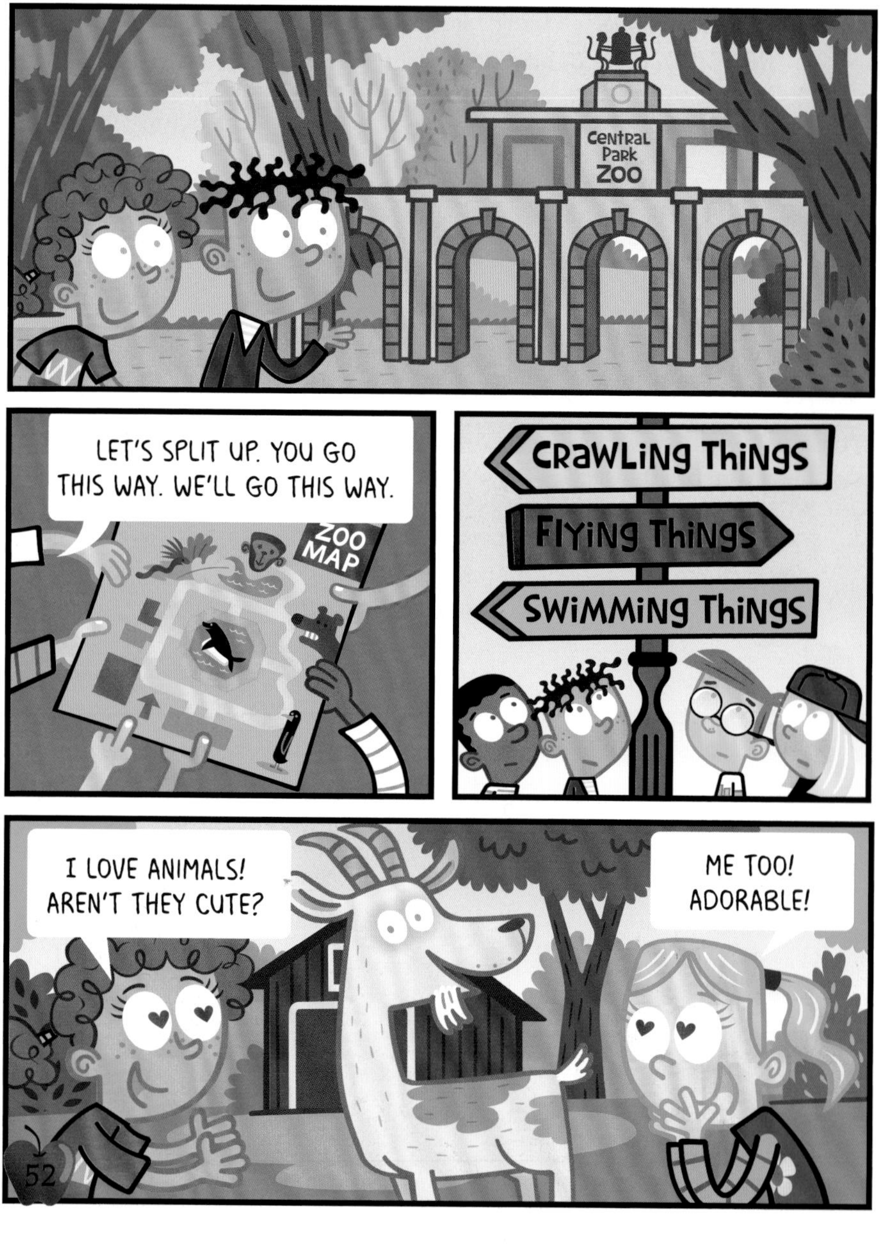
Central Park Zoo
LET'S SPLIT UP. YOU GO THIS WAY. WE'LL GO THIS WAY.
ZOO MAP
CRAWLING THINGS
FLYING THINGS
SWIMMING THINGS
I LOVE ANIMALS! AREN'T THEY CUTE?
ME TOO! ADORABLE!

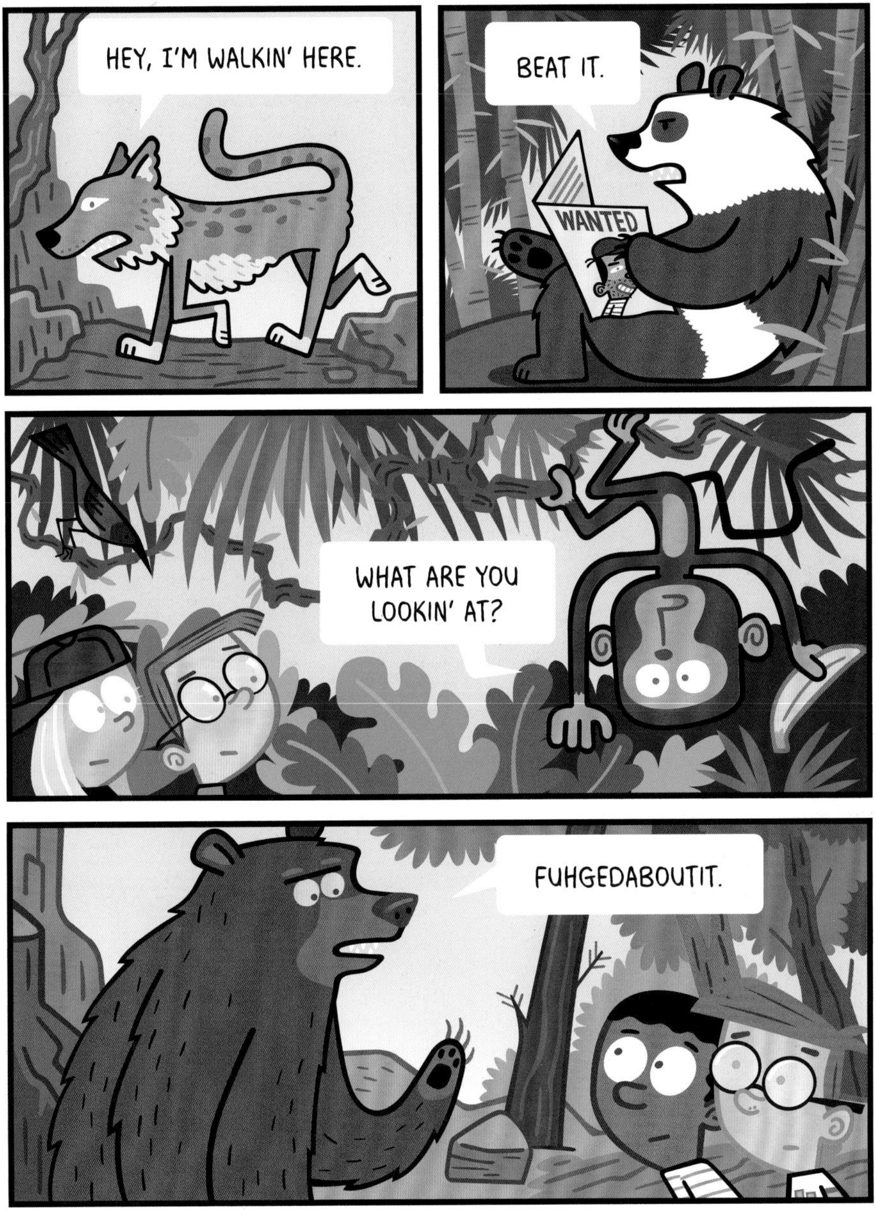
HEY, I'M WALKIN' HERE.
BEAT IT.
WANTED
WHAT ARE YOU LOOKIN' AT?
FUHGEDABOUTIT.

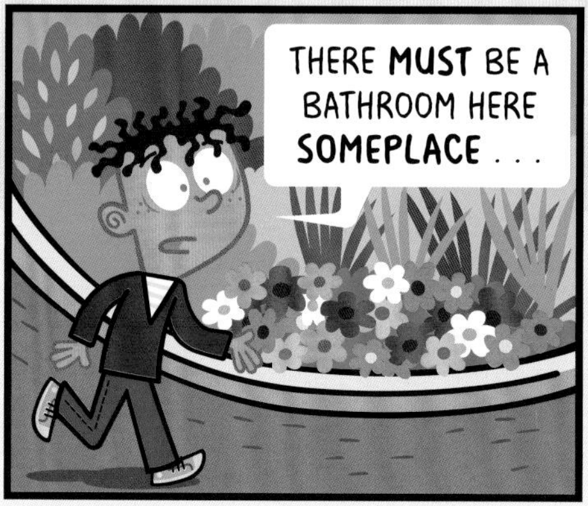
THERE **MUST** BE A BATHROOM HERE **SOMEPLACE** . . .

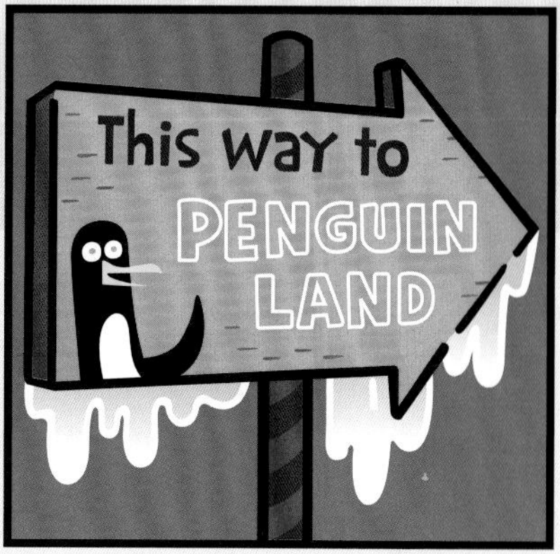
This way to
PENGUIN
LAND

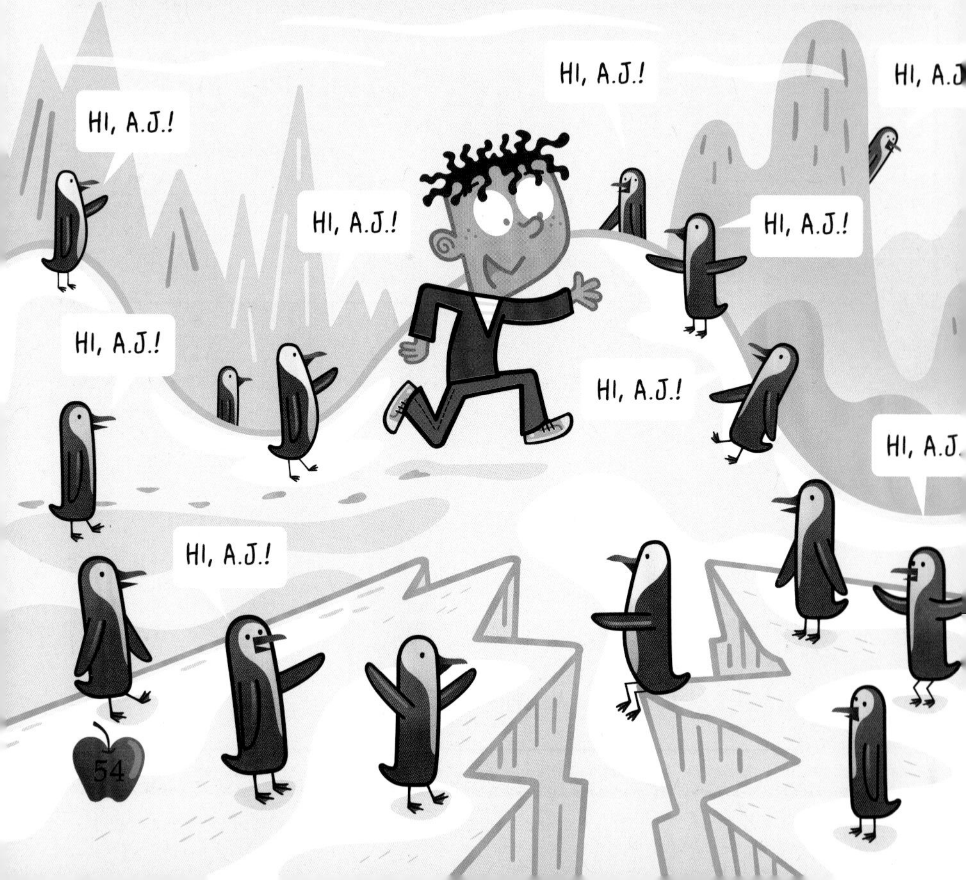
HI, A.J.!
HI, A.J.!
HI, A.J
HI, A.J.!
HI, A.J.!
HI, A.J.!
HI, A.J.!
HI, A.J.
HI, A.J.!

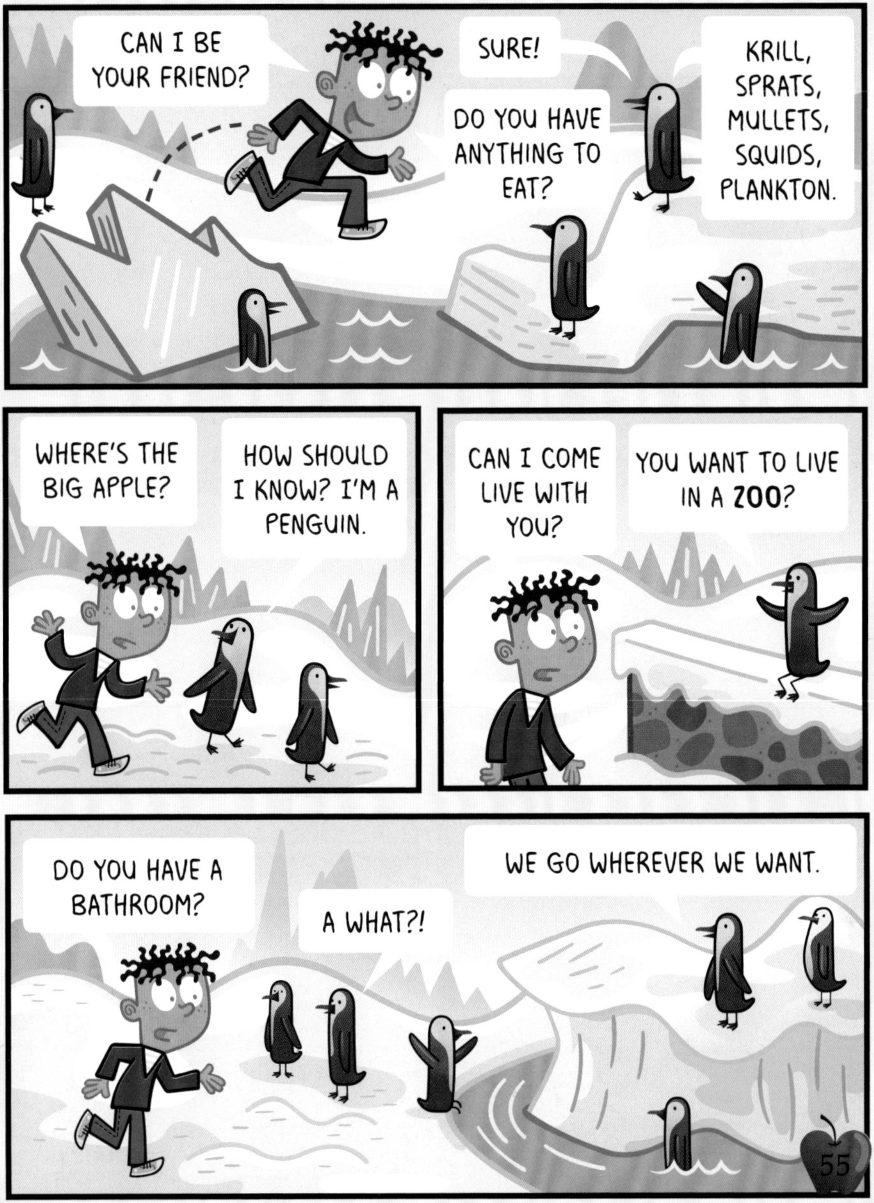
CAN I BE YOUR FRIEND?
SURE!
DO YOU HAVE ANYTHING TO EAT?
KRILL, SPRATS, MULLETS, SQUIDS, PLANKTON.
WHERE'S THE BIG APPLE?
HOW SHOULD I KNOW? I'M A PENGUIN.
CAN I COME LIVE WITH YOU?
YOU WANT TO LIVE IN A **ZOO**?
DO YOU HAVE A BATHROOM?
A WHAT?!
WE GO WHEREVER WE WANT.

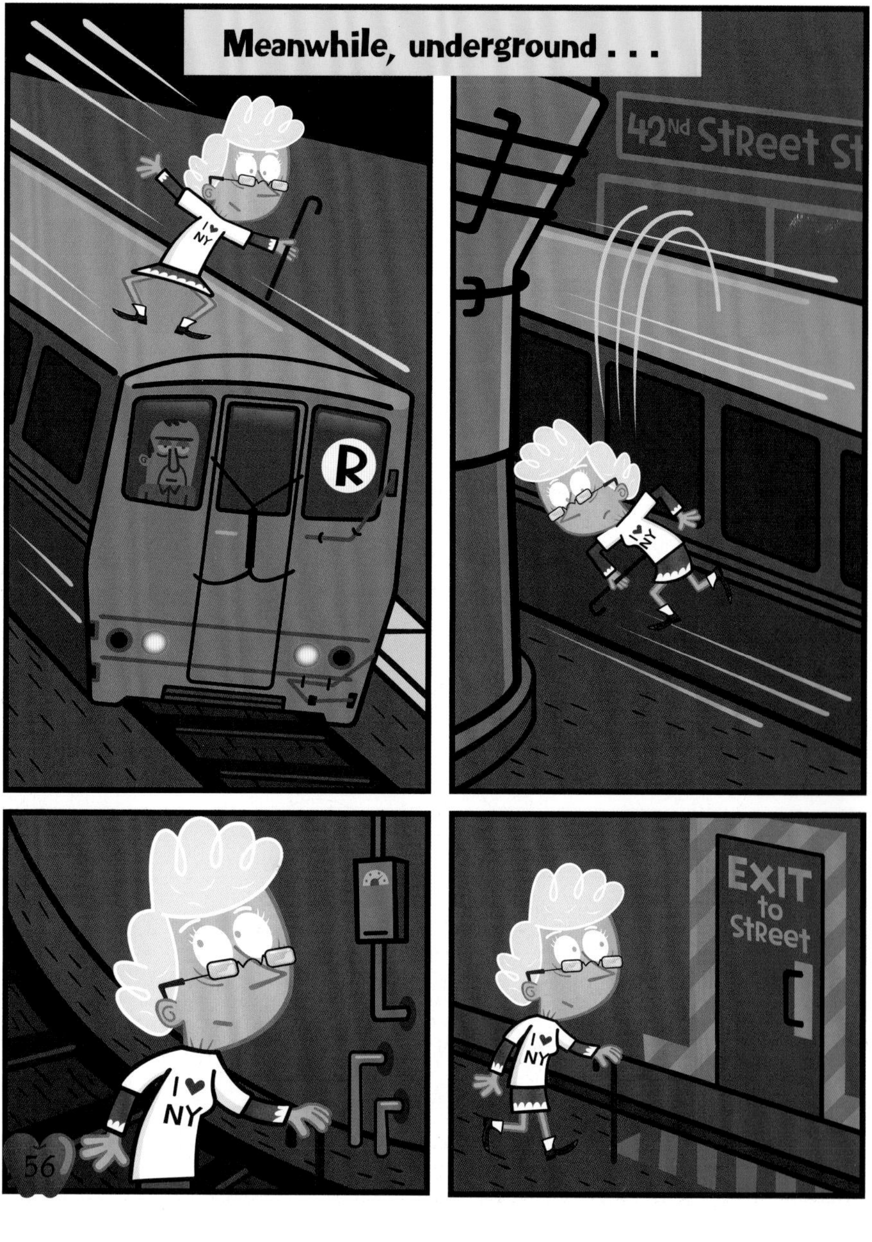
Meanwhile, underground . . .
R
42ND StReet St
I ♥ NY
EXIT to StReet

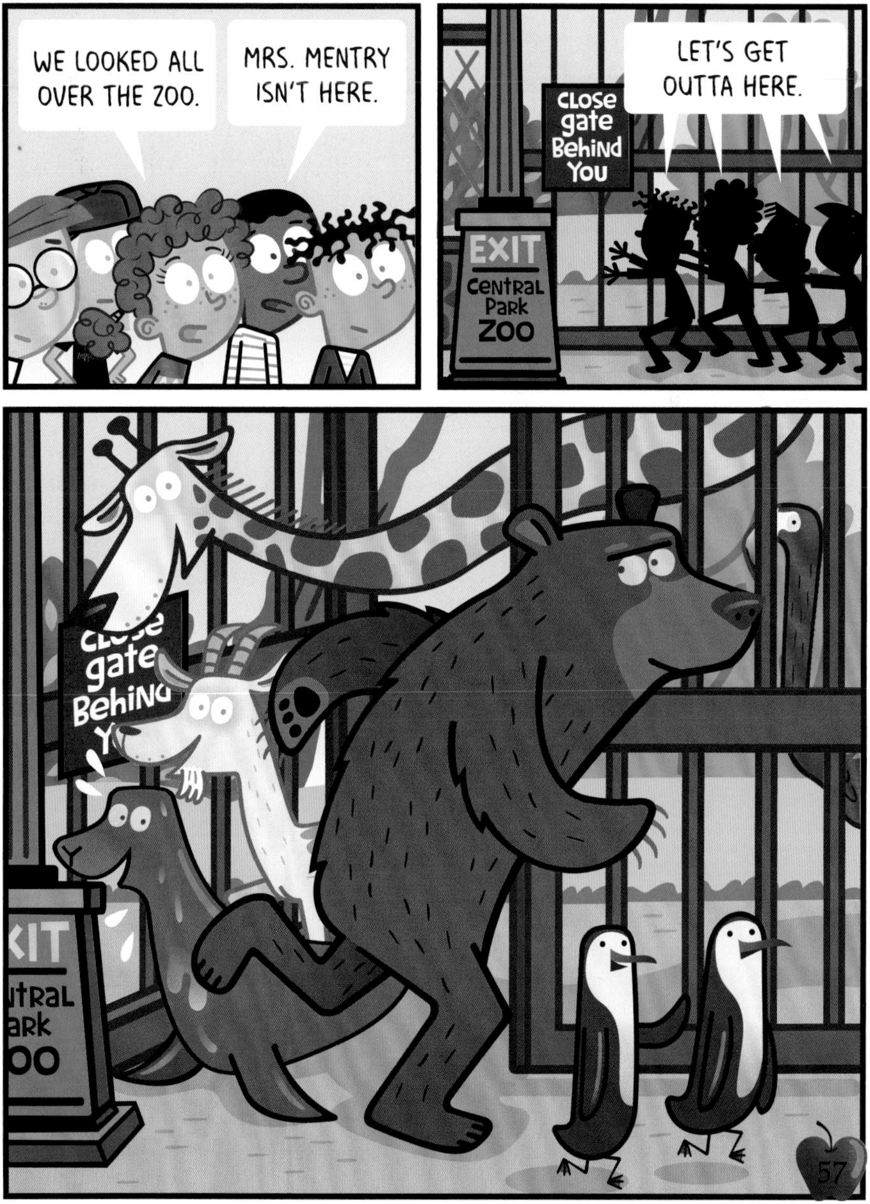
WE LOOKED ALL OVER THE ZOO.
MRS. MENTRY ISN'T HERE.
CLOSE gate BEHIND YOU
EXIT
CENTRAL PARK ZOO
LET'S GET OUTTA HERE.
CLOSE gate BEHIND Y
EXIT
NTRAL ARK OO

Help A.J. Find

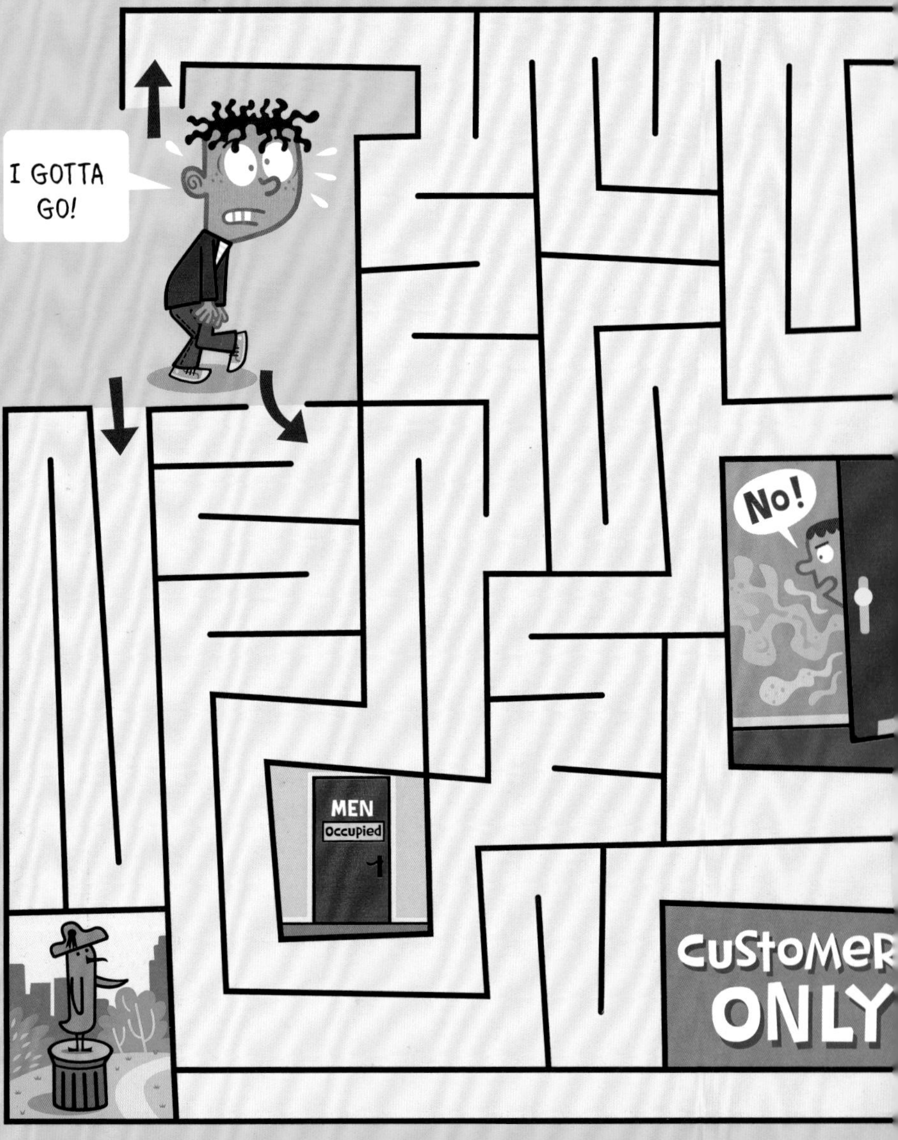
I GOTTA GO!
No!
MEN
Occupied
CUSTOMER
ONLY

a Bathroom!

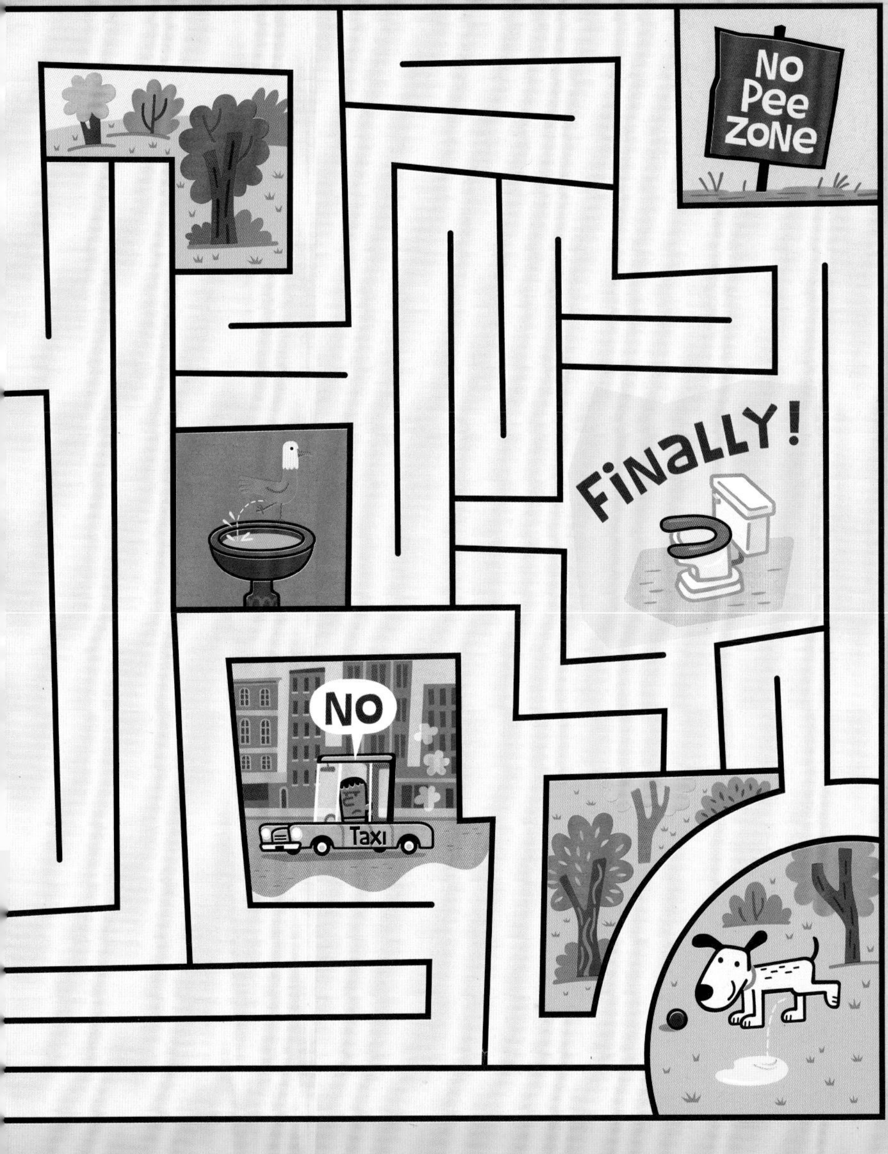
No
Pee
ZONE
FiNaLLY!
NO
Taxi

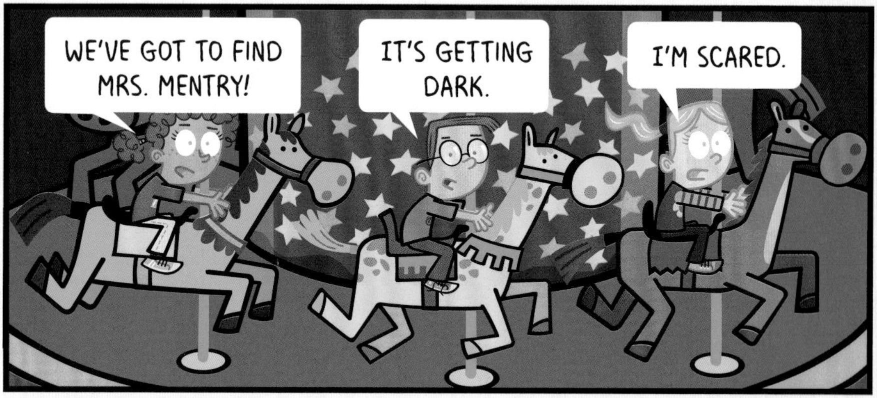
WE'VE GOT TO FIND MRS. MENTRY!
IT'S GETTING DARK.
I'M SCARED.

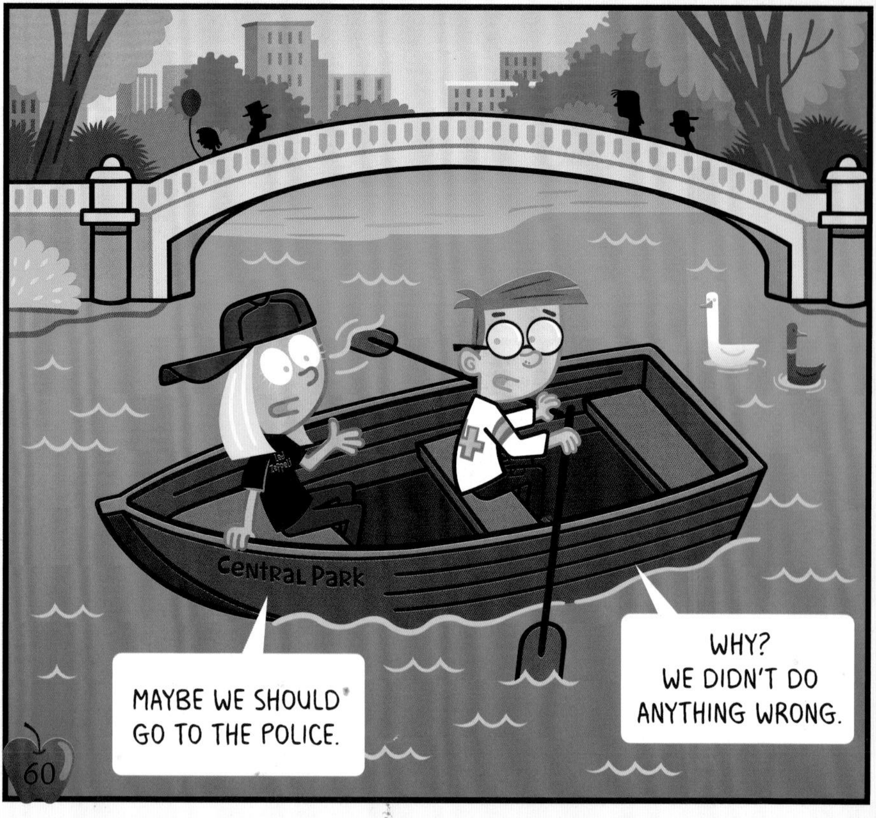
Central Park
MAYBE WE SHOULD GO TO THE POLICE.
WHY? WE DIDN'T DO ANYTHING WRONG.

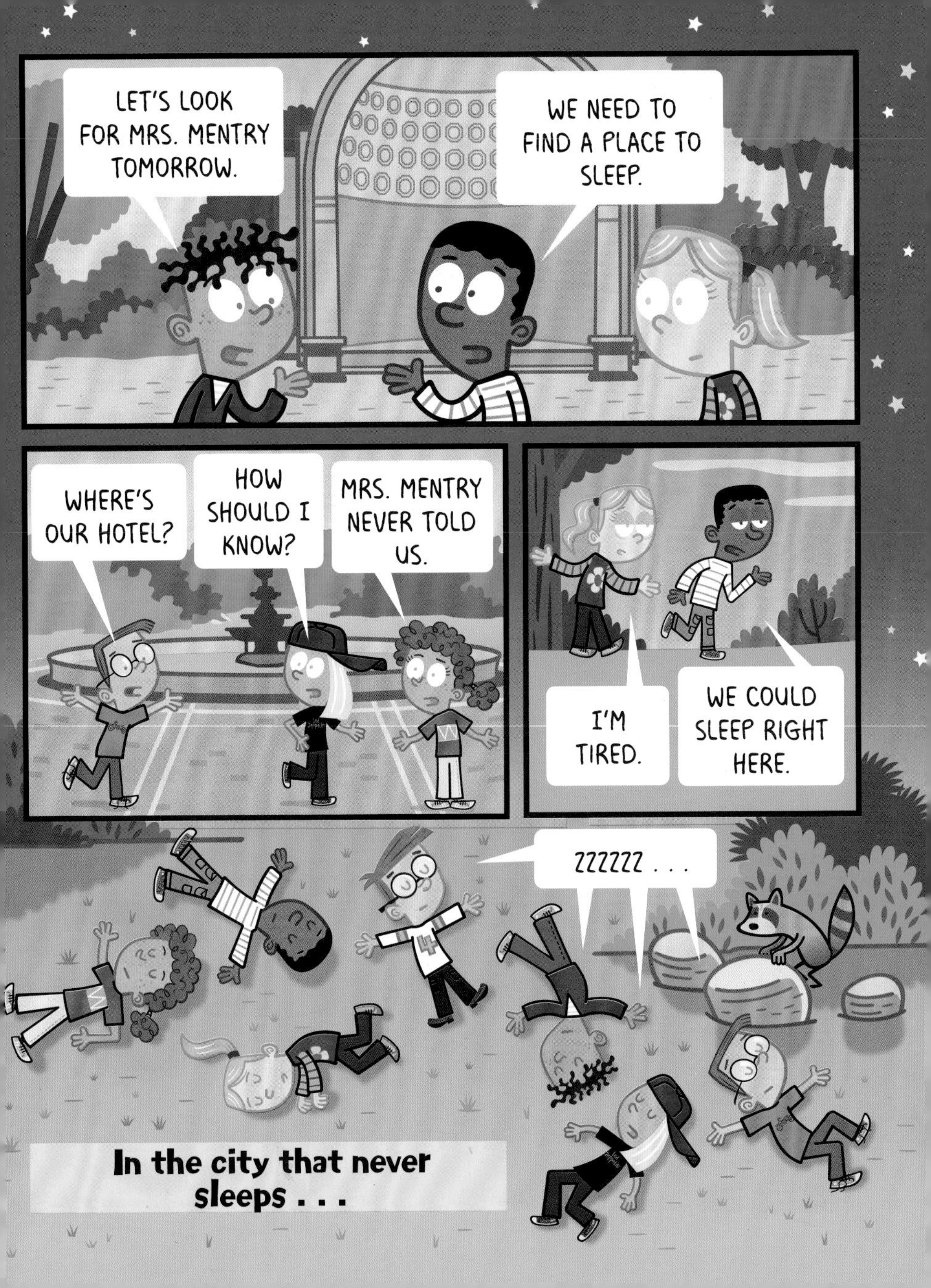
LET'S LOOK FOR MRS. MENTRY TOMORROW.
WE NEED TO FIND A PLACE TO SLEEP.
WHERE'S OUR HOTEL?
HOW SHOULD I KNOW?
MRS. MENTRY NEVER TOLD US.
I'M TIRED.
WE COULD SLEEP RIGHT HERE.
ZZZZZZ . . .
In the city that never sleeps . . .

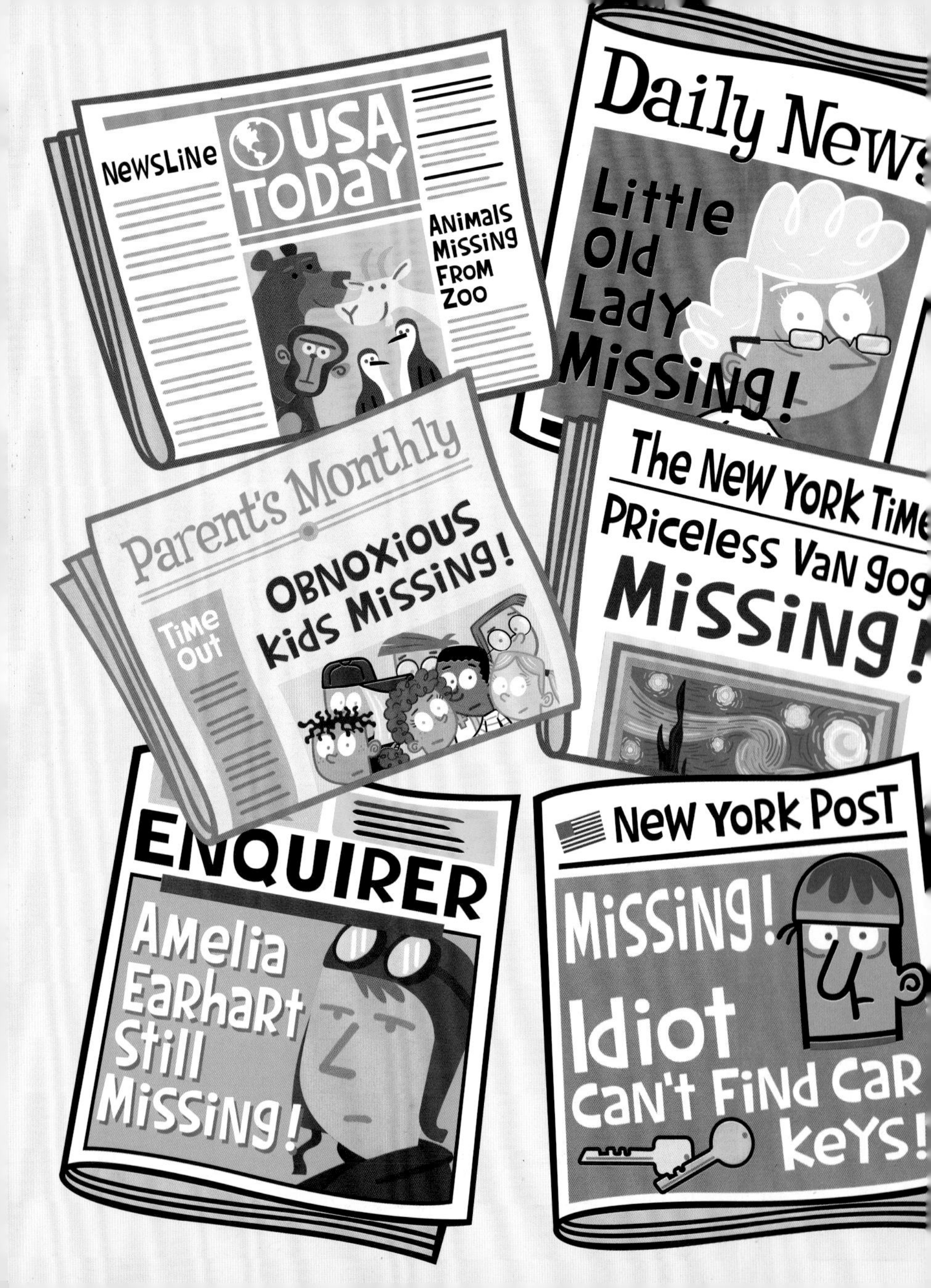

NewsLine
USA TODAY
Animals Missing From Zoo
Daily News
Little Old Lady Missing!
Parent's Monthly
Obnoxious Kids Missing!
Time Out
The New York Time
Priceless Van gog
Missing!
ENQUIRER
Amelia Earhart Still Missing!
New York Post
Missing!
Idiot Can't Find Car Keys!

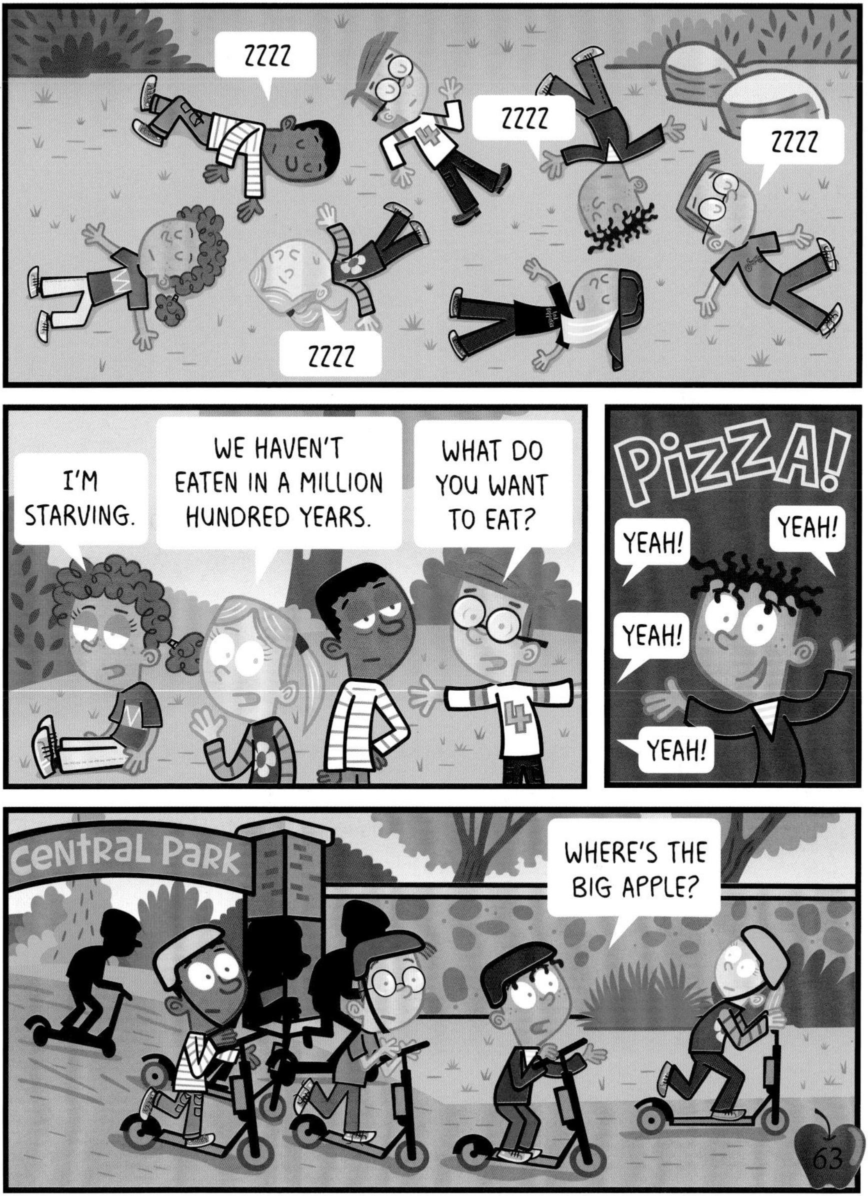
ZZZZ
ZZZZ
ZZZZ
ZZZZ
I'M STARVING.
WE HAVEN'T EATEN IN A MILLION HUNDRED YEARS.
WHAT DO YOU WANT TO EAT?
PIZZA!
YEAH!
YEAH!
YEAH!
YEAH!
CENTRAL PARK
WHERE'S THE BIG APPLE?

YUM!

WE GOTTA FIND MRS. MENTRY.

SHE SAID SHE LOVES MUSEUMS.

SO MAYBE SHE'S AT A MUSEUM.

LET'S GO!

64

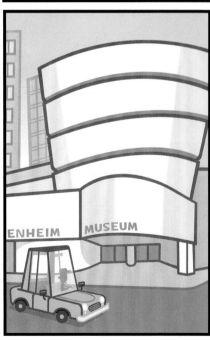

ENHEIM MUSEUM

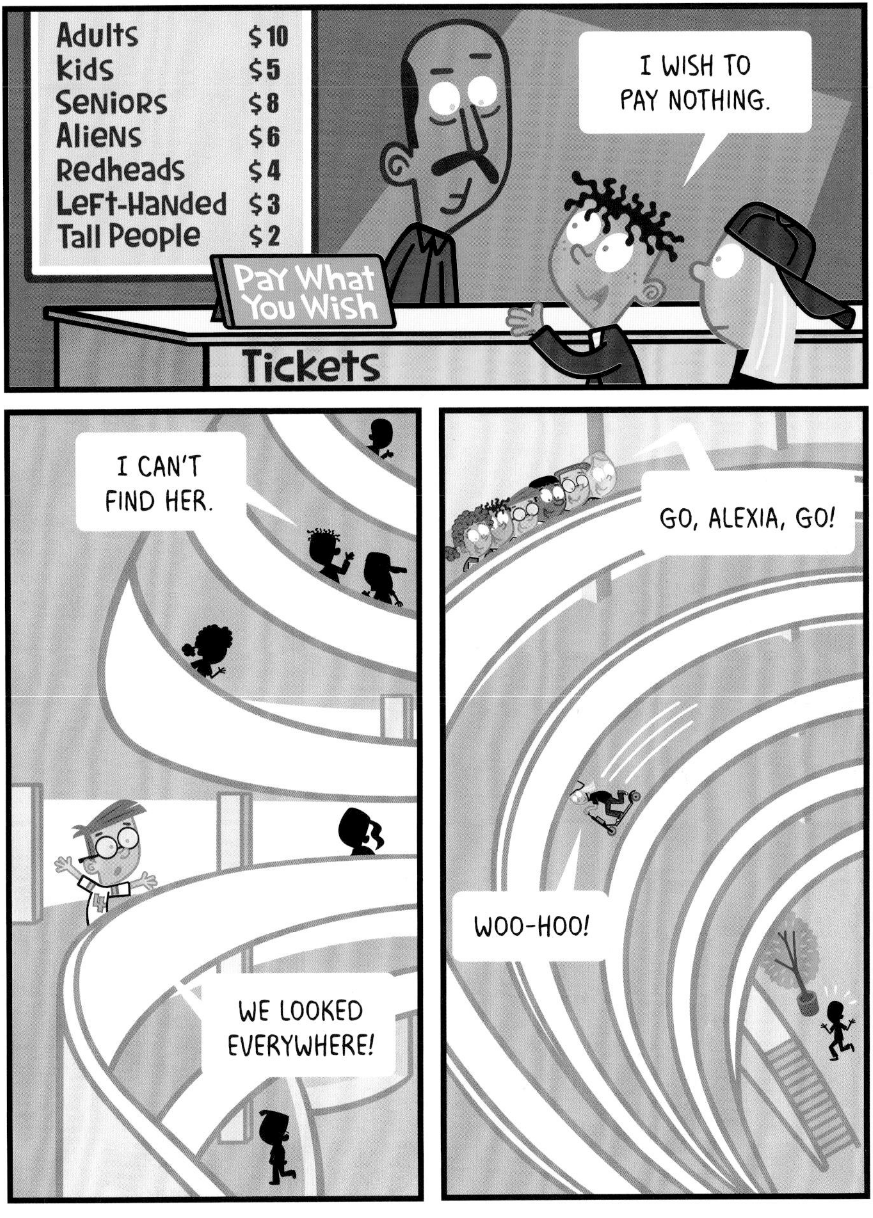
Adults $10
Kids $5
Seniors $8
Aliens $6
Redheads $4
Left-Handed $3
Tall People $2
Pay What You Wish
Tickets
I WISH TO PAY NOTHING.
I CAN'T FIND HER.
WE LOOKED EVERYWHERE!
GO, ALEXIA, GO!
WOO-HOO!

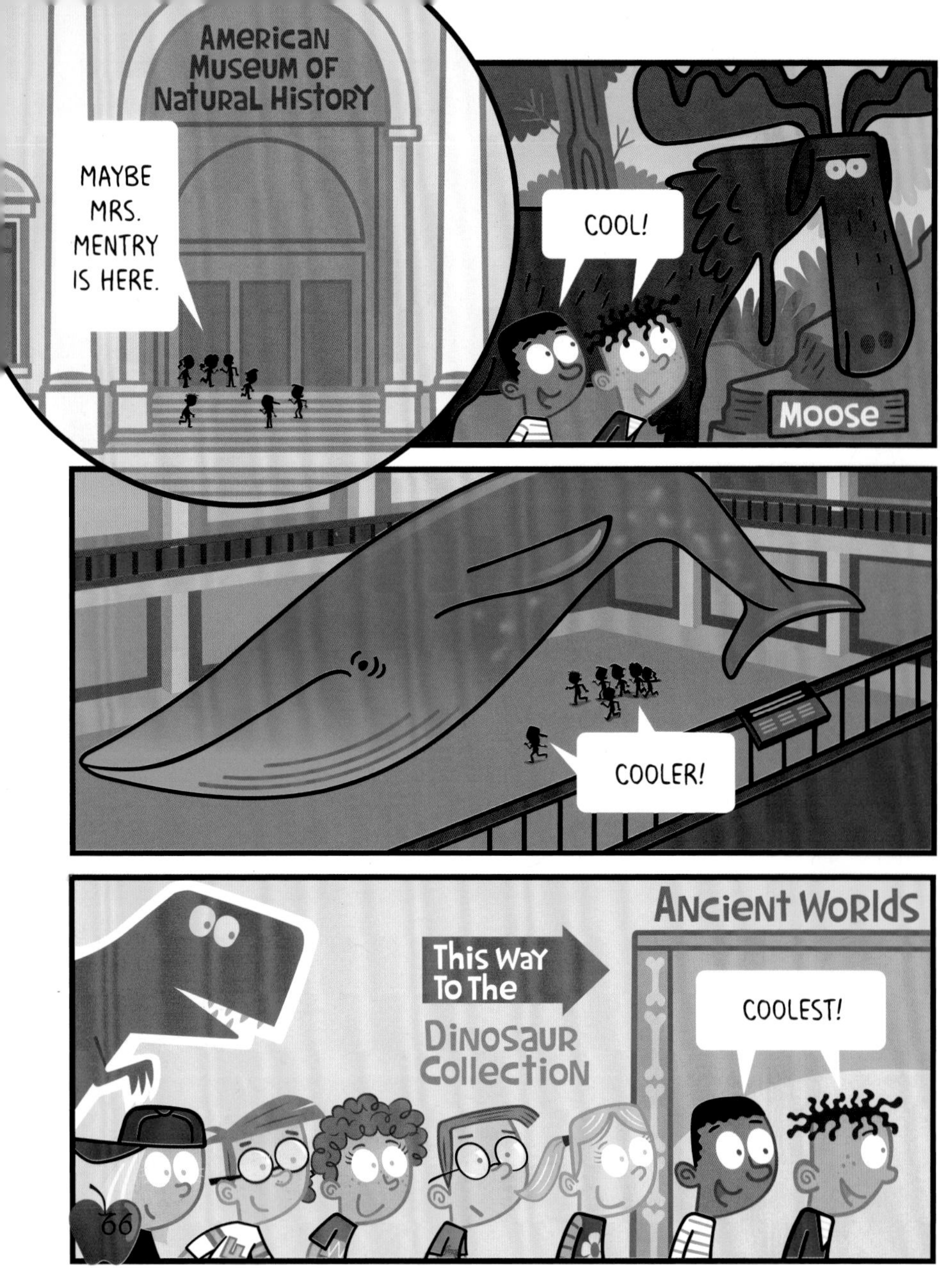
AMERICAN MUSEUM OF NATURAL HISTORY
MAYBE MRS. MENTRY IS HERE.
COOL!
MOOSE
COOLER!
ANCIENT WORLDS
This Way To The
Dinosaur Collection
COOLEST!

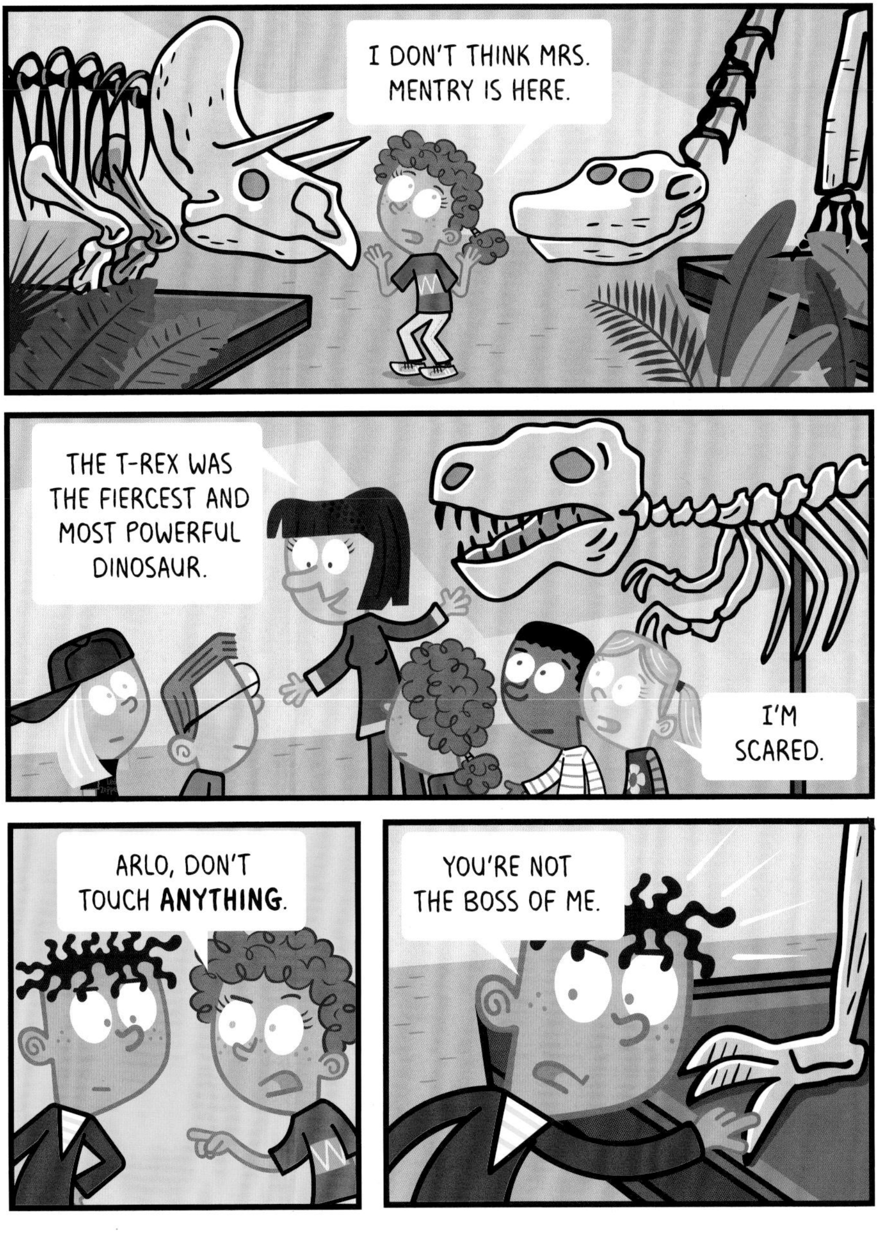
I DON'T THINK MRS. MENTRY IS HERE.
THE T-REX WAS THE FIERCEST AND MOST POWERFUL DINOSAUR.
I'M SCARED.
ARLO, DON'T TOUCH **ANYTHING**.
YOU'RE NOT THE BOSS OF ME.

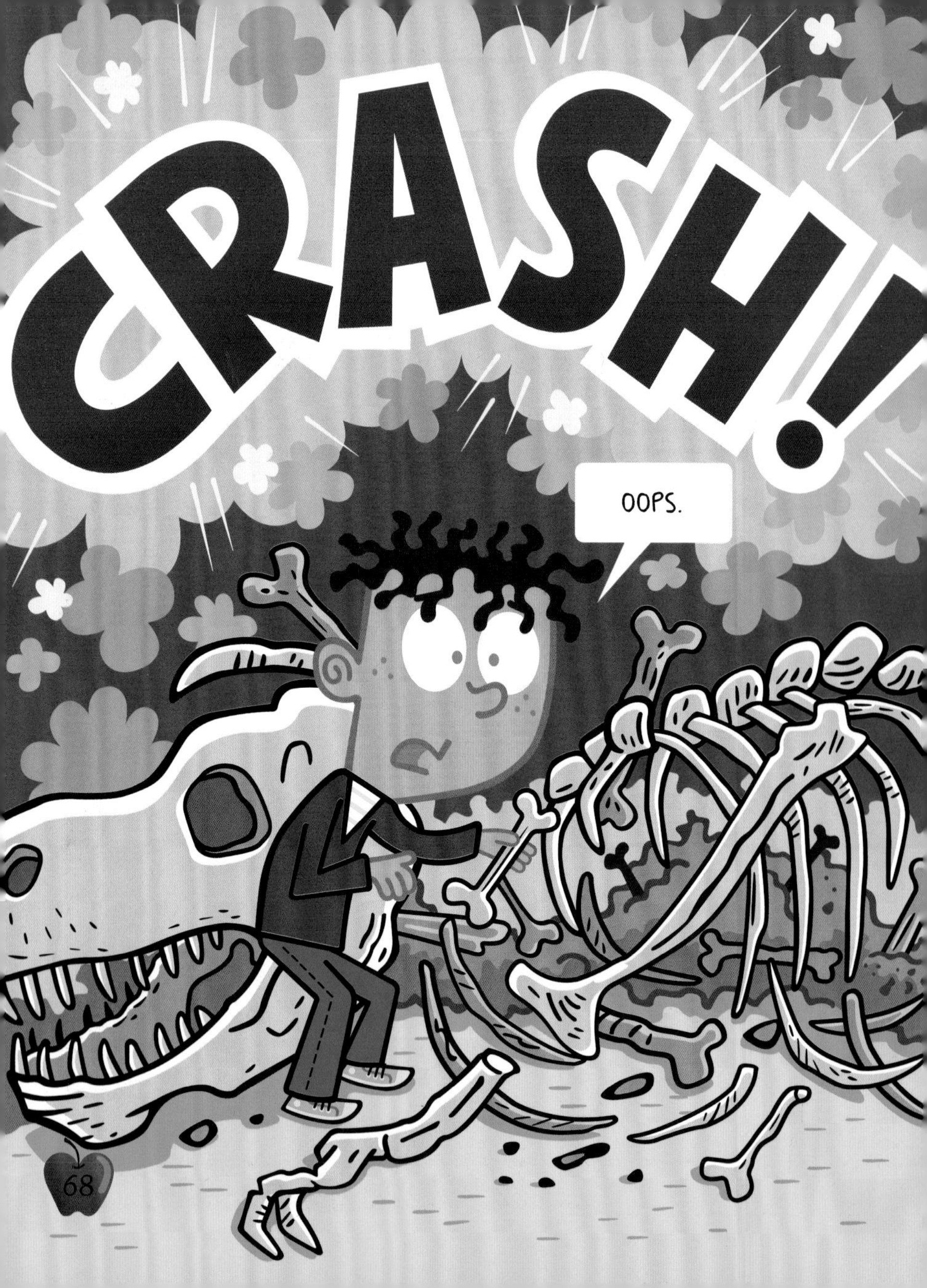
CRASH!
OOPS.

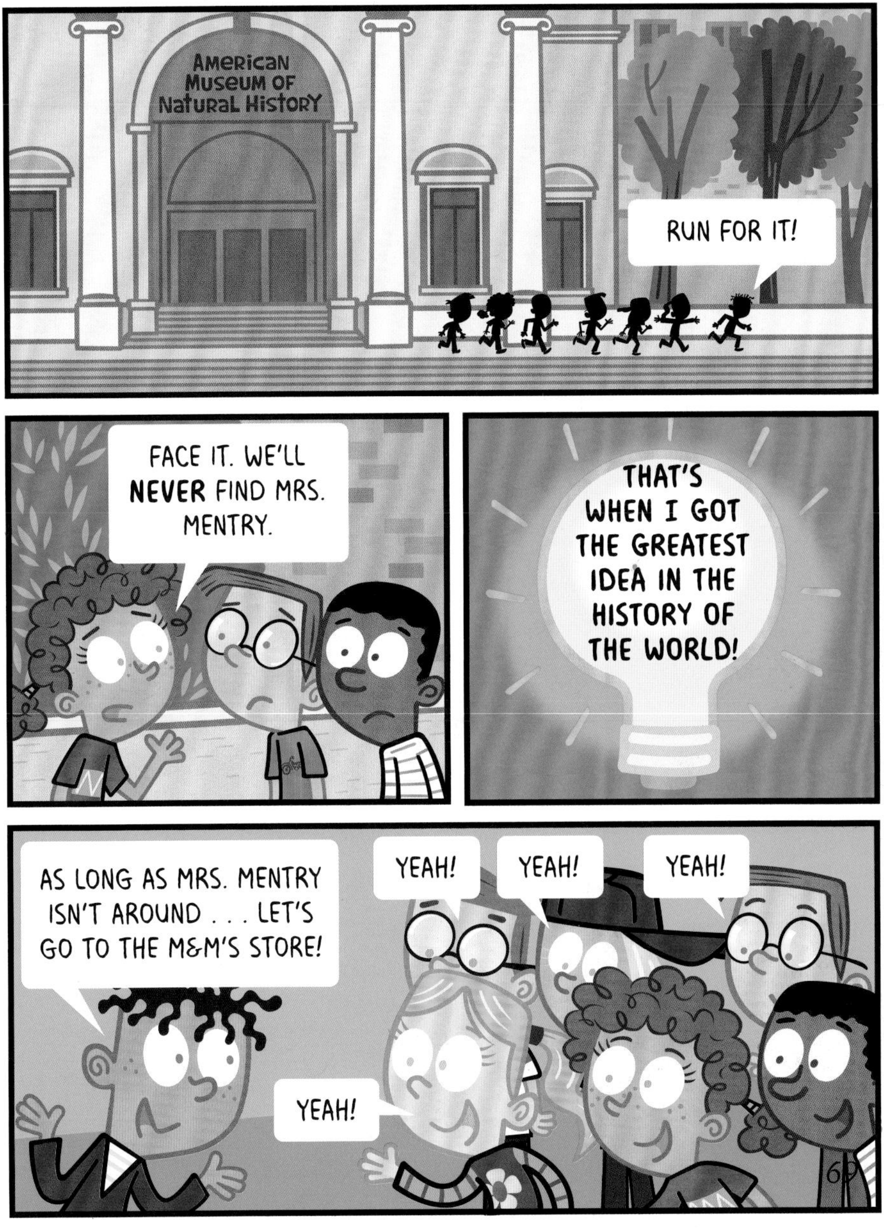
AMERICAN MUSEUM OF NATURAL HISTORY
RUN FOR IT!
FACE IT. WE'LL **NEVER** FIND MRS. MENTRY.
THAT'S WHEN I GOT THE GREATEST IDEA IN THE HISTORY OF THE WORLD!
AS LONG AS MRS. MENTRY ISN'T AROUND . . . LET'S GO TO THE M&M'S STORE!
YEAH!
YEAH!
YEAH!
YEAH!

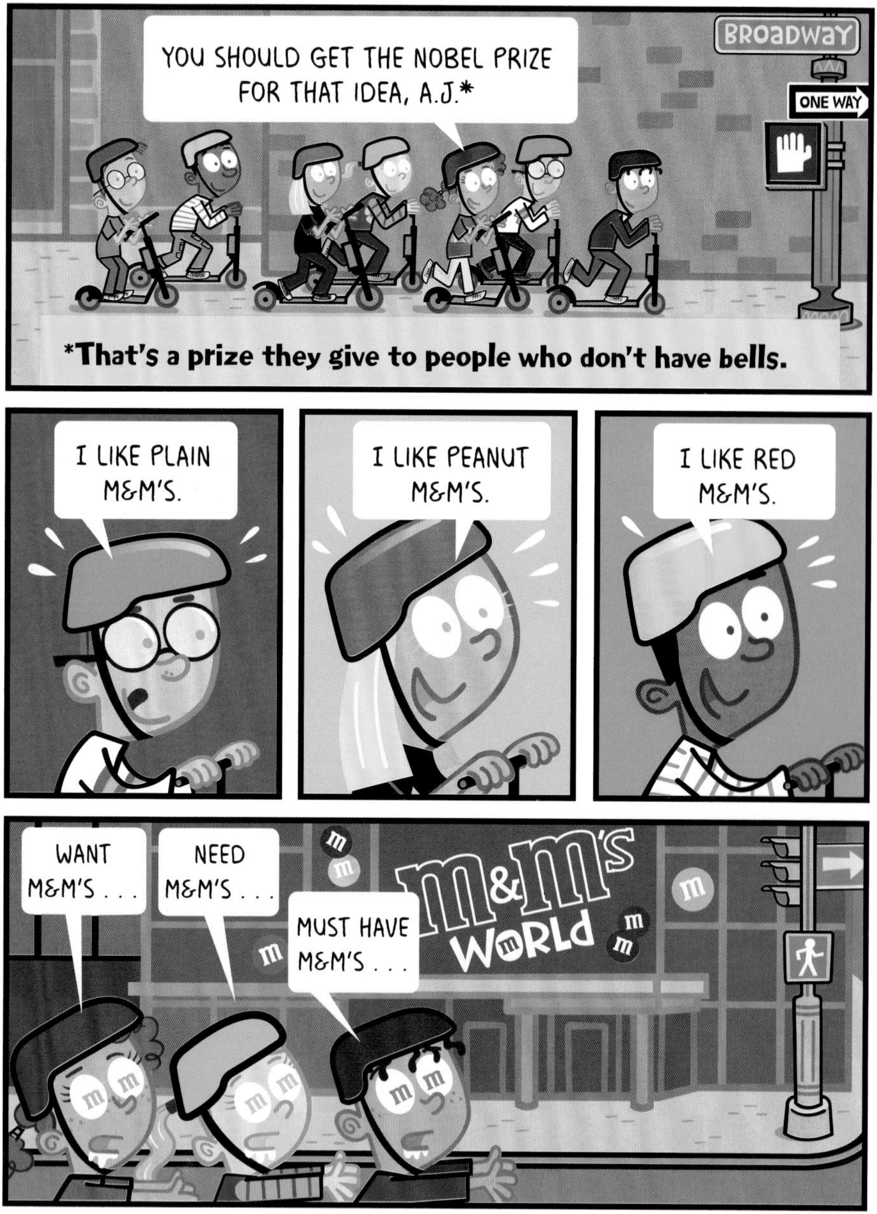
BROADWAY
ONE WAY
YOU SHOULD GET THE NOBEL PRIZE FOR THAT IDEA, A.J.*
*That's a prize they give to people who don't have bells.
I LIKE PLAIN M&M'S.
I LIKE PEANUT M&M'S.
I LIKE RED M&M'S.
WANT M&M'S . . .
NEED M&M'S . . .
MUST HAVE M&M'S . . .
m&m's WORLD

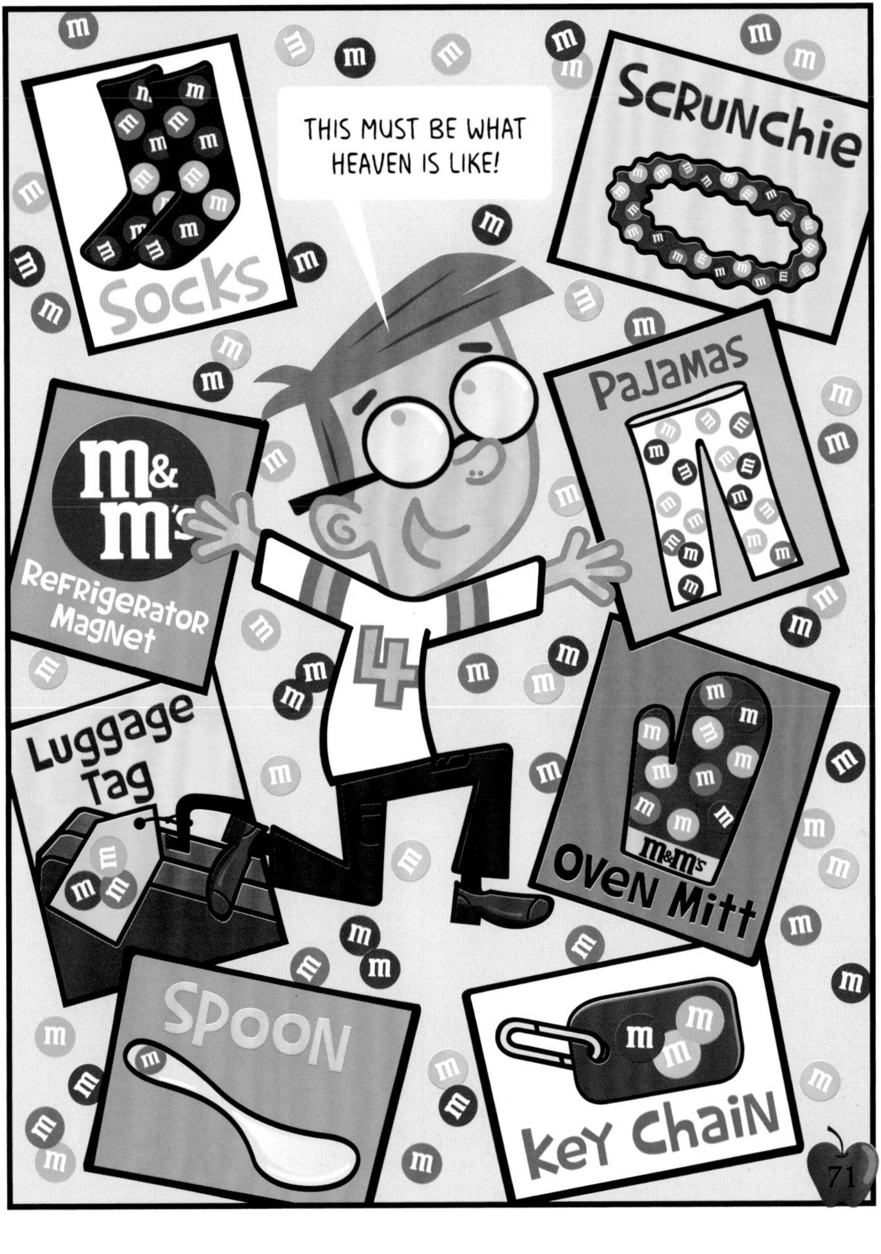
THIS MUST BE WHAT HEAVEN IS LIKE!
Socks
Scrunchie
m&m's
Refrigerator Magnet
Pajamas
Luggage Tag
m&m's
Oven Mitt
Spoon
Key Chain

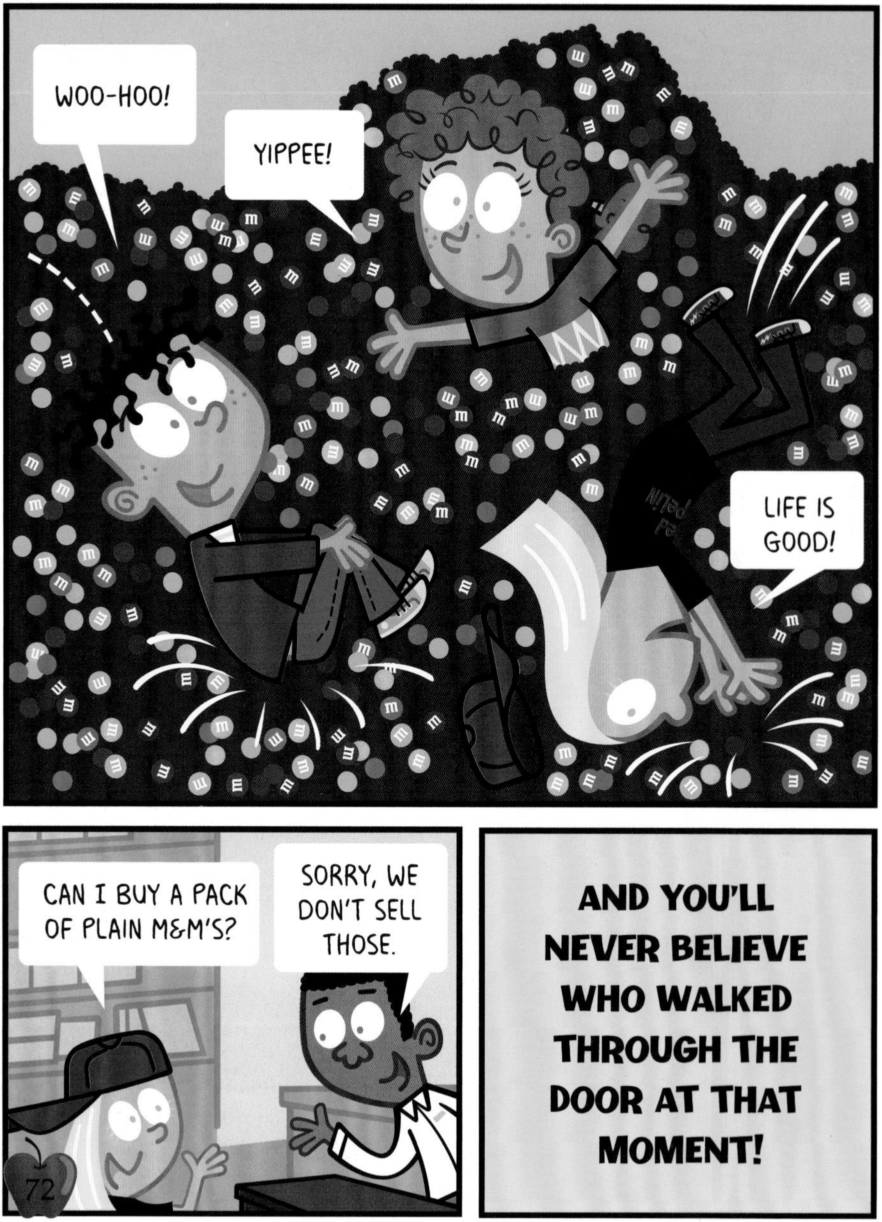
WOO-HOO!
YIPPEE!
LIFE IS GOOD!
CAN I BUY A PACK OF PLAIN M&M'S?
SORRY, WE DON'T SELL THOSE.
AND YOU'LL NEVER BELIEVE WHO WALKED THROUGH THE DOOR AT THAT MOMENT!

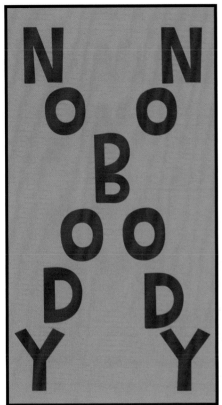

BUT YOU'LL NEVER BELIEVE WHO WALKED THROUGH THE DOORWAY . . .

HI!

It was **Mrs. Ella Mentry!**

WE MISSED YOU!

I LOOKED ALL OVER FOR YOU TOO!

WE LOOKED ALL OVER FOR YOU!

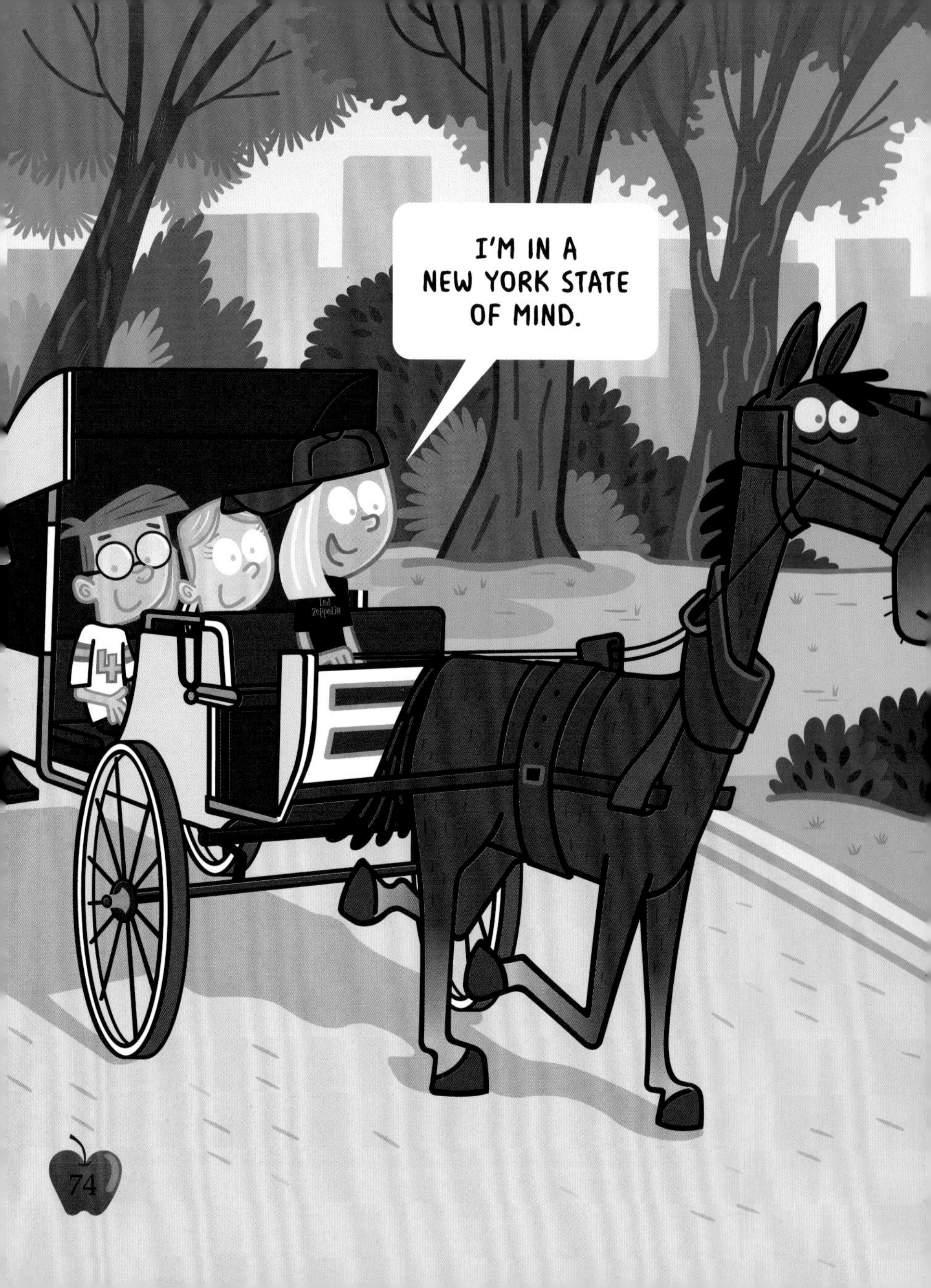
I'M IN A NEW YORK STATE OF MIND.
Led Zeppelin

CHAPTER 5

People Who Talk on Their Cell Phones Loudly in Public. People Who Don't Pick Up Their Dog's Poop. Loud Chewers. Litterbugs. People Who Put Their Recyclables in with the Regular Trash. People Who Stand and Talk to Each Other in the Middle of a Busy Sidewalk.

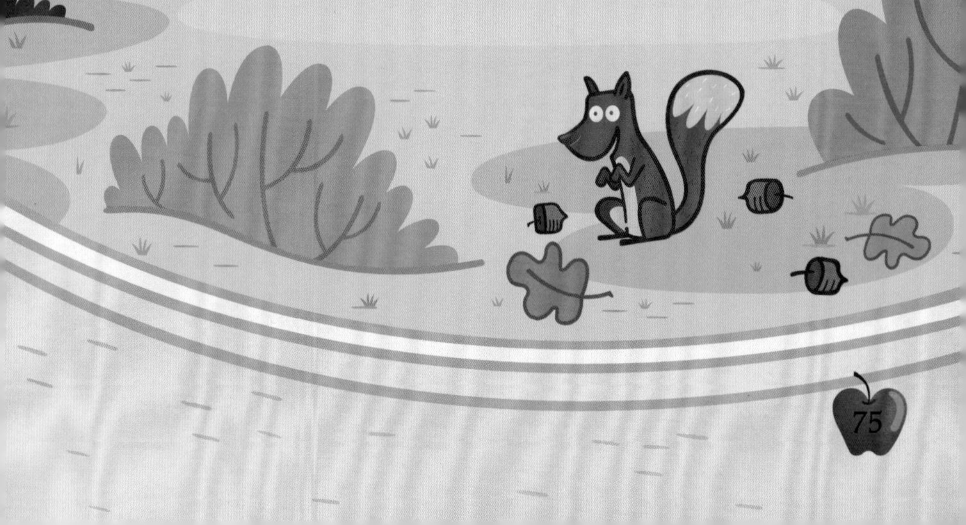

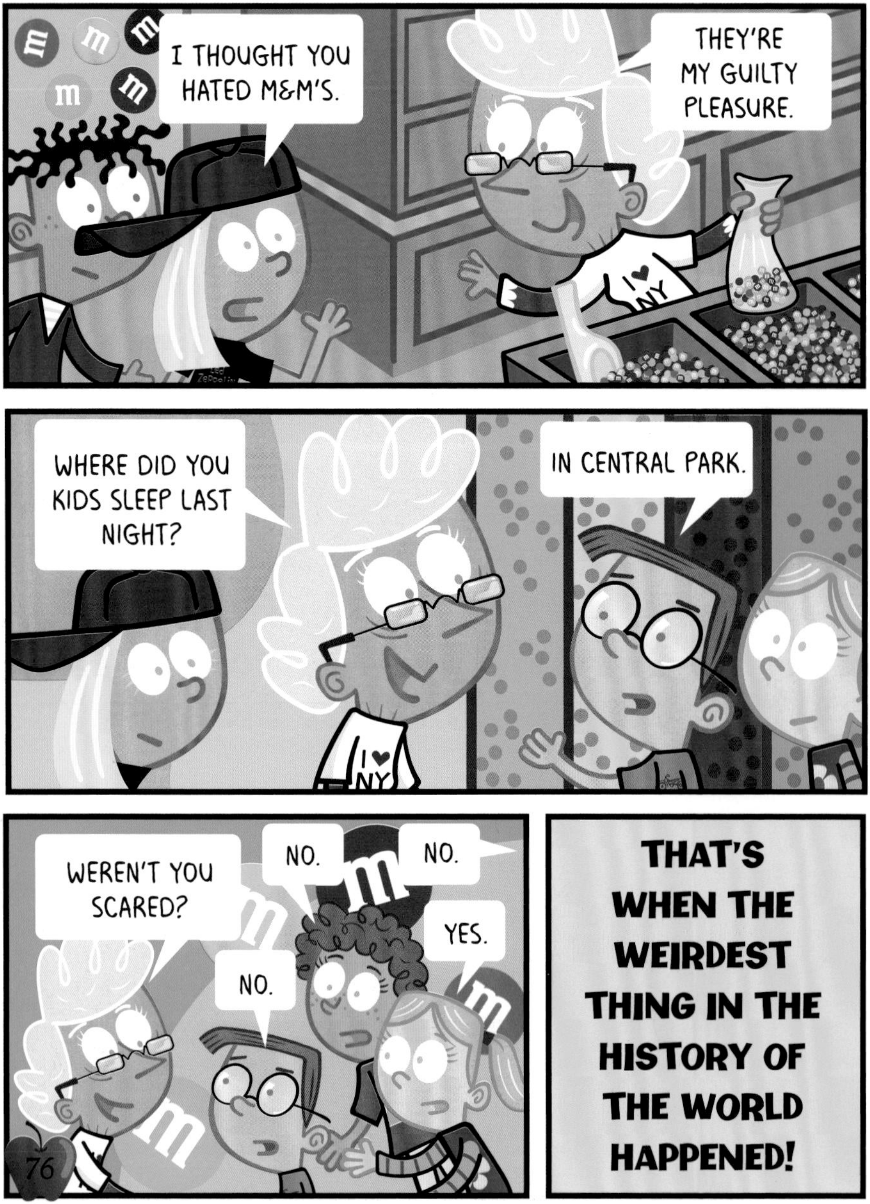
I THOUGHT YOU HATED M&M'S.
THEY'RE MY GUILTY PLEASURE.
WHERE DID YOU KIDS SLEEP LAST NIGHT?
IN CENTRAL PARK.
WEREN'T YOU SCARED?
NO.
NO.
YES.
NO.
THAT'S WHEN THE WEIRDEST THING IN THE HISTORY OF THE WORLD HAPPENED!

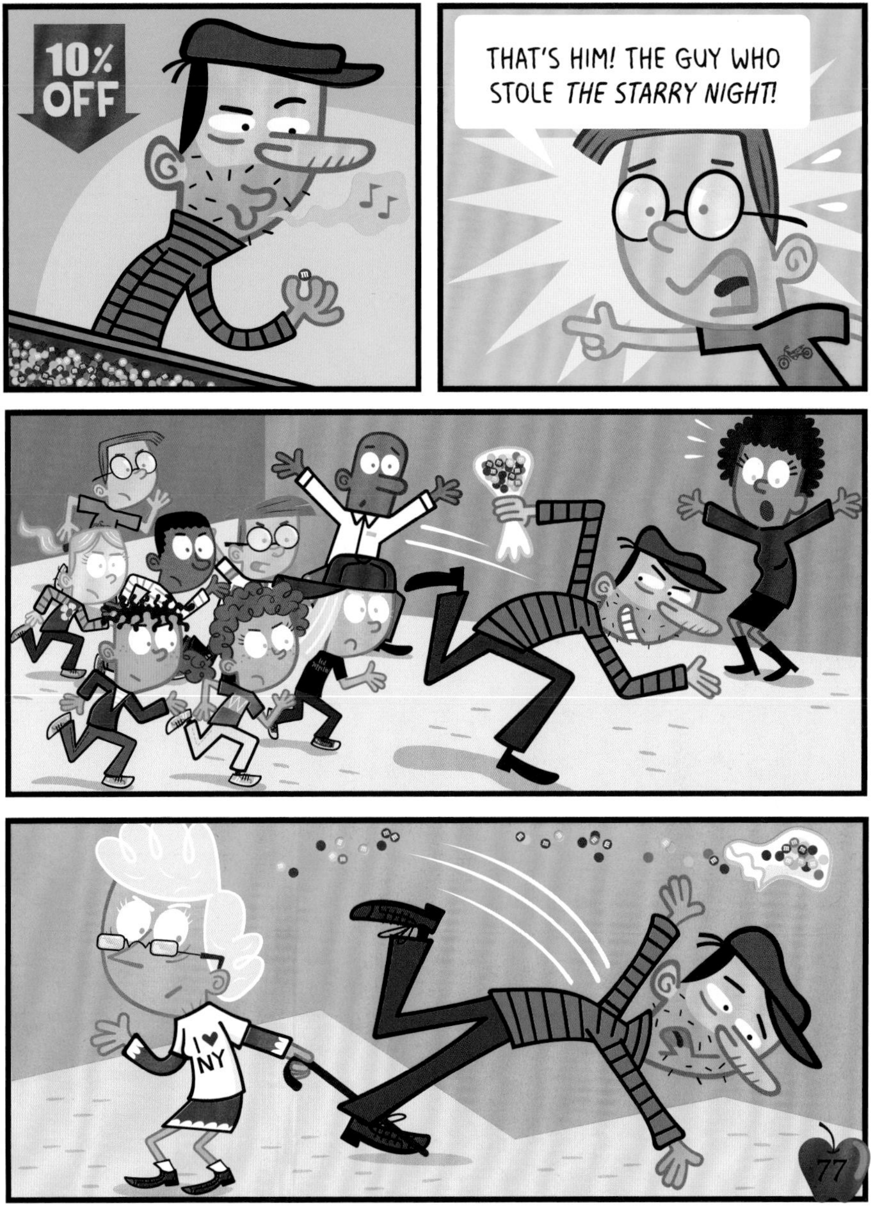
10% OFF
THAT'S HIM! THE GUY WHO STOLE *THE STARRY NIGHT*!
I ♥ NY

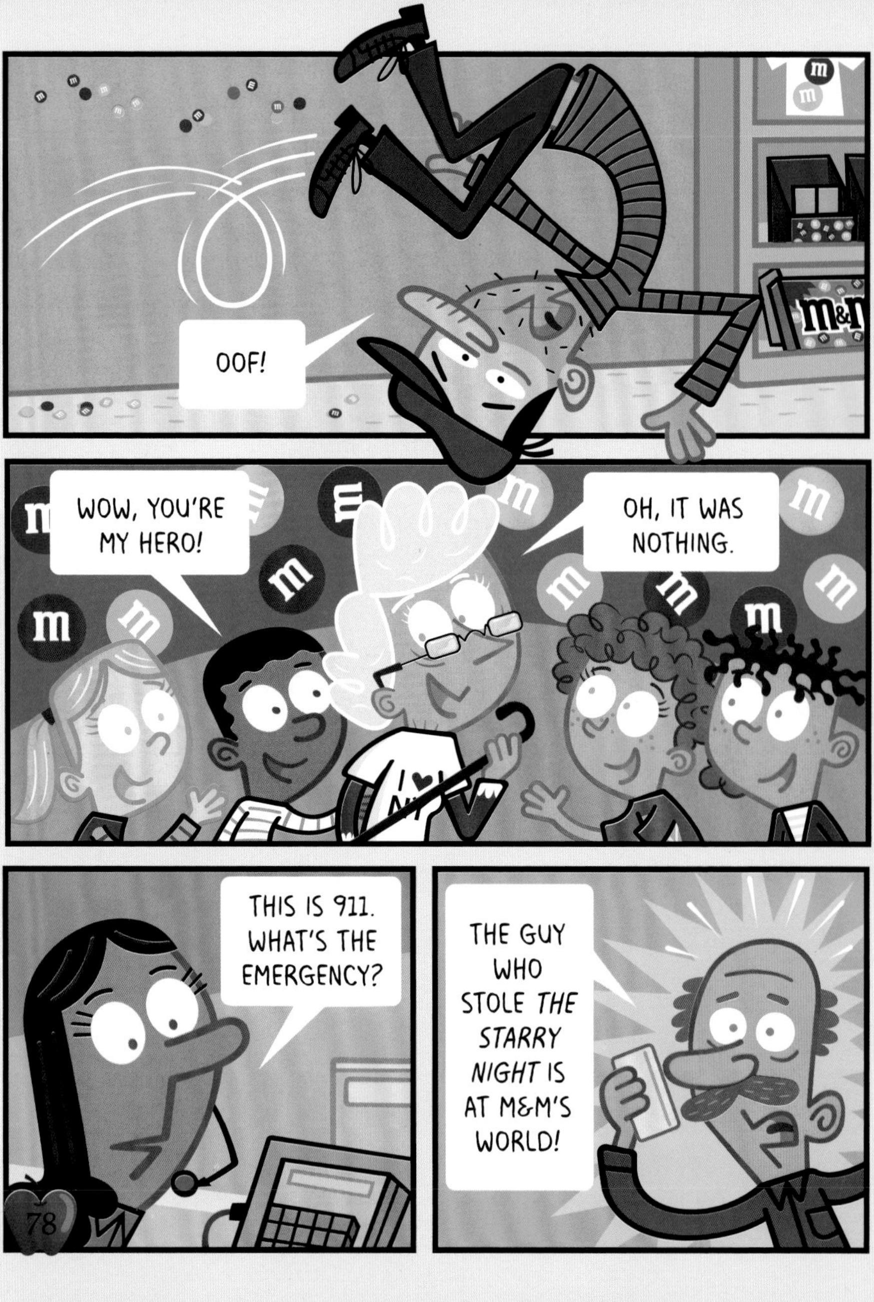
OOF!
WOW, YOU'RE MY HERO!
OH, IT WAS NOTHING.
THIS IS 911. WHAT'S THE EMERGENCY?
THE GUY WHO STOLE *THE STARRY NIGHT* IS AT M&M'S WORLD!

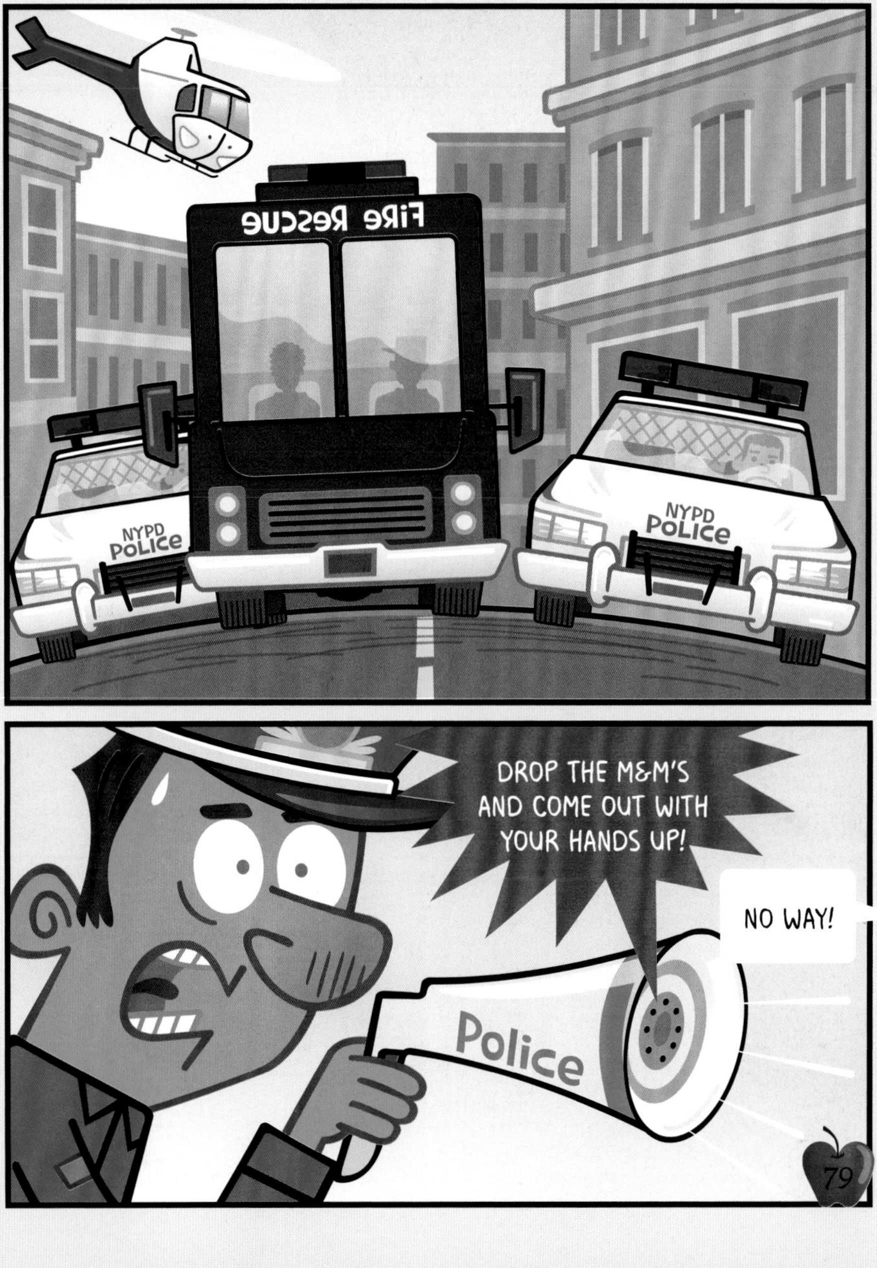
FIRE RESCUE
NYPD POLICE
NYPD POLICE
DROP THE M&M'S AND COME OUT WITH YOUR HANDS UP!
NO WAY!
Police

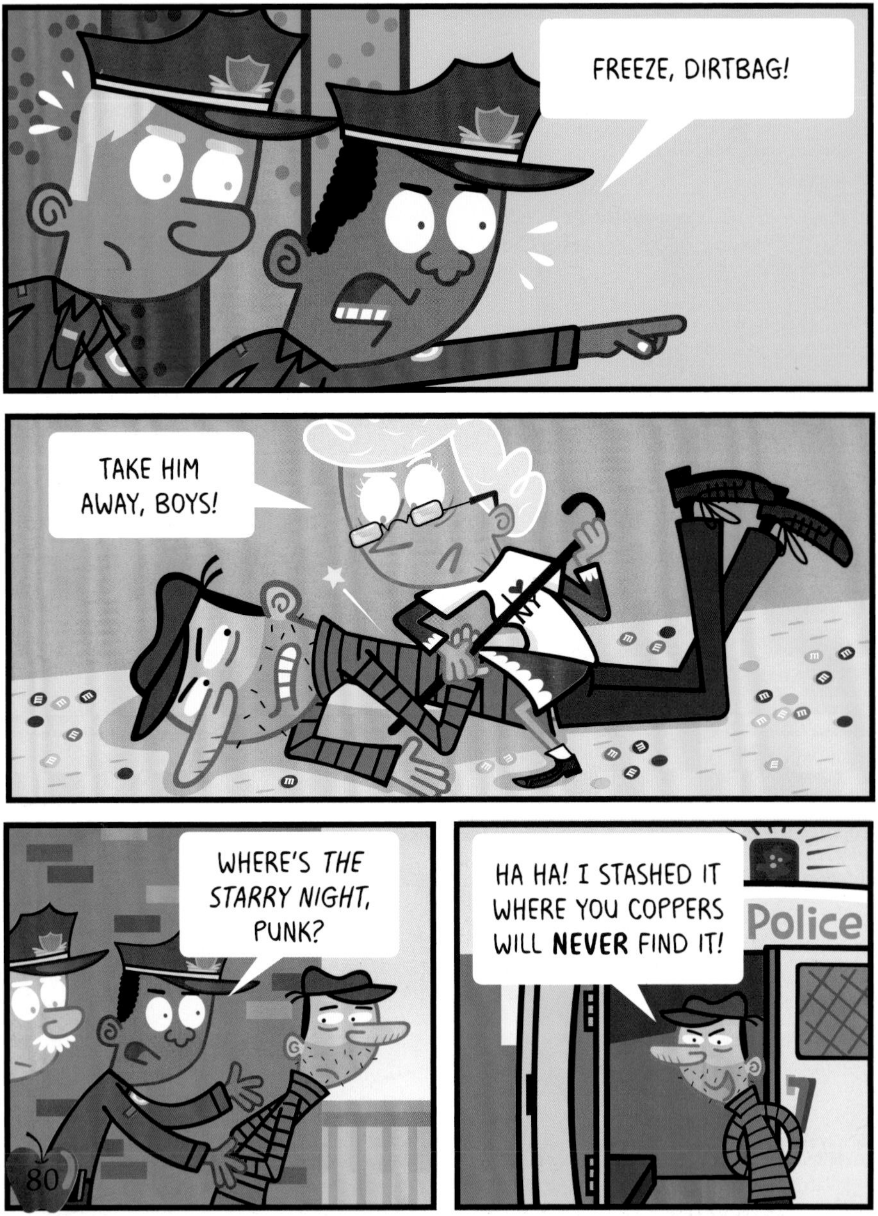
FREEZE, DIRTBAG!
TAKE HIM AWAY, BOYS!
WHERE'S THE STARRY NIGHT, PUNK?
HA HA! I STASHED IT WHERE YOU COPPERS WILL NEVER FIND IT!
Police

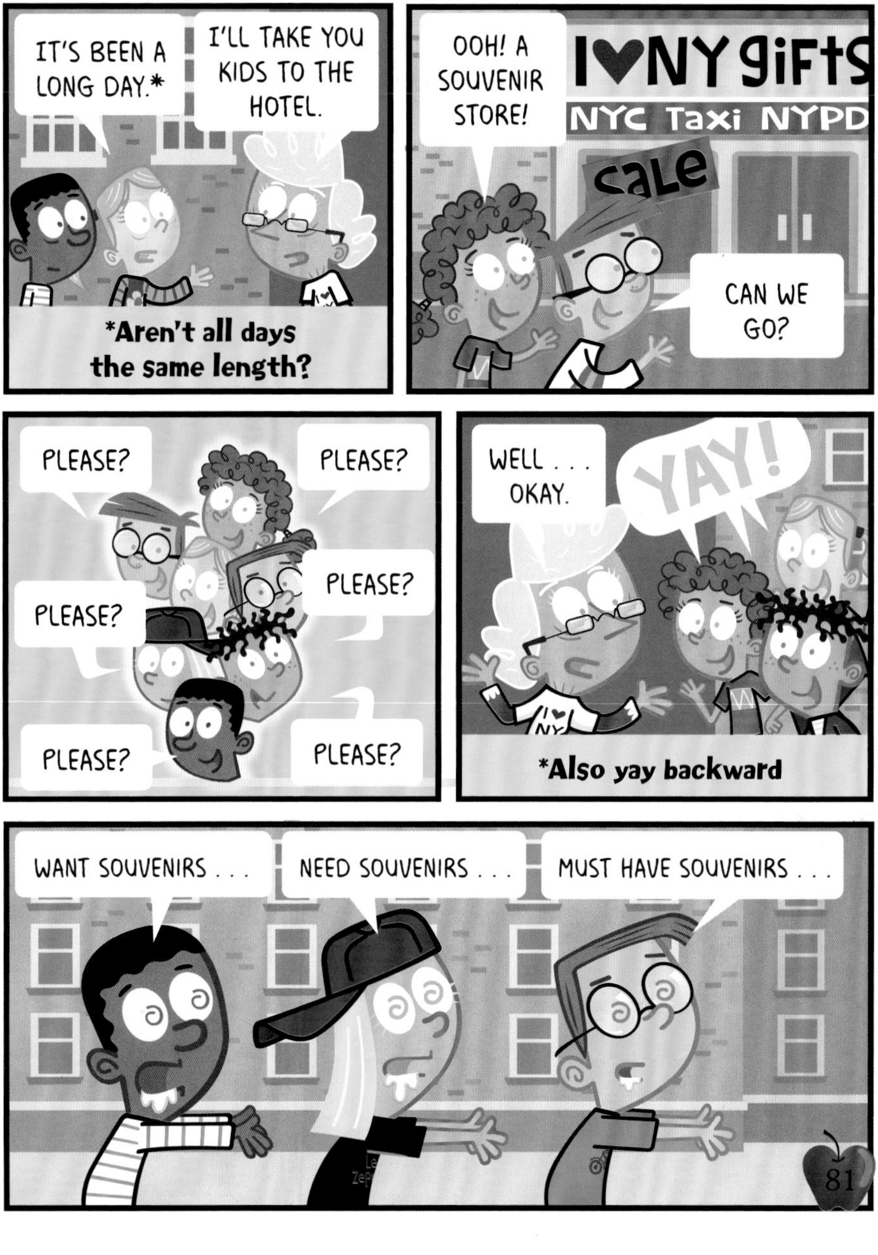
IT'S BEEN A LONG DAY.*
I'LL TAKE YOU KIDS TO THE HOTEL.
*Aren't all days the same length?
OOH! A SOUVENIR STORE!
I♥NY gifts
NYC Taxi NYPD
SALE
CAN WE GO?
PLEASE?
PLEASE?
PLEASE?
PLEASE?
PLEASE?
PLEASE?
WELL . . . OKAY.
YAY!
*Also yay backward
WANT SOUVENIRS . . .
NEED SOUVENIRS . . .
MUST HAVE SOUVENIRS . . .

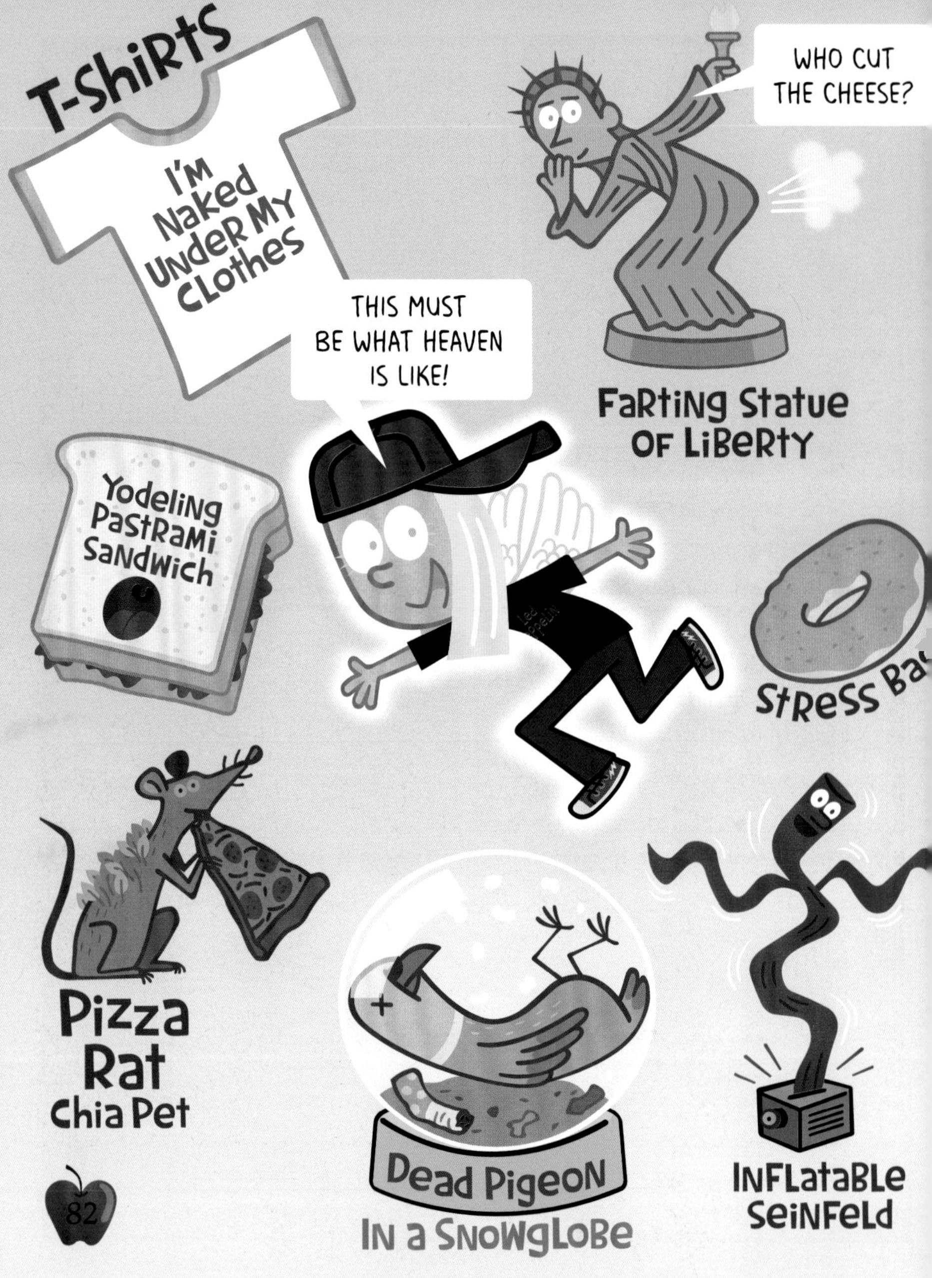
T-Shirts
I'm Naked Under My Clothes
WHO CUT THE CHEESE?
Farting Statue of Liberty
THIS MUST BE WHAT HEAVEN IS LIKE!
Yodeling Pastrami Sandwich
Stress Ba
Pizza Rat Chia Pet
Dead Pigeon In a Snowglobe
Inflatable Seinfeld

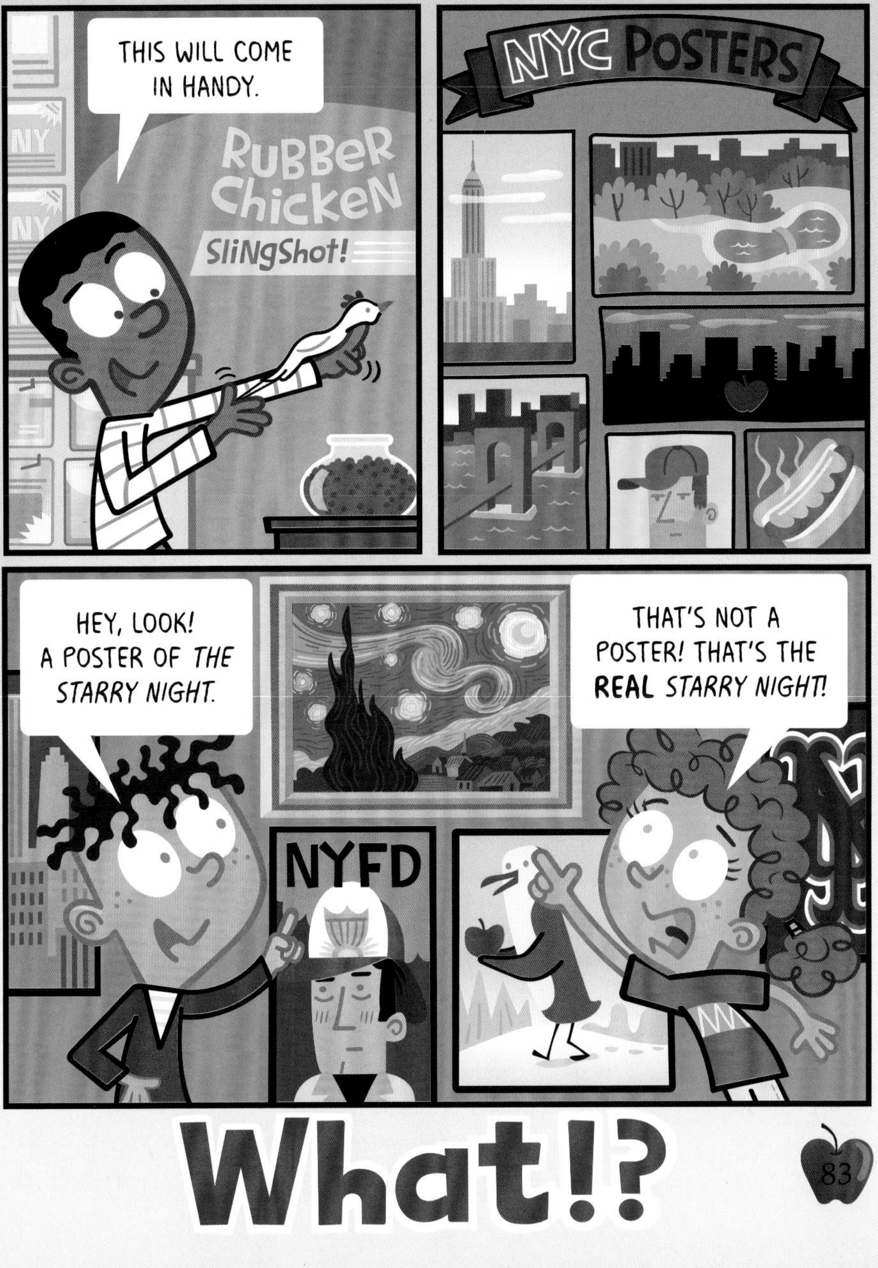
THIS WILL COME IN HANDY.
RUBBER Chicken SliNgShot!
NYC POSTERS
HEY, LOOK! A POSTER OF *THE STARRY NIGHT*.
THAT'S NOT A POSTER! THAT'S THE **REAL** *STARRY NIGHT*!
NYFD
What!?

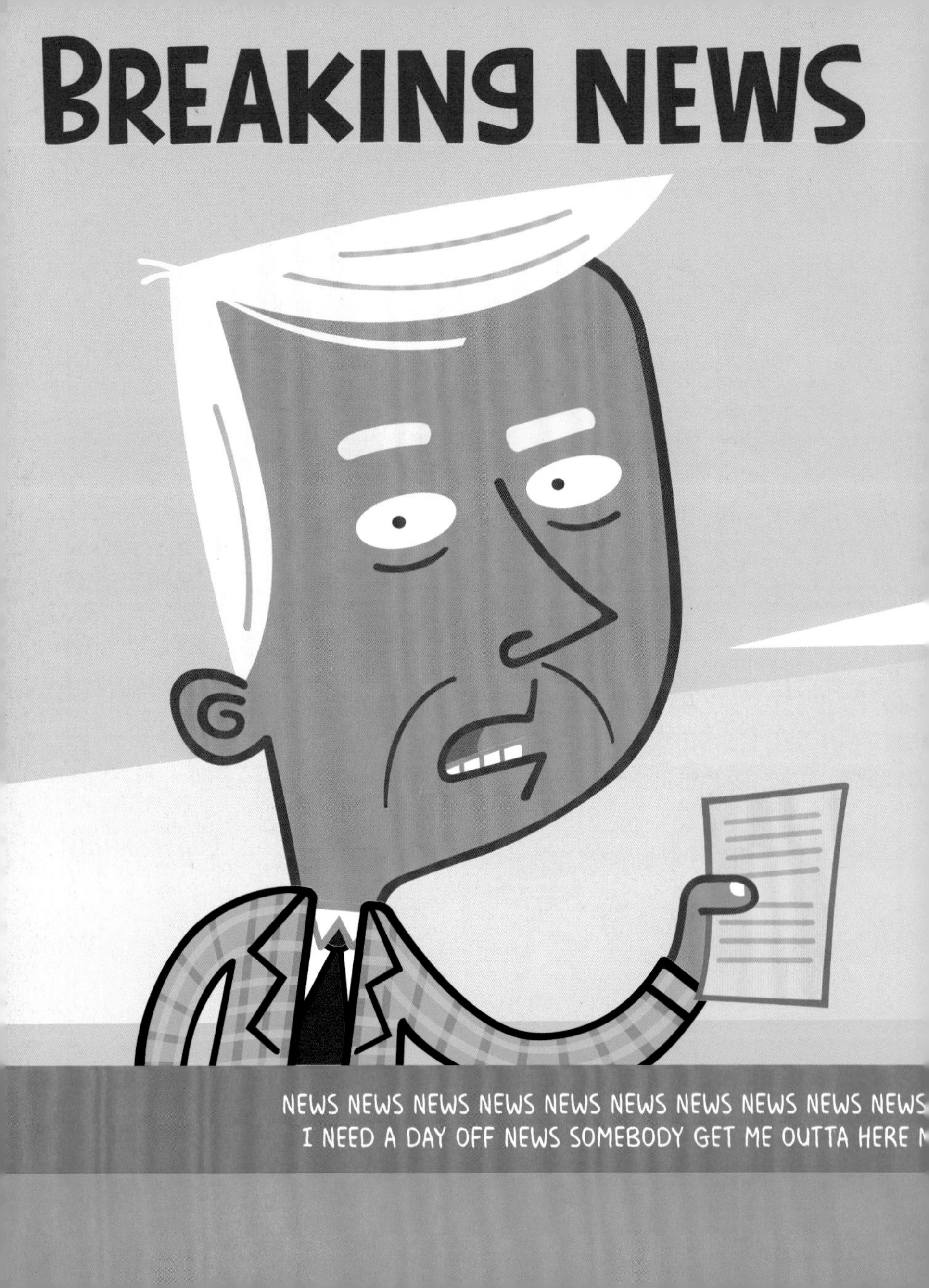
BREAKING NEWS
NEWS NEWS NEWS NEWS NEWS NEWS NEWS NEWS NEWS NEWS
I NEED A DAY OFF NEWS SOMEBODY GET ME OUTTA HERE

TOP STORY

THE STARRY NIGHT FOUND!

MISSING KIDS CATCH CROOK!

OLD LADY IS OKAY!

ZOO ANIIMALS STILL MISSING!

THIS IS TAB BATTAN WITH BREAKING
WS. IN AN AMAZING TURN OF EVENTS,
THE PRICELESS *THE STARRY NIGHT*
PAINTING BY VINCENT VAN GOGH HAS
N FOUND HANGING IN A TIMES SQUARE
UVENIR SHOP BY THE OLD LADY WHO
FELL INTO AN OPEN MANHOLE AND A
ROUP OF OBNOXIOUS KIDS WHO HAD
BEEN MISSING SINCE YESTERDAY. THE
IEF WHO STOLE THE MASTERPIECE HAS
EEN CAPTURED. SADLY, THE ANIMALS
THAT ESCAPED FROM THE CENTRAL
ARK ZOO YESTERDAY HAVE NOT BEEN
UND. BUT THE TOP STORY OF THE DAY
ONCERNS THE JARDISHIAN FAMILY . . .

LIVE
BNN

/7 UGH NEWS
S NEWS . . .

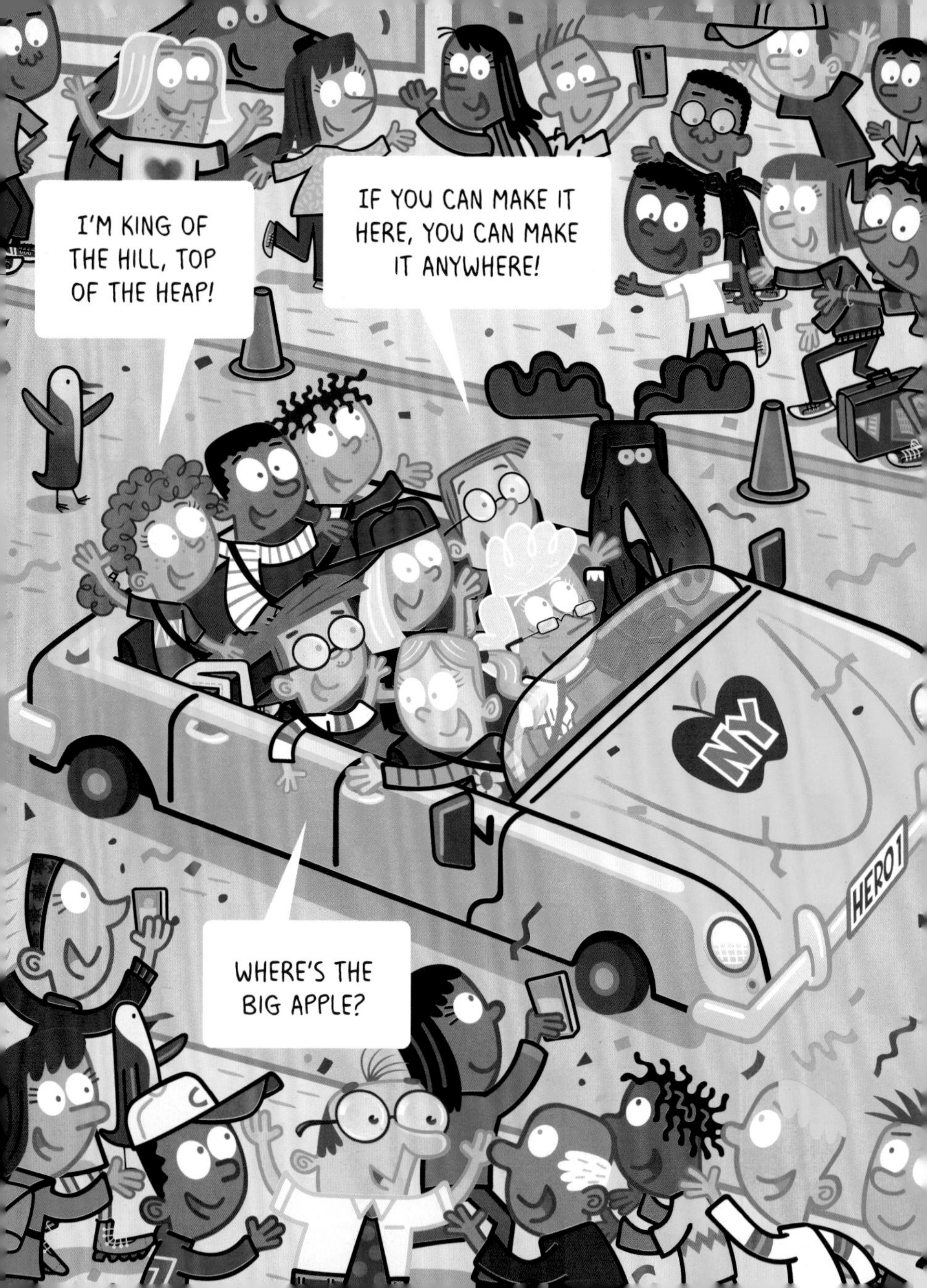
I'M KING OF THE HILL, TOP OF THE HEAP!
IF YOU CAN MAKE IT HERE, YOU CAN MAKE IT ANYWHERE!
NY
HERO 1
WHERE'S THE BIG APPLE?

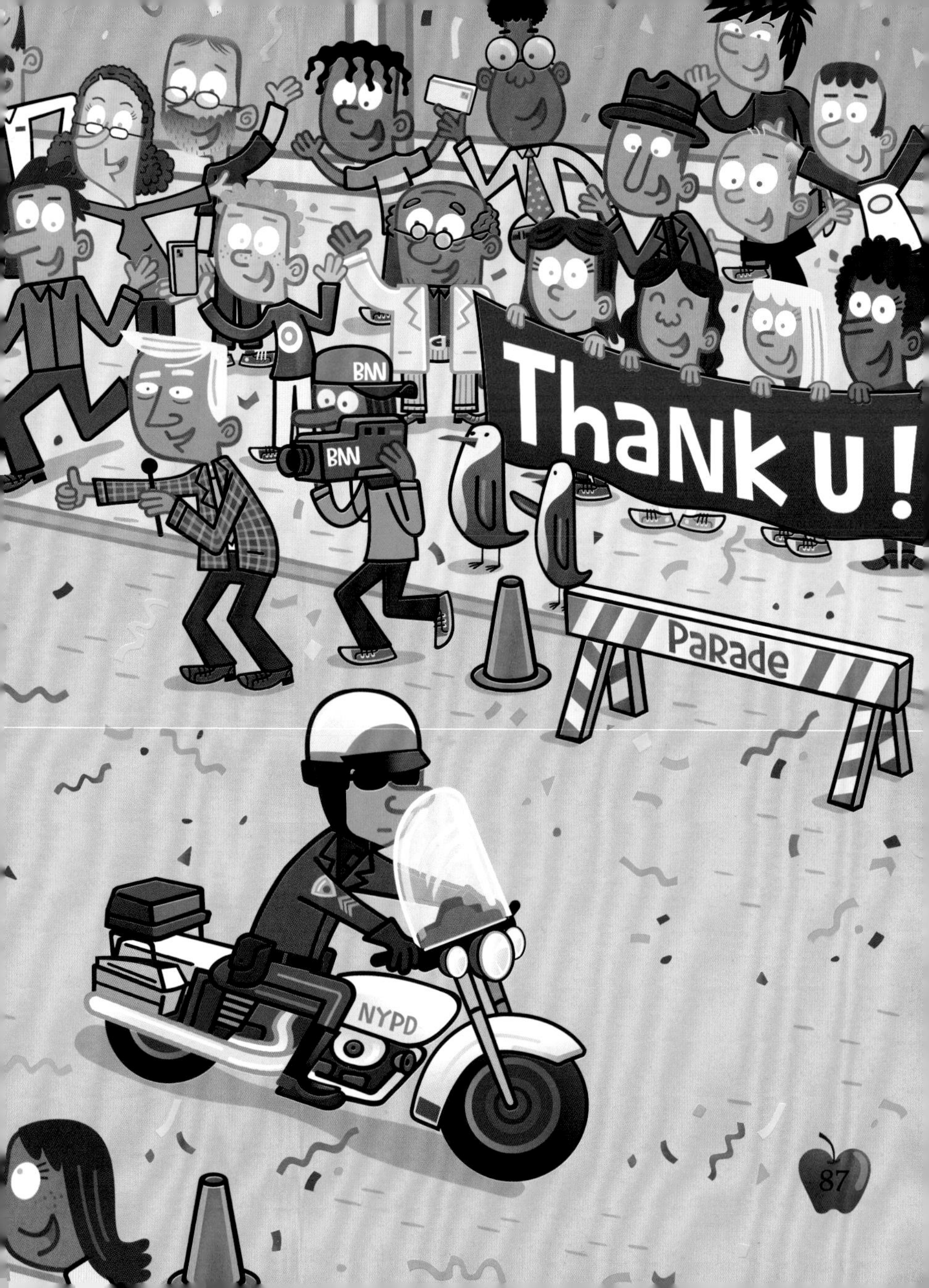
BNN
BNN
Thank u!
Parade
NYPD

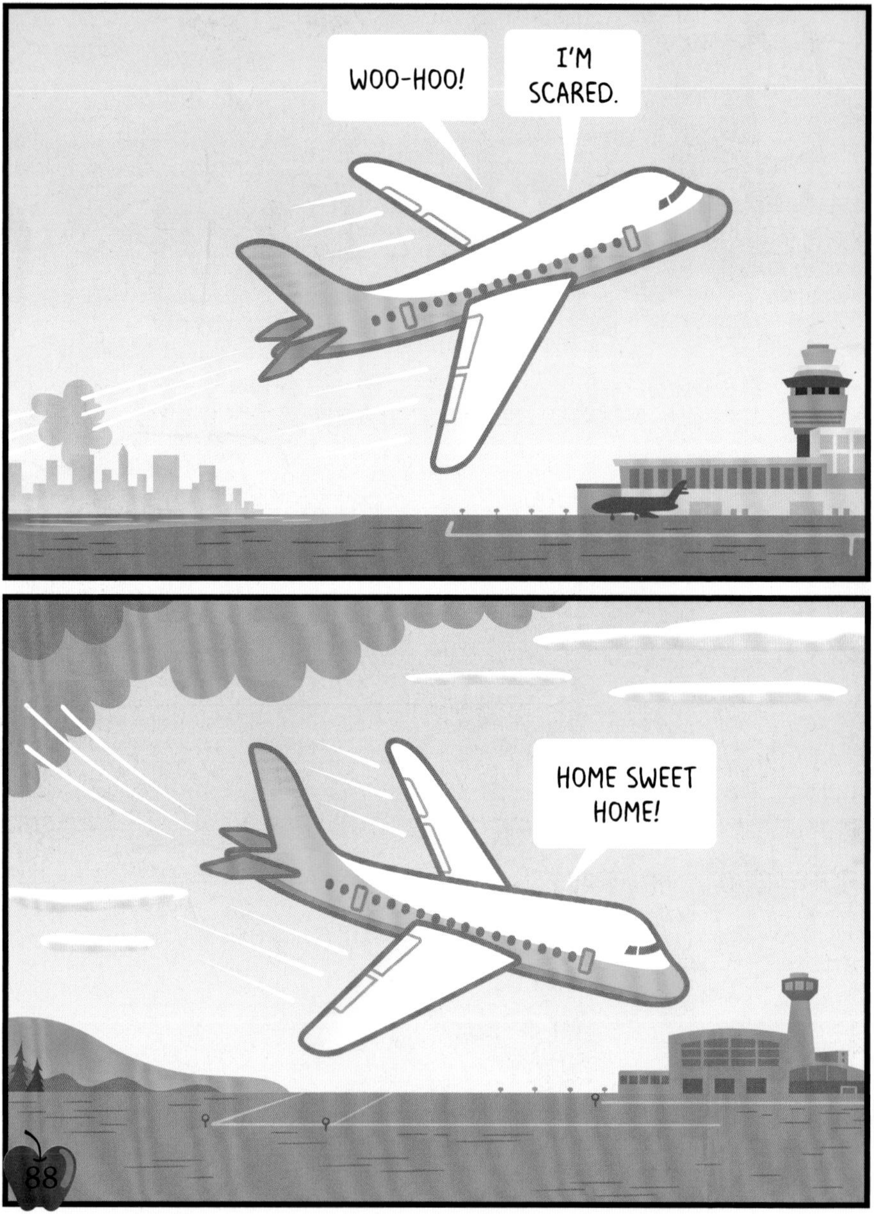
WOO-HOO!
I'M SCARED.
HOME SWEET HOME!

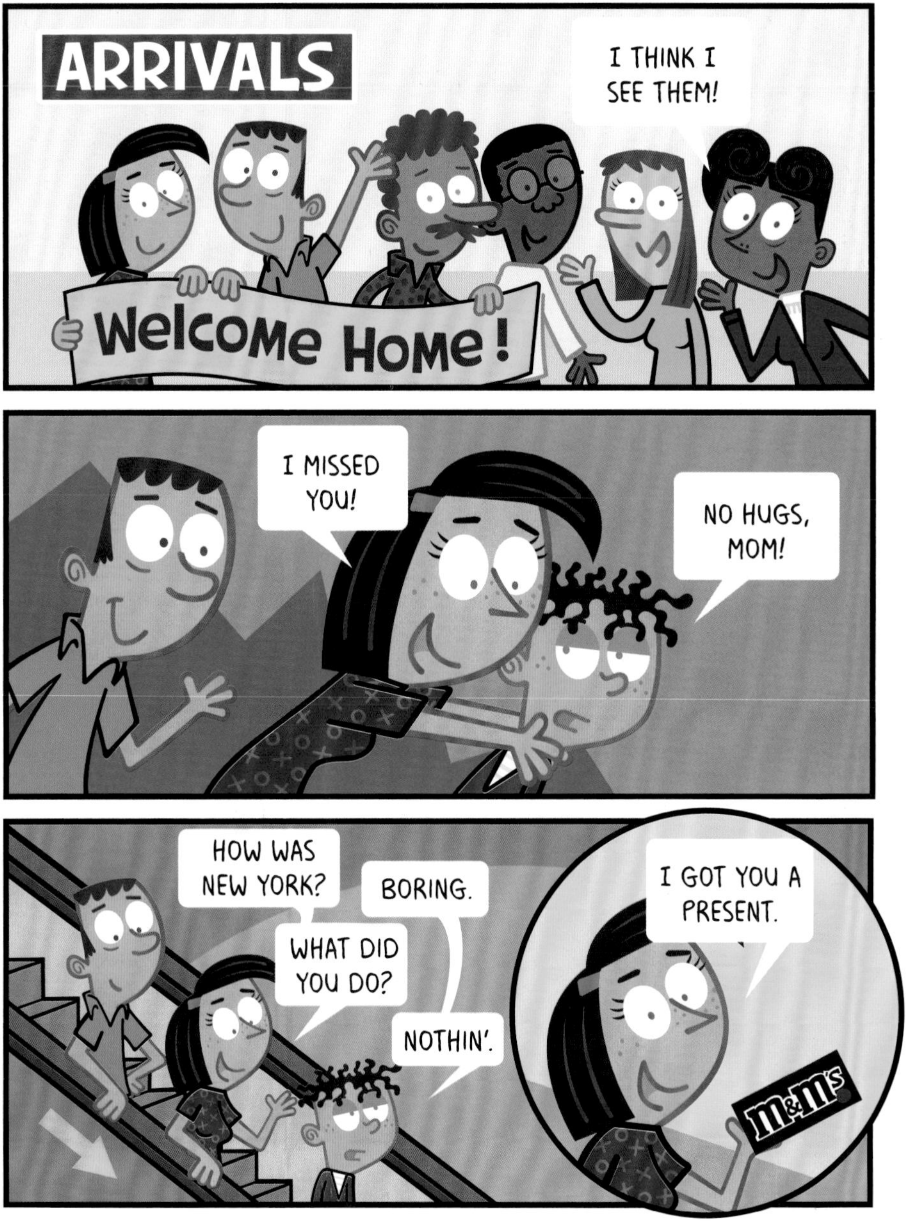
ARRIVALS
I THINK I SEE THEM!
Welcome Home!
I MISSED YOU!
NO HUGS, MOM!
HOW WAS NEW YORK?
BORING.
WHAT DID YOU DO?
NOTHIN'.
I GOT YOU A PRESENT.
m&m's

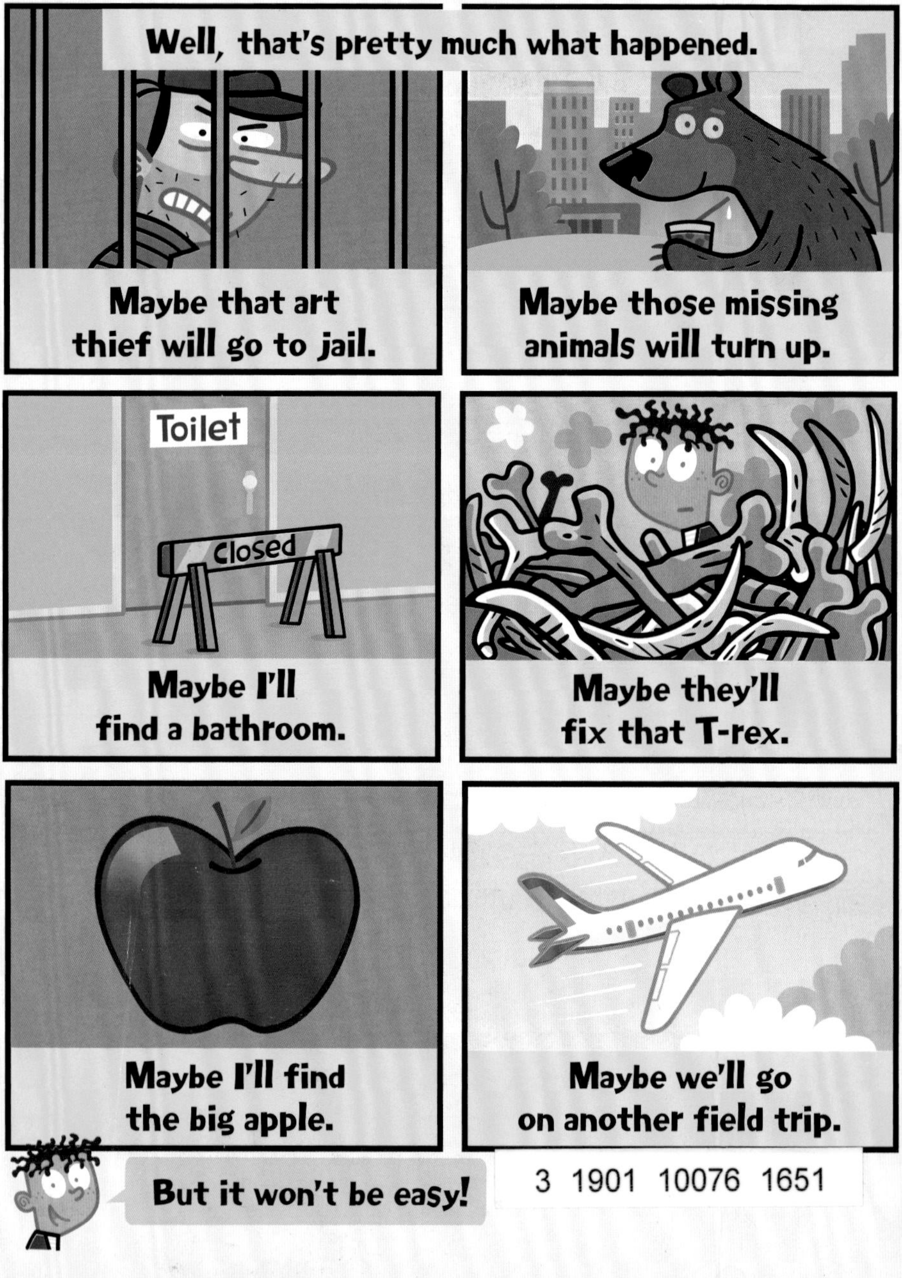
Well, that's pretty much what happened.
Maybe that art thief will go to jail.
Maybe those missing animals will turn up.
Toilet
Closed
Maybe I'll find a bathroom.
Maybe they'll fix that T-rex.
Maybe I'll find the big apple.
Maybe we'll go on another field trip.
But it won't be easy!